A little BIT Country

A LITTLE
BIT
Country

BRIAN D. KENNEDY

BALZER + BRAY

An Imprint of HarperCollins*Publishers*

Balzer + Bray is an imprint of HarperCollins Publishers.

A Little Bit Country
Copyright © 2022 by Brian D. Kennedy
 For information address HarperCollins
Children's Books, a division of HarperCollins Publishers, 195 Broadway,
New York, NY 10007.
www.epicreads.com

ISBN 978-0-06-308565-7

Typography by Chris Kwon
22 23 24 25 26   SB   10 9 8 7 6 5 4 3 2 1
❖

First Edition

For Danny, who on our very first date
asked why I had so much Dolly Parton on my iPod.

And for Dolly.

I will always love you both.

THREE CHORDS AND THE TRUTH.

—Harlan Howard, on country music

Chapter

1

EMMETT

Here's the thing about writing a good country song: It's *really* fricking hard. For starters, you can't swear. Not if you want radio play. But I don't give a "ship" about that. For me, the bigger challenge is coming up with something original to say. Anyone can put words to music, but how do you make those words sound new? I mean, the world's only big enough for so many songs about long dirt roads, cheating spouses, and drinking enough six-packs of cheap beer to crash your pontoon.

To be a good songwriter, you constantly have to be aware of your surroundings. You never know when inspiration is going to strike. Which is why—as my mom stands at the top of our driveway, sniffling into a balled-up tissue—my brain is already cycling through potential song titles:

"The Tears in Mama's Eyes."

"Mama Sobbed Like a Little Baby the Day Her Little Baby Left Home."

"Don't Cry, Mama, I'm Only Seventeen and Not Legally Allowed to Leave for Good."

Okay, so I need to keep workshopping those. The good news is I have the next nine hours to do so. I can't wait to be on the road, where

I'll have the sun on my skin, the wind in my hair, and my favorite country singer—Miss Wanda Jean Stubbs—blaring on my stereo.

"You can at least pretend to be sad, Emmett," Mom says.

"It's only for three months," I tell her, trying not to smile as I pack my guitar case and my laptop, which has the latest copy of my demo, into the back seat.

"It's the longest you've been away. Don't forget, you called asking if you could come home early from music camp—and that was only two weeks."

I didn't want to leave music camp because I was homesick. I wanted to leave because it was full of snobs. Classical music prodigies who were total dicks about my taste in music. Look, I didn't deny that Bach and Beethoven were musical geniuses. Would it have killed them to pay the same respect to Johnny Cash and Dolly Parton?

"This is different," I explain, making my way back up the driveway. "It's the opportunity of a lifetime."

"It's a job," Mom reminds me, ever the realist.

"No, it's a *gig*. My first real one. I get to perform Wanda Jean's greatest hits. In public. And someone's giving me a paycheck for it."

"I just don't want you to get your hopes up too much."

"Mom. I'm replacing someone who had to drop out at the last minute *because he signed a recording contract*. So, yeah, this is a little different than performing at the school talent show. This could be an important step toward something bigger."

Mom sighs, brushing my hair out of my face. "It's so last-minute. I'm still trying to wrap my head around it."

"You and Dad already said yes. If you change your mind now,

you'll only be crushing my biggest dream."

Behind us, the front door to our house swings open. Dad comes out carrying a plastic shopping bag. "It's a long drive to Jackson Hollow," he says. "I bought snacks for the road. And an extra package of socks and underwear. You can never be too sure."

This is exactly why I have to leave home.

"I'm not running off to join the circus," I say, taking the bag from him. "I'm staying with Aunt Karen. You have nothing to worry about."

"The circus might not be so bad compared to your aunt's house," Dad mumbles, getting an immediate head snap from Mom.

"Derek . . ."

"What? The woman lets strangers live with her. *Strangers she finds online.*"

"She only rents out her spare room when money is tight."

"Money wouldn't be so tight if she got a real job instead of selling her wind chimes."

"They're not wind chimes. They're artistic sculptures."

"Artistic sculptures people hang on their back porch. How's that different from wind chimes?"

"Well . . ." Mom pauses. "They're more expensive."

Dad's eyebrows skyrocket so far off his face, they practically orbit the earth. I love my parents, but I don't know how they're going to survive without me. I guess this summer will be good practice. Because as soon as I finish school next year, I'm leaving Oak Park for good. No offense to Illinois, but I was born in the wrong state. If I want to be a real country singer, I need to be surrounded by rolling hills and wide-open spaces. Not Starbucks drive-throughs and suburban shopping malls.

Of course, it's not only my geography that's holding me back. There's also the matter of my sexuality. There aren't a lot of gay country singers for me to follow in the footsteps of. And there certainly aren't many famous ones. But I don't take that as a strike against me. I take it as a challenge.

I like who I am.

And I like who I like.

Which is why I plan on becoming country music's biggest openly gay superstar.

It's not going to be easy. But I'm willing to put in the work. I just wish I had gotten an earlier start. Taylor Swift was sixteen when she released her debut album. LeAnn Rimes won her first Grammy at fourteen.

I'm seventeen and my dad still buys my underwear.

But all that's about to change. Because I get to spend my summer performing at Wanda World, the amusement park owned by Wanda Jean Stubbs.

That is, assuming I can leave my driveway before my parents bicker themselves to death.

"If you love her sculptures so much," Dad says, still going on about Aunt Karen, "then why are the ones we bought still in the garage?"

"I haven't found the right place to hang them yet! They have a very specific . . . aesthetic."

"I'm leaving now," I announce.

Mom takes her tissues back out; Dad pulls a wad of bills from his pocket. "Here. We'd feel better if you took this. Think of it as an emergency fund. In case you run out of gas. Or if something unexpected pops up. Like if you meet someone. . . ."

"If I meet someone?"

"Yeah. Like . . . a guy."

"Oh my God, Dad. What?"

His face turns bright pink. "I don't know what I'm saying. Just be smart. Use protection."

I take the money, carefully avoiding eye contact.

"You two are a mess," I say, giving each of them a hug. "I can't wait to see what this is like next year, when I leave for good."

"There are plenty of great colleges in state," Mom says.

Country music superstars don't have time for college. But that's a conversation for another day. Walking back down the driveway, I try to take a mental snapshot of this moment. I need to capture everything I'm feeling so I can write about it later. Except . . . if I write a song about leaving home, shouldn't it be a sad one? Or at least bittersweet? The only tears I feel like shedding right now are tears of joy.

It's finally time for me to spread my wings and fly! Which is a cliché, I know. But it's also the lyrics to one of my favorite Wanda Jean songs. And when I climb into my car and turn the ignition, it's the song that kicks off the playlist I created for this trip.

Who am I to keep you?
Who am I to cry?
My love for you is not a cage
It's a flame. Burning bright
One I'll never let die
So spread your wings, my lil' darlin'
And fly, fly, fly

Before I can fly, I have to obey a twenty-five miles per hour speed limit as I drive past all the well-manicured lawns and pink fairy-tale playhouses in our cul-de-sac. But once I'm out on the freeway, with the Chicago skyline in my rearview mirror and my future before me, I floor it.

Next stop: country music stardom.

Or, at the very least, Tennessee.

Chapter

2

LUKE

I like having a brother and sister. Really, I do. But there's nothing like the first day of summer vacation to make me miss being an only child. It doesn't matter how well behaved they are during the school year. Once classes and homework are out of the picture, their inner demons are unleashed and we're lucky if no one's bleeding or tied to a banister by the end of the day.

"Luke!" Gabe shouts, running into the kitchen with a bedsheet wrapped around him, like a drunk frat boy at a toga party. "I don't got any clean underwear."

"Gabe, buddy. I did laundry last night."

"Well, my drawer's empty."

"Check on top of the dryer, then."

Amelia enters, her long dark hair wet from the shower. "Do I even wanna know?" she asks, looking at Gabe and using the sarcastic tone she's adopted ever since starting fifth grade.

Gabe sticks out his tongue and leaves. Amelia grabs a box of cereal and plops down on a stool at the counter. She's wearing her soccer jersey, even though practice won't begin for another week.

"Bean," I say. "I'm fixing breakfast this morning."

She wrinkles her nose. "What is it?"

"Eggs."

At least, I hope it is. I open the fridge to check if the carton I bought earlier this week is still there. It is. Along with a jumbo pack of shredded cheese, three kinds of lunch meat, and plenty of RC Cola. Keith must've gone shopping on his way home from work this morning.

"I'd rather have cereal," Amelia says, opening the box to pour a small mound of Lucky Charms on the counter in front of her.

"Seriously, Bean?"

"My name is Amelia."

"Sorry, Bean. But c'mon, you'll always be a Bean to me."

She narrows her eyes. "That's sexist."

I take out the frying pan and turn the burner on. "How's that sexist?"

"You only give me a nickname because I'm a girl."

"I call Gabriel 'Gabe,' don't I?"

"Gabe is an actual name. Bean's a vegetable."

"Actually, a bean is a legume."

Shit. Now I'm being sexist *and* mansplaining.

"Okay, sorry. From now on, I shall only refer to you as Amelia."

"Thank you." She crushes a green marshmallow under her thumb. "Treating me like I'm not a little kid anymore is the least you can do. If I'm old enough to babysit Gabe all summer . . ."

"You ain't babysitting me," Gabe says, returning to the kitchen in his actual clothes. Hopefully with clean underwear on underneath.

Amelia snorts. "Yeah, I am. Not that anyone asked if it was okay with me."

☆ 8 ☆

"*Luke*," Gabe whines. "Tell Bean I'm old enough to take care of myself."

"My name's Amelia. Not Bean."

"Beanie the meanie!"

"Quit being ugly," I snap. "Y'all are gonna wake your daddy."

Keith, my stepdad, works the overnight shift at the automotive plant. It'd take an army of bulldozers to rouse him from his slumber down in the basement. But Bean and Gabe had still better hush.

I go back to fixing breakfast while Gabe takes a seat at the table. It doesn't matter how cranky or tired I am, there's something about the sizzle a cold slab of butter makes when it hits a hot frying pan that puts a smile on my face. When I'm cooking, the only thing I've got to worry about is making sure food gets on the plate. Sometimes, if I want to challenge myself, I'll pretend I'm a cook in a Michelin-starred restaurant or a contestant on *Top Chef*.

I'm not saying I'm good enough to be either of those things. But maybe someday I could be. We've got a shelf of my nana's old cookbooks in the kitchen that I've slowly been making my way through. A lot of the recipes are dated—apparently, cheese logs were big in the seventies—but some aren't bad. Despite Amelia and Gabe having picky palates, I got them to eat asparagus after it was baked into a quiche.

Even when I'm fixing simpler dishes, I do what I can to dress them up. If this were last summer, I'd run out to Mama's garden and grab a tomato or some parsley to give my scrambled eggs a pop of color. This summer, however, the only things growing in there are weeds. Mama was too sick to plant anything.

After serving Gabe and Amelia their breakfast, I set a third plate of eggs on a tray with a glass of orange juice and some toast. "Y'all are in charge of washing your own dishes," I say, leaving them to eat. "And make sure you actually scrub."

The floorboards on the staircase groan as I head upstairs. Our house is a big old farmhouse. Emphasis on the *old*. It's drafty as heck, and we have to line the upstairs hallway with Tupperware containers whenever there's a heavy rain. But as Mama likes to remind us, we're just blessed to have a roof over our heads. Besides, except for the cookbooks, this house is about the only thing we've got left that belonged to Nana.

Heading down the hallway to Mama's bedroom, I peek through the crack in her door. She's sitting up in bed with her eyes closed. The TV's on, but the volume's turned down low. Mama just likes the company.

"Knock, knock," I say, nudging the door open with my foot.

Mama smiles, opening her eyes. "Hey, honey."

"I made breakfast." I set the tray down on her side table, knowing there's a good chance it'll still be sitting there, untouched, when I get home later tonight. "How you feeling, Mama?"

She sits up a bit. "Like I'm 'bout ready to get out of this bed."

Mama wasn't officially diagnosed with multiple sclerosis until after Gabe was born. For years before that, Mama would complain about feeling tired and having dizzy spells. She'd even experience the occasional numbness, but the doctors couldn't figure out what was causing it. She spends most of her time in remission now, until this spring, when she caught the flu and had a bad relapse. Amelia and Gabe are a bit young to fully understand her condition, but while Mama's been off her feet the past month, we all do our best to keep the house from falling apart.

"I'm sure I could use a trip to the salon," Mama says. "Heck, I've been avoiding looking in the mirror for days now."

"You look fine, Mama. Besides, Dr. Collier said you shouldn't—"

Mama swats her hand in the air. "I've been getting all my infusions. And I haven't felt dizzy in weeks. Dr. Collier just likes being cautious. He'd keep me on bed rest forever if he could."

Unfortunately, because Mama only works part-time at the Craft Barn, they don't give her any sick leave. Keith's job at the auto plant pays decent enough, but his insurance doesn't cover the full cost of Mama's treatments. As a seventeen-year-old, I didn't think I'd have to know anything about deductibles or out-of-pocket expenses. But we're a family, so I made it my business to learn. Mama and Keith shouldn't have to take on the burden alone.

"Luke," Mama says. "You've got that look on your face again."

"Huh?" I reply, snapping out of it.

"Like you've got the weight of the world sitting on your shoulders."

"No, Mama. I'm fine."

She grabs my hand. "Don't take this the wrong way, honey. But I wish you'd learn to have more fun."

Fun's not going to put breakfast on the table. Not that I'm bitter. I like doing my part to help out. It's more than my father or granddad ever did. Except for Keith, the men in my family don't have great track records.

I give Mama's hand a gentle squeeze and sit on the edge of her bed. "You don't gotta worry about me, okay?"

"I do worry. You're always so serious."

"Would you rather I be out drinking and gallivanting all the time?"

She shrugs. "I wouldn't mind if you cut loose now and again. Especially if it got you to stop using words like 'gallivanting.'"

Maybe Mama has a point.

"You planning on seeing Vanessa this summer?" she asks. "Haven't heard you mention her lately. . . ."

Of course, she's also still stuck on me having a girlfriend.

"I told you, Vanessa and I are just friends now."

Well, that might be a stretch. Friends usually text each other and hang out.

"I still don't understand why you two broke up," Mama says. "It made me so happy to see you with her."

Before she can guilt me any further, Mama gets distracted by something behind me. Romantic music's playing on the TV, and two men lean toward each other, sharing a PG-rated kiss. Mama shakes her head and lets out a "tsk." As she grabs the remote to turn it off, I try not to react. I don't need to look at the cross hanging on the wall behind Mama's head to be reminded her church thinks it's a sin to be gay. And while Mama's never said that's what she believes, too, her actions have always made it clear.

Mama sighs, running a hand through her rumpled blond hair. "Are your brother and sister behaving themselves?"

"I think we both know the answer to that."

She frowns. "I hope they don't give you too much trouble today."

"I'm starting back up at the factory this morning. Speaking of which, I don't wanna be late."

I stand, giving her a kiss on the top of the head.

"How'd I get so lucky to have a son like you?" Mama asks.

If she were lucky, she'd have a son who didn't prefer sneaking around with boys. Mama's had enough disappointment in her life. I don't want to be yet another thing that didn't turn out right for her.

After leaving her bedroom, I grab my work boots and head downstairs. Gabe's dirty dishes are on the table and Amelia's still at the counter, watching something on her iPad, which has a crack running across the screen.

"Believe it or not, our next performers grew up in the same small town together. And trust me when I tell you Nashville's forever gonna be indebted to Jackson Hollow, Tennessee, for these pretty little ladies."

I don't have to look over Amelia's shoulder to know who the announcer is talking about. But I can't help myself.

"If you've tuned in to any of our shows recently, you'll surely recognize our first guest. Ladies and gentlemen, please welcome Miss Wanda Jean Stubbs!"

The audience applauds as a woman with about ten pounds of bright red hair piled on top of her head walks out. She's wearing a purple jumpsuit with sparkly rhinestones running down the legs. Even without the stage lights, you can tell she'd brighten any space she was in.

"And making her Grand Ole Opry debut tonight is a name that I believe will soon be just as popular. Folks, put your hands together for Miss Verna Rose!"

A petite woman with long blond hair joins her. She's wearing a white jumpsuit with pink roses stitched into it. The two women take a second to smile at each other before holding up their long, skinny microphones to sing.

Mama made it look so easy
As she tied a bow in her apron strings

But what Mama never told us
Is that being someone's wife comes with a list of things

The dishes need washin'
And the pork needs roastin'
Shirts can't iron themselves
And that party needs hostin'

Your legs need shavin'
And your hair needs dyein'
Makeup ain't cheap
And . . . Oh no, is that the baby cryin'?

It ain't always pretty
But we do what we can
'Cause when you're a woman
You gotta keep a smile on your man

Yeah, if you wanna be a woman
You gotta keep a smile on your man

"Amelia . . ."

I don't mean to startle her, but she jumps.

"What?" she says, pausing the video real quick.

"You shouldn't be watching that."

"Why not? She was my nana, too."

My heart wrenches and I get an ache in my chest, like there's an empty space that won't ever be filled. I can't blame Amelia for being curious. It's not like I haven't searched message boards and fan sites for more information about our nana, too.

"You know Mama doesn't like that crap," I tell her.

Bean works her big brown eyes for maximum sympathy. "But it's not fair. I never got to know her."

"Neither did I," I tell her. "Not really."

"At least you were born," she mutters.

"I was five."

When I think of Nana, I can't tell if my memories are real, or if I'm inventing them from the few photographs we still have of her. Either way, I guess it doesn't matter. Mama says it's best not to live in the past.

"Can you please just wash your dishes and not give me a hard time?" I say.

With a dramatic eye roll, Amelia slides off her stool and makes her way to the sink.

"Thank you, Bean."

"My name's not—"

"Thank you, *Amelia*."

After grabbing my lunch from the counter, I run outside and hop into my truck. But when I turn the engine, country music starts blaring from my radio. Amelia or Gabe must've been playing around in here again. I snap the dial back off, shaking my head.

Country music ruined my nana's life.

There's no way I'm letting it into mine.

Chapter 3

LUKE

"Holy balls!" Whizzer bites into his Hot Pocket as I enter the break room. "Look who decided to return for another summer."

Tossing my lunch in the fridge, I mentally prepare myself for what's coming next. It doesn't matter who your coworkers are: When you work in a rubber hose factory, you're going to hear a few dick jokes. Unless your coworkers are two ex–football jocks who never matured a day past high school and still insist on being called Whizzer and Bulldog. Then you're going to hear *nothing but* dick jokes.

Whizzer flashes me a cocky smile. "Bet you couldn't wait to come back and fondle all the merchandise, huh, Lucille?"

Yup. There it is.

It's not even one of his better ones.

Thanks to last summer, I've learned how to handle myself in these situations. I know not to insult Whizzer back, or deny whatever he says, because he'll only come at me harder. It's better to play along. But you can't play along *too much*. You've got to be the right amount of sarcastic. Like you're in on the joke, but not actually gay.

"You got me, Whizzer," I deadpan. "I missed touching phallic-shaped tubes for eight hours a day."

"Yeah. Because it reminds you of touching a dick."

Bulldog looks up from his phone and grunts. "That's literally what 'phallic' means, dumbass."

"Sorry for not being all slick like you and College Boy here," Whizzer says, inhaling the rest his breakfast and talking with his mouth full. "Hey, you still thinking about going to that fancy school? The one where you cook all day?"

"Culinary school," Bulldog says.

"Yeah, I knew it had a prissy name."

I try not to wince. Mentioning culinary school to them was a mistake. Not only because I should've known they'd make fun of me, but because the idea of going to college turns my stomach into knots. Would I like to go? *Sure.* But how can I help my family out if it means taking on more debt?

"Damn." Whizzer shakes his head. "Our boy thinks he's too good to work in a factory. Wants to be all sensitive and bake cupcakes for a living."

I pretend to laugh it off. But as we leave the break room, his comment sticks. Part of me wants to keep my head down, do what's asked of me, and prove I'm no different from any other guy in Jackson Hollow. But then there's part of me that wonders if he's right. There's nothing wrong with this job, of course. I just don't think it's what I want to do for the rest of my life.

The knots return to my stomach. Whenever I imagine my future, an even bigger worry weighs down on me: *Will I always be alone?* I've had girlfriends in the past, though nothing too serious; I think I always knew I was more attracted to guys. But I can't ever see myself having a boyfriend. I didn't even think I'd fool around with another guy.

Not until last summer.

Not until Cody.

As we walk out onto the warehouse floor, my nose wrinkles. I'd forgotten how overwhelming the scent of fresh rubber is. When you work here, you get used to it pretty quick. But the amount of testosterone and unchecked masculinity that permeates this place? That takes longer.

"Lucille," Whizzer barks, tossing me a tape gun. "Time to assume the position."

Since Whizzer and Bulldog work here year-round, they stick me with the boring jobs. Today I'm taping up boxes. It's not a task that requires a lot of brainpower. My first few hours tick by so slowly I'm not sure how I'm going to survive one day of this, let alone an entire summer.

Out of habit, I keep checking my phone, hoping to find a text from Cody. But Cody was last summer. And he was supposed to be a one-time thing—something to get out of my system. We met at a party over in Rayburn, when I might've a had a little too much to drink. Okay, I had *a lot* too much to drink. My inhibitions were gone and when he looked at me, it was like he could see right through me. Through the me I was pretending to be. It was unnerving at first. But after enough trips to the keg, I finally started looking back.

The next morning, I thought I'd feel shame or regret over what had happened between us. And there was some of that. But mostly, I was just excited Cody had texted, asking when we could hang out again.

Our relationship was only supposed to be about the sex. He was heading off to college; I wasn't ready to be out. By the end of the summer, though, I was so attached to my phone that Whizzer—of all people—had to lecture me about the dangers of being distracted while working in the warehouse.

Scrolling through our old texts, I tune out the hissing of the machines around me and remember what it was like to be with him.

> Three more hours until my shift ends.
> **You mean three more hours until you get to kiss me.**
> Don't say that. You'll make it go slower.
> **Guess I shouldn't mention all the humping then?**
> Oh my God. Cody. Stop.

"Hot date tonight, Lucille?"

Shit. I try to hide my texts, but fumble and drop my phone.

"Whoa," Whizzer says. "Why so jumpy?"

"I'm not . . . I just . . . It's nothing . . ."

A weasel-like grin spreads across his face. "It's that girl again, isn't it? The hot one? What was her name?"

"Vanessa," I mutter. She swung by the warehouse a few times last summer. We were still just friends then. I didn't start dating her until the beginning of the school year, after Cody left.

"Right," Whizzer says. "She was one *spicy chica*, huh?"

"Whizzer, you can't say shit like that."

"What? She was Spanish, right?"

"Mexican American. But you're playing into stereotypes."

He crosses his arms, looking self-satisfied. "See, this is how I know you're going to college. Because you give a shit about this PC crap."

"You don't have to go to college to not wanna be an asshat," I say.

Whizzer gets right up in my face, like he's going to fight me. But then he quickly throws his arm around my shoulder instead. "Relax, Lucille. I'm just busting your chops. Now tell me, are you finally dating this girl? Because if not, your boy Whizzer here is ready to swoop in."

"You know she's sixteen, right?"

"She got an older sister?"

"Nope."

"Damn. Well, she's lucky to have you. You're an upstanding guy, Luke. Even if it means you're a pain in the ass half the time."

I get a small ache in the back of my throat. Despite the fact that Whizzer can be a dick, it's still nice to have someone treat me like a friend every once in a while. Most everyone from school took Vanessa's side after the breakup. And I can't blame them. Vanessa deserved a real boyfriend, not someone who was distant and unavailable.

"Hey," Bulldog snaps. "Will you two get back to work?"

"Aw, don't be jealous," Whizzer says. "He's just my work wife."

Bulldog doesn't crack a smile. Doesn't even grunt.

"Cut that shit out. It's not funny."

Whizzer chuckles. "What, the idea that Lucille and I could get hitched? It's hilarious! And hey, we already know which one of us would be the woman. I hope you like housework, Lucille. Because I'm a fucking slob."

Bulldog slams his fist on the table.

"Quit acting like a couple of fags."

The air in the room suddenly changes. Bulldog's staring right at me, like he's about ready to punch a hole through my chest.

Does he know? How could he?

Whizzer drops his arm from my shoulder. "Jeez. We were only messing around."

Bulldog doesn't acknowledge him, and our workstation stays uncomfortably silent for the rest of the afternoon. Whizzer doesn't even try cracking any more jokes.

When the end of the workday finally arrives, I head straight for the parking lot. Sitting in my truck, my mind replays all our conversations. *Did I slip up and give myself away? Did Bulldog see my texts?*

The knots in my stomach are now the size of basketballs. I take out my phone, ready to look up what the symptoms of an ulcer are, but my fingers are too jittery to type.

How can I come back here tomorrow? Or any day after that? I'll constantly be looking over my shoulder, wondering if Bulldog knows my secret. Even if he doesn't know, he made it clear how he feels about someone like me. How am I supposed to work here and still feel safe?

Looking at my phone, I consider texting Cody. But I don't even know if he came home for the summer. He probably stayed at school, where he has a life. And maybe a boyfriend.

There's only one other person I can think of. I doubt she'd want to hear from me, either. But it's not like I have any other options at this point.

Hey, I type, taking a breath before hitting send.

I toss my phone on the passenger seat, wishing I hadn't just done that. But half a second later, my phone vibrates.

She sent me the emoji of a face with a raised eyebrow—one of her favorites.

Guilt presses down on me like a ton of shipping crates. Vanessa and I broke up three months ago. It shouldn't have taken me this long to reach out to her. I have no right asking her to be here for me now.

My phone buzzes again. It's an emoji of a hot dog and an ice cream cone. I smile, sending back an oyster and a fortune cookie. It's this game we used to play; see who could come up with the grossest food combinations.

Vanessa responds with the green-faced vomit emoji.

Sorry to text out of the blue, I type. I just needed someone to talk to.

You okay?

Yeah. Just having a rough day.

When she doesn't respond right away, my thumbs hover over the screen. I should tell her to forget it. As much as I'd like for us to be friends again, Vanessa's probably happier without me.

Sorry, she texts. **It's a shit show here.**

Half the kitchen staff walked out today.

My shift ends in 20. Call you then?

Wait—*kitchen staff*? I thought Vanessa was supposed to be in Nashville this summer. Doing some fashion design thing. We've known each other since freshman year, and Vanessa's never had a job before. Never had a need for one, really. Her family's well off.

Hey. You like cooking, right?

Shit. Gotta run. Call you soon.

I send her a thumbs-up emoji, then reread the part about the kitchen staff walking out. Is that why she asked if I like cooking?

Vanessa's nice. But she has no reason to be *that* nice. I was a terrible boyfriend to her. And maybe even a worse friend. Even if she were suggesting there's a job opening where she works, I couldn't take it. No matter how much I wanted to.

Chapter

4

EMMETT

If you saw a picture of my mom and Aunt Karen when they were kids, you'd assume they were twins. Same hair. Same dimples. Same funny dresses, with big lacy collars and too many bows. But now that they're adults—and no longer styled by my grandma—you'd never even guess they're related.

My mom's the sensible one. She wears neutral-colored business suits that say, "Hi, my name is Amy and I'm here to help you refinance your mortgage today." My aunt Karen, on the other hand is, well . . . Aunt Karen.

"Emmett!" she screams, running across her front lawn in bare feet and a pair of paint-spattered overalls. Her hair is blonder than when she came to visit for Thanksgiving last year, and I catch a glimpse of a feather tattoo on her arm that definitely wasn't there before.

"Holy shit," she says, attacking me with a bear hug. "Did you grow even more? No, wait—don't answer that. That's a question only old people ask."

"It's nice to see you, too," I say, trying to keep my balance.

Releasing me from her grip, she takes a moment to look me over. "Don't take this the wrong way, because you've always been my cute little nephew, but you've really grown into your looks. I mean, can we talk about your hair? Those curls! Seriously, how many boyfriends do you have back home?"

"No boyfriends," I say, blushing.

"Well, I'm guessing you left behind a trail of broken hearts, then."

As if. Between creating content for my YouTube channel, trying to write original songs for my demo, and going to school five days a week, I hardly have time for homework, let alone dating. Which is fine. Have I kissed a few boys? Sure. But I've already made peace with the fact that winning my first Grammy is more important than losing my virginity.

"Listen to me," Aunt Karen says, finally catching her breath. "Let's bring your things inside before I embarrass myself and try pinching your cheeks."

No offense to my dad's side of the family, but Aunt Karen has always been my favorite. She used to stay with us for extended periods of time when I was younger. My parents would frame her visits as a fun vacation, but Aunt Karen always told me the truth: There was the time she broke things off with her boyfriend in Cincinnati after discovering he already had a fiancée in Cleveland. The time she moved to Santa Fe to sell healing crystals and immediately ran out of money. And, perhaps most famously, the time she was kicked out of her apartment complex in Tampa after she threw a singles mixer and accidentally set the pool area on fire with a tiki torch.

Aunt Karen was also the one who introduced me to country music. Staying in our guest room, she'd crank up Reba McEntire or Sugarland and sing along. I'll never forget the moment I heard my first Wanda Jean song. Even if I didn't understand all the lyrics, I could feel the emotions behind them. It was like Wanda Jean was right there, speaking directly to me. I didn't know a song could make you feel that way.

Wanda Jean's the reason I want to write my own lyrics, too. It might not be my strength yet, but I'm working on it. I just love the idea that a song can tell a story. *My story.* Fame and fortune would be nice—I can't lie. But nothing beats having an audience. People who want to hear what your music has to say.

When Aunt Karen announced she was moving to Jackson Hollow a few years ago, I was obviously the happiest nephew in the world. My parents no longer had an excuse not to take me to Wanda World. And we did visit. But only once. Now when I drop hints about wanting to see my aunt again, Mom just buys a plane ticket and flies her to Chicago.

"Okay then," Aunt Karen says, after we bring in my bags. "Grady's out back, grilling dinner. I hope you like veggie burgers. I also hope you like Grady. No pressure, but I happen to think he's great."

I've never met any of Aunt Karen's boyfriends before. According to my mom, I haven't missed out on much. But Grady, as far as I'm concerned, is already the best. He's the senior VP of entertainment management at Wanda World, which is an extremely fancy title. Fancy enough to pull a few strings and get me a job performing in Wanda's Good Time Jamboree.

There are a lot of different performance groups at Wanda World. But the Jamboree is the biggest and the best. They only hold auditions twice a year. It's very competitive, and a lot of the performers stick around for a few seasons. But this year, when someone dropped out right before rehearsals began, instead of holding emergency auditions, I guess they were desperate enough to trust Grady's word about me.

"Babe," Aunt Karen calls, opening the sliding door. "Emmett's here."

When Grady enters carrying a platter of imitation meats and an empty bottle of beer, I'm surprised by how young he is. I mean, he's probably not *that* much younger than my aunt. I guess I just expected a senior vice president to be more, well, senior.

"So this is the famous Emmett Maguire," he says.

Aunt Karen lets out a squeal. "I told Grady you're going to be bigger than Wanda Jean someday. And when that happens, he'll be lucky to be working at *your* amusement park."

My face grows warm. "Um, let's not get too ahead of ourselves. I'm just happy to be working at Wanda World for now."

"Don't be so modest! Grady and I watch all your videos. That cover of 'Cowboy Take Me Away' you posted last night? I had tears in my eyes. Didn't I, babe?"

Grady nods. "I showed your videos to some of the performers in the Jamboree. They were impressed."

Really? I've been nervous about meeting the rest of the cast. We're supposed to have two weeks of rehearsals before performances begin, but I missed the first one because school wasn't out yet. I'll have a lot of blocking and choreography to catch up on. Not to mention all the cast bonding and funny inside jokes. But it's not like I haven't been practicing my ass off since I got our script. I know my parts inside and out.

"Everyone's eager to meet you," Grady says. "You'll be a fine addition to the team."

"Are you kidding me?" Aunt Karen shoots me a wink. "He's going to be the fucking star of the show."

♪

The next morning, Grady accompanies me to Wanda World for my first day of rehearsal. Even though we have to enter through the employee entrance at the back of the park, where all the buildings are nondescript and gray, the asphalt beneath my feet still feels sacred. I can't believe I get to work here. I can't believe I get to *perform* here. I would've taken a job scrubbing toilets if they'd offered it to me.

The other employees walking in with us are dressed in bright yellow polo shirts or old-timey costumes. They smile and greet each other like they're all one big family. And in the distance, the Smoky Mountain Scrambler slowly climbs its rickety wooden slats, before dropping back down and setting off a symphony of screams. Even the air smells sweeter—a mixture of funnel cakes, kettle corn, and happiness.

With my script in a three-ring binder, where all my parts are highlighted and color coded, I'm ready to start. But Grady informs me I need to sit through orientation first, during which human resources has me watch a ninety-minute "Introduction to Wanda World" video that I could probably narrate myself.

Placing my phone discreetly in my lap, I check my YouTube page. I wouldn't say I have an exorbitant number of subscribers. But there are enough to know that it's not just my parents and Aunt Karen who are watching. My most popular video—a cover of my favorite Wanda Jean song—is just shy of ten thousand views. That's about five million away from going viral. But I'm still proud of it.

I click over to my latest video, the cover of "Cowboy Take Me Away" by the Chicks that I uploaded before leaving. It only has 427 views so far. But I do have three new comments.

Hey_its_Jenna: omg, i love your curly hair. do you have a girlfriend?

5nB0dTB1Vq: Have you ever wanted to work from the comfort of your home? I make $40/hr from taking online surveys in my pajamas. Visit easymoneyfrom-home dot com.

boner jamz: damn. this shit is gay.

Okay, so maybe this one isn't going viral anytime soon, either.

By the time orientation ends, my stomach is growling. Grady offers to take me to any of the restaurants in the park, but I opt for a foot-long corn dog on the way. I don't want to miss another second of rehearsal. Eating and walking as fast as I can, we arrive at the Little Red Barn, which, contrary to its name, is an amphitheater that seats over five hundred people.

Looking up at the empty stage, I picture myself in the spotlight. The audience is applauding. Chanting my name.

"Emmett," Grady says, tapping my shoulder. "Rehearsal room's this way."

When we enter the rehearsal space, my dreams of stardom quickly fade. I count eight other performers, who all appear to be in their early twenties. I figured I'd be the youngest one here, but these people are full-on professionals. Watching them perform an intense country line dance, I'm mesmerized by their megawatt smiles and synchronized moves.

After they finish the number, Grady claps and all heads turn toward us. "I didn't think y'all could top the show from last summer," he says. "But it looks like you already have."

I haven't completed a single do-si-do yet, and I'm already sweating. These people all performed together in last summer's show? Do they even *need* to rehearse again?

At a table off to the side, a white lady wearing bifocals on a beaded chain stands up. "Thank you, Grady. You're sweet as a packet of sugar. I presume this must be the Mr. Maguire we've all been waiting for?"

"Y'all," Grady says, pushing me a step forward. "Give a warm Wanda World welcome to your newest team member, Emmett."

They greet me in perfect unison.

Almost like . . . a cult?

I get an uneasy feeling in my stomach. And I don't think it's just from eating my corn dog too fast.

"It's a pleasure to have you," the woman says, rearranging the bright silky scarf she's wearing. "I'm Miss Trish, lead entertainment coordinator for the show." She pauses, looking at her watch. "We're about to take our mandatory ten-minute break, then we'll pick back up at the top, with our medley of 'Tennessee Sunrise' and 'Proud to Be a Mountain Girl.' You've got a lot to catch up on, Mr. Maguire. But Grady here assures me you're up to the task."

I've never called anyone "ma'am" before. But I "yes, ma'am" Miss Trish so fast I don't even realize it until the words are out of my mouth.

"Don't worry," Grady tells me. "You're in good hands. I'll swing by at the end of the day when I'm done at the office."

Before he can leave, one of the performers comes running over. And if Carrie Underwood wasn't a multiplatinum megastar who *definitely* doesn't need to be working at an amusement park for the summer, I'd swear it was her.

"Grady!" she says, using a singsong voice with the perfect amount of Southern twang. "Is this your nephew you were telling us about?"

"My girlfriend's nephew."

"Oh, silly me! Now why do I keep forgetting you have a girl-friend?"

Okay, maybe this is Carrie Underwood's evil, flirty twin.

"Grady played one of your videos for me," she says, placing a del-icate hand on my arm. "I absolutely loved it. I'm Cassidy, by the way. Cassidy St. Clare." She pauses. Like maybe I should recognize her name? "Now, Grady, don't you worry. I'm gonna take Emmett here under my wing and make sure he feels right at home."

Grady matches her smile. "Thanks, Cassidy. I appreciate your help."

"Anytime," she replies, giving him a little wave as he goes.

Clutching my binder to my chest, I try to play it cool. "You were amazing in the last number," I tell her. "Everyone was. I saw this show when I was freshman, and I've been dying to be part of it ever since. I'll be a senior next year. Um . . . in high school. Not college."

Cassidy's probably only a few years out of college herself. But standing her in front of her now, it seems very clear to me that she's an adult, while I'm still a kid.

"Have you ever performed in a show like this before?" she asks, grinning.

"I played the Teen Angel in our school's production of *Grease* this year?"

Not to brag, but my friend Sophie, who's a total theater snob, said I was the highlight of the show. The review in our school newspaper agreed, despite me only having one song.

Cassidy's smile grows tighter. "Well, I'm not gonna lie. You've got your work cut out for you. But I'm serious about my offer. I'm here to help if you need it."

She does seem sincere. Maybe I judged her too quickly.

"Thanks," I tell her. "I should look over my lines before we start back up."

Pivoting away from Cassidy, I come face-to-face with another one of my new castmates. Well, more like face-to-chest. To be a male country singer, you basically have to look like a rugged, handsome cowboy. One who can mend hearts as easily as he breaks them. And this guy definitely fits that description. He's white, with a chiseled jawline, the shoulders of a linebacker, and pale blue eyes that are piercing yet tender.

"Hey," I say. "I'm Emmett."

"Jameson."

"It's nice to—"

"Sorry, kid. We only get ten minutes to piss and smoke."

"Oh. Yeah. Neat."

Neat? Shut up, Emmett! I get out of Jameson's way, taking a seat against the back wall to study my script. Since I'm a last-minute replacement, and only here for one summer, I knew I wouldn't have any lead roles. And that's fine. Honestly, I'm lucky to be in this show at all. Compared to someone like Jameson, it's no surprise that I'm playing only side characters and children.

Thankfully, there is one song I get a solo in: "A Little Red Fire Engine for Amos." The song's about how Wanda Jean's family was too poor for Christmas presents, but always rich in love. It sounds depressing. And, really, it kind of is. But no one wants to be sad when they go to Wanda World, so they've upped the tempo and Santa arrives on his sleigh to give Amos his toy fire engine at the end.

Except now that I'm thinking about it, Miss Trish said they were starting with a medley of "Tennessee Sunrise" and "Proud to Be a Mountain Girl." My heart sinks as I frantically flip through the rest of my pages.

Fuck. I don't have either of those songs.

"Um, Miss Trish?" I raise my hand, like we're in a classroom now. "I think there's been a mix-up. I'm missing some songs." I bring my binder to her table and show her.

"Where'd you get this?" she asks.

"You mailed it to me along with my welcome packet."

She looks down at me over the top of her bifocals. "You think I have time to personally send out welcome packets?"

I gulp, and I'm pretty sure the entire park can hear it.

Miss Trish sighs. "Didn't you read through these pages? 'A Little Red Fire Engine for Amos' is a Christmas song. Did you really think that was part of our summer show?"

"I . . . uh . . ."

Oh my God. Why didn't I think that was weird? Well, I *did* think it was weird. But this is Wanda World. They have a year-round Christmas shop. Plus, anytime you walk into a Target after, like, the second day of fall, they already have their holiday decorations out on the shelves.

My stomach turns. The ten-minute break must be over because everyone's back in the rehearsal room, staring at me. Except for

Cassidy. When I try to make eye contact with her, she averts her gaze to the floor.

"I'm sorry," I say. "I don't know what I was thinking."

Miss Trish shakes her head. "It's fine. But we can't start rehearsing the medley yet. It's too complicated for you to learn on the fly." She consults the massive stack of papers in front of her. "We'll do 'Calamity Joe.' Your part's easy enough for that one."

That song is about a stubborn old mule.

I'm afraid to ask which part I play.

My fears are confirmed when they bring out a mule costume. And just when I think it can't get any worse, I realize it's a two-person costume. I don't have to ask which end I'll be wearing.

Chapter

5

LUKE

Texting Vanessa was a mistake. So was not showing up for my shift at the factory this morning. If I hadn't done either of those things, I wouldn't be standing here now, next to an animatronic opossum that's violently jerking back and forth.

"Look, Mom!" a little girl in pigtails and face paint yells.

The mom, who also has her face painted, takes a sip from her sixty-four-ounce Wanda World souvenir cup. "Aw, isn't she cute?"

The opossum is wearing granny glasses, a white bonnet cap, and the ugliest floral dress I've ever seen. *She* is a robotic nightmare.

"Excuse me." The woman gives me a wave. "Would you mind taking a photo of us in front of this kitty cat?"

"Um . . ." I say, struggling to fold up the map I was reading. If she thinks that's a cat, I pray they never meet an opossum in real life.

She hands me her camera. "It'll just take a second."

As they pose in front of the opossum, music pumps through hidden speakers around us. It's the same song over and over. Something about Granny's front porch. I guess the opossum is supposed to be Granny? Since she's standing on a front porch? Or rather, a one-dimensional cutout of one. This is an amusement park, after all. Nothing's real.

"Smile, y'all." I snap the picture and hand her camera back. "Ma'am, you don't happen to know which direction Bootstrap Junction is in, do you?"

"That's on the other side of the park," she tells me.

Dang. There's no way I'm not going to be late. I reach for my phone to text Vanessa, but there's already a message from her: **Where are you?**

"My eyes were closed!" the woman says. "Can you take another?"

Lost, I type. Be there soon.

I told you to be on time for a reason, Luke.

"Shit," I say, forgetting I'm in the presence of someone young enough for pigtails. The woman's eyes go wide. "'Scuse my language, ma'am. I've got a job interview that I really can't be late for."

"This is a family establishment," the woman calls out as I take off running. "They shouldn't be hiring anyone with a mouth like that!"

She's right. I shouldn't be applying for this job. But not because I swore. Because it would kill my mama if she ever found out. Wanda World's completely off-limits for my family. No exceptions. It didn't matter how many year-end field trips I was supposed to take here—Mama would never let me go. Because it wasn't just country music that ruined my nana's life. It was also Wanda Jean Stubbs.

I wasn't planning on going behind Mama's back like this. But when I talked to Vanessa last night, she offered to put in a good word with the manager for me. Which was really nice of her—I would've felt bad saying no. Besides, the idea of working in a kitchen, learning new recipes, getting away from Whizzer and Bulldog . . . How could I say no to that?

Of course, if I don't find this restaurant in the next few minutes,

I'm going to be back at the warehouse tomorrow, begging for them not to fire me.

I'm by a food stand that's shaped like a giant ear of corn, I text. *Is that close?*

Vanessa doesn't answer. I take off running again, navigating my way around park-goers who are too occupied with their selfie sticks to watch where they're going. And kids. *So many kids.* Dodging a middle-aged man who's carrying an ice cream cone in one hand and a massive plate of cheese fries in the other, I reach for my phone again, hoping Vanessa has texted back. But the second I glance down, I run smack-dab into someone.

"Oof," I say, trying to regain my balance. "Sorry, I didn't see you there."

"Ughhh," replies the furry gray lump crumpled in front of me.

I know I should help them back up, but . . . *how?* There's no front half to this creature. It's just a rear end, sticking straight up. The only thing I can grab on to is its tail. And that just seems rude.

The lump rolls over onto its side. Onto *his* side. It's a guy, probably around my age, with dark, curly hair and a dazed look.

"Corn dog," he says.

"Excuse me?"

"*Corn. Dog.*"

I kneel down next to him, wondering if he's concussed.

"You okay?" I ask. "I'm sorry, I didn't mean to run into you."

He groans. "If I knew I'd be stepping into a fifty-pound costume with a limited air supply today, I never would've had a corn dog for lunch. Do you have any idea how hot it is in here? It's really hard to see, too. I mean, I hate it when performers make excuses—but it wasn't my fault I kept missing my cue. If I hadn't had that corn dog, then I wouldn't have started to feel sick. And if I hadn't started to feel sick, then I wouldn't have run out of the rehearsal room. And if I hadn't run out of the—"

"Yeah, I got it," I say, cutting him off.

I don't mean to be a jerk. But I'm in a rush.

"Sorry," he says, still curled on his side. "Just leave me here to die."

I offer him my hand. "C'mon. Let me help you up."

"Oh . . ." He pauses, finally looking at me. "I was wrong."

"What?"

"I didn't think this day could get any more embarrassing. But this . . . I mean, you're . . ." His face goes bright red. "Never mind, I have no idea what I'm saying right now."

I grab on to his elbow. "I'm gonna lift, okay?"

He winces as I pull. With only a thick pair of suspenders to hold up his cumbersome costume, he looks unsteady on his feet, like the slightest breeze could knock him back down. Underneath the swath of curls falling over his forehead, there's something dark and wet. Without thinking, I reach to brush his hair aside, but he takes a step back, almost tripping over himself.

"Sorry," I say. "I think you're bleeding."

He touches his forehead. His fingers come back with a smudge of red on them.

"It's fine," he says. "I need to get back to work before they fire me."

"Wait, you work here?"

His eyebrows shoot up, pushing his gash farther underneath his curls. "You think I dress like this for fun? I'm literally the ass of an ass."

He makes a good point.

"Can you tell me where Bootstrap Junction is?" I ask. "I'm late for a job interview in one of the restaurants there."

"Yeah, it's just past the Bone Rattler. But if you reach the Great Coal Mining Disaster of 1904, you've gone too far."

"Uh . . . I don't know what those are."

He smiles. "The Bone Rattler is the giant roller coaster behind us. And the Great Coal Mining Disaster of 1904 is an interactive ride about, well . . ."

"Right. Got it. Um, thanks. And again, I'm sorry about the . . ."

"I'm fine. Don't worry about me."

I should turn around and leave. But for some reason, my feet aren't moving yet.

"Do you want me to take you there?" he asks.

Now that he's upright, I notice how cute he is. Despite the fact that he's dressed as a donkey from the waist down. Or maybe because of it. Not everyone can pull off that half human, half barn animal look. But on him, it's kind of adorable.

"No, I'm good," I say, a little too quickly. "But thanks."

"Yeah. Sure."

Before things can get any more awkward, I turn around and start running again.

"Good luck with your interview," he calls after me.

"Thanks," I shout. "You too!"

You too?

Good gravy.

I need to focus. Having a paycheck's more important than talking to some guy in a donkey suit.

♪

By the time I arrive at Granny's Cupboard, the restaurant Vanessa works at, my shirt's damp with sweat. But maybe it doesn't matter. The place is a mess. Empty dishes need bussing; hungry customers need feeding; and servers are running around everywhere, carrying enormous trays of food while dressed like . . .

Oh no.

They're dressed like the animatronic opossum I saw earlier.

"Finally! What took you so long?"

I spin around. My panic over being late is quickly replaced by the desire to laugh my damn ass off.

"Don't you dare," Vanessa warns, pointing a finger at me.

I can't help it. Ever since I've known her, Vanessa's cut photos out of fashion magazines and wallpapered her bedroom with them. She already has plans to attend some fancy design school after we graduate. So to see her like this . . .

"Nice bonnet," I say, bracing myself for a slap upside the head.

"It's not a bonnet. It's a mop cap. And don't get me started on this fucking pinafore. My abuelita wouldn't be caught dead in this shit."

"You look like you're about to milk a cow," I say.

Her eyes narrow. "Do I need to remind you who got you this interview?"

"Sorry. That wasn't fair. You could also be churning butter."

"I'm serious, Luke. Rodney's a pig. I don't like asking him for favors."

My defenses immediately go up. "What d'you mean? Has he done anything to you?"

"What, you mean other than make inappropriate comments and act like he's God's gift to women?" She rolls her eyes. "Please. Like I haven't spent the first sixteen years of my life living in a world full of entitled men."

I'd like to think I'm not just another man who's mistreated Vanessa. But who am I kidding? I couldn't even be honest with her while we were dating. Or when we broke up three months ago. Maybe if I had been, we wouldn't have spent all this time avoiding each other.

"Vanessa, I'm sorry. I feel like I still owe you—"

"What the hell's on your feet?" she asks.

I look down at my boots. They're my nice ones, the ones Mama and Keith bought me for my birthday last year.

"What? You told me to dress respectable."

"Yeah, respectable for *working in a restaurant*. You think anyone wears boots in a kitchen?" She glances over her shoulder. "Shit. Here comes Rodney. Just pucker up and get ready to kiss some ass."

With a boyish face and a receding hairline, Rodney looks like a thirteen-year-old stuck in a forty-year-old's body. He puts his hands on his hips as he approaches us, attempting to look authoritative, I guess.

"Vanessa, sweetheart, if you've got time to chitchat with friends, then you've got time to help out in the kitchen. You know it's a disaster back there."

Vanessa gives him a smile that's all sugar on the outside, but a million poisoned daggers on the inside. "Rodney, perfect timing! This is my friend Luke. The one I was telling you about?"

Rodney quickly changes his demeanor. "Oh, yes. Of course." He offers me a firm handshake and nods toward Vanessa. "Not only is she one of our most beautiful employees, she's also one of our most dedicated."

Gross. Looks like it's more than just the uniforms that are outdated around here.

"Speaking of dedication," Vanessa says. "If y'all will excuse me, I have some tables to attend to."

She flips Rodney off behind his back as she leaves. Rodney smiles obliviously, pleased with his managerial skills. "So, Luke," he says. "I assume you've worked in restaurants before?"

"No, sir. But I cook all the time at home. My mama's been sick and my stepdaddy works late, so most nights supper only makes it on the table if I step in. I'm a fast learner and a real hard worker. And, sir, based on everything Vanessa's told me, it'd be an absolute pleasure to work in an establishment such as yours."

How's that for a good Southern ass-kissing?

"Well, I'm sure Vanessa also told you we're short-staffed at the moment. So I don't have the luxury of being picky. If you can start today, you're hired."

"Today? As in *now*?"

"No time to jump through corporate hoops. I need to throw someone back there ASAP."

"Yes, of course. It's just . . . don't you need to see me cook first?"

"Cook? I just need to know if you can scrape food off a plate."

"Um, sir?"

He slaps a hand on my back, leading me toward the kitchen. "Welcome to Wanda World, son. I hope you brought a more comfortable pair of shoes to wash dishes in."

Chapter
6

EMMETT

There are dozens of places to eat in Wanda World. Hundreds of foods to try. I could spend my summer hitting up a different area of the park every day and never have the same thing twice. However, I'm so exhausted by the time our morning rehearsals get out each day that I've yet to make it past the restaurants in Bootstrap Junction.

Okay, fine. Maybe I'm eating over here because this is where that guy was headed.

The hot one.

The one I *literally* ran into.

It's cheesy, but I've started thinking of him as my Dream Cowboy. I mean, the way he was hovering over me. In his checkered shirt. And his tight blue jeans. And his actual cowboy boots! It was like I had passed out and woken up in the middle of a country music video.

But this wasn't a dream.

Nope. It was a living nightmare.

Whatever. I'm pretty sure my Dream Cowboy is straight anyhow. When I offered to help him, he seemed weirded out. Like he didn't want to be seen with me. Of course, it could've been the costume that scared him away.

Either way, it's pointless to speculate. Rehearsals are a disaster right now. *I'm* a disaster. I know Wanda's songs inside and out. But a few of the arrangements are different, and I keep messing up my choreography. For the next week, my focus has to be on getting ready for opening night.

Besides, I don't even know if Dream Cowboy got the job or if this is the restaurant he works at. So then why do I keep spending my lunch break here? Why do I keep scanning the crowd, hoping to see him again?

Over in the buffet line, I spot Avery and Jessie—two of my cast-mates. Avery is muscular, tall, and Black. He has a great baritone voice that fills up the entire rehearsal room. Jessie's shorter and Chinese American. She plays the front half of Calamity Joe and looks oddly familiar to me. I probably recognize her face from last year's promo videos.

As they bring their trays into the dining area, I look back down at my food. I don't want them to feel obligated to sit with me. So far, everyone's done a pretty good job of avoiding the show's only fuckup.

Much to my surprise, they make their way over anyhow.

"Want some company?" Avery asks, dropping a textbook on the table. The cover shows a human body covered in exposed red muscle.

"Um . . . sure."

Rehearsals always leave me starving. Jessie and Avery, however, don't appear to share my problem. They only have two biscuits on their plates, and a side of gravy each. After glancing around the restaurant, Jessie takes a Tupperware container from her bag and splits a pile of cold noodles between the two of them.

"You must be tired of the food they serve here," I say.

"Are you kidding? The food's amazing."

Avery tears off a hunk of biscuit. "Yeah, have you not tried these things?"

"We just can't afford to eat here for every meal," Jessie explains, pouring gravy over her noodles. "You know, starving artists and all."

"But we get a fifteen percent discount," I say.

She raises an eyebrow. "Great. Tell that to my next bounced rent check."

Oh, right. They're older than me and probably not living with their aunt. I wonder how many plates of cold noodles are waiting for me in my future. I'd have to be deluded to think I'll land a record deal and start going on tour anytime soon.

It's just, if there's anything I've learned from Wanda Jean, it's that you have to believe in yourself. Wanda was a woman in the sixties. In the very male-dominated world of country music. She must've heard "no" hundreds, if not thousands, of times. And if she had listened to just one person who told her she didn't have what it takes, well, then she wouldn't be the legend she is today. I'm not saying I'm anywhere near as talented as she is. But I'm also not saying I'm *not* talented. Because if I don't believe in myself, I might as well go back home now.

However, I can't ignore the fact that Jessie and Avery are better performers than me. And if they're still working at Wanda World . . .

I push my plate toward the center of the table. "There's no way I can finish all this."

"Don't offer if don't you mean it," Avery says. "We're not above free handouts."

"Please. Help yourselves."

I've never tried to buy anyone's friendship with meat loaf and an absurd mound of mashed potatoes before. But it's nice to have someone to talk to. In my friend group back home, I'm the only one who really loves country music. Some of them are casual fans—and that's fine. But I feel like they're always tolerating me when I make them listen to whatever song I'm currently obsessed with, or do a deep dive of some of Wanda Jean's older lyrics.

"So, Emmett," Jessie says, eagerly digging in. "How are you feeling about the show?"

"Um . . ." I press my finger into the prongs of my fork. "In case you haven't noticed, I'm dragging everyone else down."

Jessie and Avery shoot each other a look. I wasn't fishing for a denial, but I don't know if I can stomach hearing the truth, either. Everybody knows I was hired because of Grady. Me included.

"It's only been a few days," Jessie says. "No one expects you to be perfect yet."

Avery nods. "Yeah. We all remember what it's like to be the new person."

"I spent my last two summers playing the back half of Calamity Joe," Jessie says. "It wasn't until you came along that I finally graduated to the front."

Avery covers his mouth to laugh. "You should've seen her. That part where y'all spin around in a circle? She used to get so sick. How many times did you throw up in that costume?"

"Wait, is that what that smell is?" I ask.

Jessie wrinkles her nose. "Sorry."

"Be glad you're not performing any duets with Cassidy," Avery tells me. "If you take so much as one wrong breath, she'll be in Miss Trish's ear about it."

Jessie rolls her eyes. "Unless she's too busy being up her ass."

"Is that why Cassidy gets all the best parts?"

They look at me as though I asked if the Grand Ole Opry was in New York City.

"Cassidy gets all the best parts because she's pretty, blond, and white," Jessie says.

Avery lets out a *tsk*. "Welcome to country music."

I might complain about the lack of gay country singers, but there are even bigger roadblocks in this industry. The statistics don't lie. Men get way more play than women on the radio. And if you're not white, the numbers only get worse. A lot worse. So while I may not be straight, I still have a leg up by ticking two of the other boxes.

"That sucks," I say, hoping I don't sound too ignorant. "Have you tried saying anything to Grady? He might be able to help."

Avery shakes his head. "It's bad enough that some people already think we're the diversity hires. As if we didn't have to work twice as hard and be twice as talented to get these jobs."

"Performing at Wanda World is a great opportunity," Jessie says. "But it can also be a trap. I thought I'd only be here for a summer, you know?" She frowns. "This will be my third Jamboree now. And my last."

"*What?*" I ask, unable to hide my shock. "But why?"

"I'm a glorified chorus member. I promised myself that if I didn't get any lead roles this year, I wouldn't come back." Her brow furrows as she stabs her fork into a slab of meat loaf. "I peaked years ago. Right before I ruined my career on national television."

Oh shit. The reason Jessie looks so familiar suddenly clicks into place.

"You were on *Make Me a Star*," I say.

"For, like, a minute."

"Yeah, I remember you. You were really good!"

"Emmett. I choked."

Well, she did. *Literally.* She was inhaling to yodel in the middle of her song, and she accidentally swallowed a strand of her hair. She recovered and finished her performance just fine. But the judges voted her off at the end of the episode.

"You were still good," I tell her. "They don't let just anyone on that show."

"A lot of people are good," Avery says. "You'll learn that soon enough. And when you do, you'll start thinking about your backup plan." He points to his textbook. *Goldman's Physical Therapy Rehabilitation, Third Edition.* "Being a personal trainer was supposed to be my side hustle. But you know what? I'm good at it. And if I have a talent, I might as well get paid for it. That's why I'm going back to school this fall. So I can become a physical therapy tech."

"Oh," I say, trying to sound upbeat. "Yeah. Cool."

"It's good to have other interests," Jessie says. "Otherwise you'll burn out too quickly. Don't get me wrong, I love performing. But you know what else I love? Curling up with a good book. Or watching an artsy French film and using it as an excuse to drink wine and eat an entire cheese plate by myself."

"Exactly," Avery says. "Having five hundred strangers clap for you is a rush. But the applause my younger sisters give me when I agree to take them river tubing for an afternoon? That's hard to top."

But I don't want a backup plan or other interests.

I want to be country music's biggest gay superstar.

Avery smiles. "Sorry. Don't listen to us. We've been here too long.

The Jamboree's awesome. You're gonna love it."

I understand why Avery and Jessie are frustrated about not getting lead roles. They more than deserve them. But it makes me sad to know they don't want to do the show anymore.

"What about the person who quit before rehearsals began?" I ask. "Wasn't he poached by a talent scout?"

"Hayden?" Jessie asks. "He wasn't discovered at the Jamboree. He was discovered at the Rusty Spur."

The Rusty Spur? That's either the name of a drink or a sex act.

"It's a music venue in town," Avery explains. "They have an open mic night every month."

"Legit talent scouts come to it," Jessie says. "Which is why Hayden's in a recording studio this summer, under contract, instead of back onstage with us, performing the same old songs again."

I sit up straighter. This is new information. Information that could help further my career.

"When's the next one?" I ask.

"At the end of the month," Avery says.

"Can anyone sign up? Is there an age restriction? Shit. It's not at a bar, is it?"

Avery laughs. "Relax, cowboy. All you need is a guitar and a song."

"We're planning to perform at it," Jessie says. "If you want to join us?"

This is exactly why I needed to be in Tennessee this summer. Because this is the type of opportunity that I'd never get in Chicago. The only open mics I've done have been at small coffee shops where half the audience is my friends.

"I'm in," I tell them, trying to play it cool.

"Do you write your own music?" Jessie asks. "A&R scouts like that kind of thing. You know, so they can see you're more than just a performer. Take Cassidy, for example. She's great in the Jamboree. But only because she's doing an imitation of someone. Put her on a bare stage with an acoustic guitar . . . and, well, she's hollow and dead behind the eyes."

I slump back in my chair. That's why I'm always posting covers of other artists' songs on my YouTube channel. Whenever I try working on my own stuff, I end up with a page full of scribbles.

"Don't worry," Jessie says, reading my thoughts. "You still have plenty of time."

"If you're not counting rehearsals," Avery says.

"Or costume fittings and promotional appearances around the park."

"Or three shows in a row on performance days."

Jessie and Avery definitely sound like they're over the Jamboree. Maybe I'll be just as jaded by the end of the summer. But for now all I want to do is eat, live, and breathe country music. And if that means working on an original song in between shows, then I'm ready.

Jessie takes her Tupperware back out, scooping the last of my mashed potatoes into it as she lets out a dejected sigh. "And my friends all wonder why I'm still single."

"Maybe you spoke too soon," Avery replies, making a face like he just smelled something rotten.

Jessie and I follow Avery's gaze across the room to where Jameson is walking toward us with his tray. Jameson, as it turns out, is the male version of Cassidy. He gets all the lead parts in the show because he fits the "look" the audience is expecting.

"Great," Jessie mutters.

Jameson smiles as he approaches our table, and it's like looking directly into the sun. Those *cannot* be his real teeth.

"'Sup, Jessie?" he asks, puffing out his chest.

Jessie adopts an exaggerated pout. "Oh no, we were just about to leave."

The smile falls from his face. "Yeah. Whatever. I was just saying hey."

"Okay, cool. See you in rehearsal, then."

Jameson curls his lip into a snarl, pivoting to go sit at a different table. I'd say I felt bad for him, but in three days of rehearsals, that's the most he's ever said to me. And even now, he obviously wasn't talking to me. He was looking at Jessie the entire time.

"So," Avery says, once Jameson's out of earshot. "I take it there's not going to be a showmance this summer?"

"Not a chance," Jessie replies. "You know how some people spend a year saying yes to everything? Well, I'm taking a year to say no. No more Jamboree. No more compromises. And no more falling for Jameson's mediocre charm."

"Did you two date last summer?" I ask.

Jessie grimaces. "We hooked up a few times. And I've regretted it ever since."

"Jameson's a tool," Avery says. "But sometimes you gotta let off a little steam."

"Yeah, well, this summer when I need to let off steam I'll take up running," Jessie says. "Or drink a margarita the size of my head."

Avery nods, licking his fork clean. "What about you, Emmett? Is your social life as depressing as ours?"

"Oh. I don't know anyone in Jackson Hollow. Other than my aunt."

He smirks. "That'll change. Park-goers tend to hang around after the show. I'm sure you'll have plenty of girls asking for your number."

Jessie elbows him. "Or maybe some guys. If that's what he's into."

I smile. "That's definitely what I'm into. But I'm not looking for a boyfriend. I'd rather concentrate on my music and the show."

"Good call," Jessie replies. "We're all pretty much married to Wanda World at this point."

When the three of us finally leave the restaurant, it hits me that I forgot to keep an eye out for Dream Cowboy. But that's probably for the best. I'm only here for the summer. And if I'm doing the Jamboree *and* the open mic, I definitely don't have time to sit around and flirt.

Still, though, the thought of never seeing him again does make me a little sad. My heart's never beat so fast around a guy. But that doesn't mean our running into each other has to be pointless. Maybe instead of falling in love with him, he's supposed to be the inspiration for something bigger.

Something like a song.

Chapter 7

LUKE

Anyone who thinks pigs are the filthiest creatures on earth clearly hasn't worked in the service industry before. I'll never eat at another restaurant in my life and not finish every last bite of food that's on my plate. With the amount of leftovers I've scraped into the garbage these past few days, it's not an exaggeration to say I could re-create Mount Rushmore out of uneaten mashed potatoes.

Surprisingly, the food at Granny's Cupboard is good. Not that I've been eating off dishes that make their way back to me. Well . . . it happened once. It was a piece of berry cobbler that was only missing one bite, so I just scooped that part out. It was absolutely delicious, and I can never do it again because that seems like a very slippery slope to slide down.

It's hard, though, because everything smells amazing. Slow-cooked pinto beans. Gooey mac 'n' cheese. Warm, buttery biscuits that melt in your mouth. It's intimidating to watch the chefs in action. When I'm cooking, my nose is buried in one of Nana's cookbooks, following every last step. But these guys, despite having close to a hundred different menu items to make, don't use recipes. It's all in their heads.

I'm jealous of their skill. And their versatility. While the food's all

Southern, not every chef is. I'm sure a lot of our diners' heads would spin if they realized the grits they're eating were made by Paulo, a laid-back surfer dude from Brazil, or Bjorn, who's tall enough, and blond enough, to look like the seafaring Vikings he's probably descended from.

So far everyone's been pretty nice. Some of the guys even sneak me food to try. I can't decide if they're really that friendly, or just feeding me so I won't quit. Their daytime dishwasher was part of the walkout that happened earlier this week.

I can understand why someone wouldn't want this job, though. Not only am I responsible for every plate that comes back from the dining room, I've got a mountain of dirty pots and pans to scrub, too. Every time I turn my back on it, the pile grows. And I haven't quite mastered how to use the spray hose yet without getting water all over myself.

Still, it beats working with Bulldog and Whizzer.

"Order up," Bjorn yells, tapping the service bell with his knife.

The cooks only use the bell when food's been sitting out too long. But every time I hear it, I have to smile. It doesn't matter that I'm up to my elbows in soapsuds and getting a face full of steam when I open the dishwasher hood, working in a real kitchen is pretty damn cool.

Bjorn dings the bell a second time and the swinging doors fly open.

"Yeah, yeah," Vanessa says, tucking a loose strand of hair under her mop cap. "I heard you the first time."

Paulo and another chef share a look, wiggling their eyebrows. And in that respect, I guess the kitchen's not all that different from the warehouse.

"How's the new guy working out?" Vanessa asks, giving a nod in my direction.

"¿Tu amigo?" asks César, the head chef, who's Mexican.

"Sí. ¿No está quebrando tus platos?"

"Todavía, no. Dejalo. Estoy mirándolo."

Even the non-latinos in the kitchen understand some Spanish. It's embarrassing how limited mine is. But I think that was a semi-decent review.

"If you want to thank me," Vanessa tells César, "I wouldn't say no to an order of biscuits. My shift ended five minutes ago." She balances two plates on her arm and takes a third in her hand. "Hey, Luke. Come find me when you're done?"

I give her a nod and half the kitchen hoots or whistles.

"Oh please," Vanessa says, backing her way out of the swinging doors. "That boy already missed his chance."

The guys hoot even louder. My face goes warm. Half from embarrassment, half from shame. Though I guess it's a good thing Vanessa can joke about it now.

Glancing up at the clock, I see my shift's over, too. But when I look at all the scorched pots and greasy pans still in the sink, I feel bad for the evening dishwasher. Rodney told me he doesn't approve overtime, because it only encourages people to be lazy and work slower. So I clock out first and then get back to scrubbing.

When I'm finally finished, César motions me to his station and hands me a to-go bag. "Thanks for staying late, güero. Make sure Miss Vanessa shares those biscuits with you."

I thank him and head to my locker in the communal break area.

Opening the bag, I see César also gave us some chicken-fried steak and two slices of pecan pie. Maybe I'm delirious from standing in a hot kitchen all day, but I get a little emotional. No one looked out for me like that at the warehouse.

After changing out of my uniform, I throw on my ball cap and exit the restaurant through the back. Vanessa's waiting for me outside. She's wearing frayed jean shorts and a yellow top. You'd never guess she spent the last eight hours sweating under a starchy floral dress.

"What took you so long?" she asks, putting her sunglasses on top of her head.

I hold up the bag. "I scored us a free meal."

"Us?" She crosses her arms. "A bit presumptuous, don't you think?"

"Oh. Sorry. I didn't . . ."

"Luke, I'm kidding. I smell like creamed corn and gravy. I clearly don't have plans."

"Right. So you wanna eat, then?"

"Yes. But not by the dumpster. Come on, I know a spot."

Vanessa leads me to the back entrance of some building, where we jump over a set of turnstiles. Once we're inside, we sneak into a stairwell and come out at the top of a large amphitheater. Down below, the front of the stage is made to look like a barn.

"Doesn't anybody care if we're in here?" I ask.

She shrugs. "Looks empty to me."

Taking a seat on one of the aluminum benches, we get straight to eating, not even bothering with plates and silverware. "So," Vanessa says, inhaling a biscuit. "Are you finally going to tell me what's going on? Or do I have to drag it out of you like always?"

"What d'you mean?"

"Something's up with you, Luke. Why else would you text me out of the blue?"

"I already told you," I say, licking gravy off my thumb. "I was having a bad day."

"Yes. But you didn't tell me why. Which is very on-brand for you."

I shrug. "I didn't feel like working at the warehouse again this summer."

She gives me a look. "Right. Because working as a dishwasher at Wanda World sounds so much more rewarding."

I wish I could be honest with Vanessa. But if tell her why I left the factory—to escape Whizzer and Bulldog, and their homophobic comments—I'd have to tell her why I broke up with her, too. And I don't want to hurt her any more than I already have.

"What about you?" I ask, changing the subject. "Weren't you supposed to be in Nashville this summer? At your fancy design job?"

"It was an internship, not a job. And I decided not to go."

"Why?"

She takes another bite of chicken-fried steak. "Didn't seem like it was worth all the fuss. If I want to be a stylist, I should just go out there and do it, right? Do I really need to learn how to make a photocopy and take someone's coffee order first?"

"Yeah, I guess not."

"For example . . ." She waves her hand in my direction. "I could do wonders fixing this."

I look down at my outfit. "What's wrong with jeans and a T-shirt?"

"For starters, there's a hole in your shirt. And you should stop wearing hats. They cover your best feature, which is your eyes."

I take off my cap. "Whatever. All my features are my best."

She hits my shoulder playfully and a silence falls between us. But it's more familiar and comfortable than awkward. Vanessa pulls her long hair to the side to cool off her neck. In the distance, shrieks of delight erupt from a roller coaster as it flips riders upside down.

"Why'd you tell me about the job opening at the restaurant?" I ask. "You didn't have to do that. Not after . . . uh, everything that happened."

"I know." She offers up a half smile, like maybe these wounds are still a little too fresh. "But you were my friend first. And I don't give up easily on my friends."

I try to match her smile, but it feels forced. I'd like to think I would've helped Vanessa if the situation were reversed. But ever since our breakup, I've done my best to avoid her.

"Hey," Vanessa says. "I've been meaning to ask about your mama."

"Oh. Yeah, thanks. She's . . ." I clear my throat, trying not to sound too glum. "She's on bed rest again."

"Did she have another flare-up?"

"A few weeks ago."

"Luke, I'm so sorry to hear that."

"It's okay. She's home from the hospital now. It's just hard not knowing when the next one's gonna happen. Or if things will get worse before they get better."

Vanessa places her hand on my knee. "I know that's not easy for y'all. Please tell your mama I said hello, and that I'm thinking about her."

"I will, thank you."

When she takes her hand away again, it makes me kind of sad.

Sometimes I forget what it feels like to be touched. Even platonically.

"What'd your mama say about you working at Wanda World?" Vanessa asks.

I look down at my feet. "Uh . . ."

"Don't tell me she doesn't know."

"I just started working here. It hasn't come up yet."

"Luke Reginald Barnes!"

"You *know* that's not my middle name."

"I know, but it sounds better when I'm yelling it at you."

"My family's got history with Wanda Jean," I remind her. "I don't want Mama knowing my nana's probably rolling over in her grave right now. I'll tell her eventually. When she's feeling better."

Vanessa gives me a dubious look, and I can't say I blame her. Taking a job here was not my brightest move. There are dozens of other restaurants in Jackson Hollow I could've applied at. But this seemed so easy. I didn't have to pad my résumé or spend a week running around filling out applications first.

"Don't worry about me," I say. "I'll figure it out."

"I do worry about you, Luke Reginald Barnes. Way more than I should."

When she says my name this time, it's much softer. And it leaves an ache in my chest. Vanessa really cares for me. And I care for her. I hate that *I'm* the reason things didn't work out between us.

"Believe it or not," she says, handing me my slice of pie, "I'm glad we're working together this summer. Maybe we'll quit being so stubborn and hang out like this more often."

"I'd like that," I say.

After we're done eating, I don't trust myself to leave the park with her. I'm afraid I'll end up doing something I'll regret later, like suggesting we try getting back together. I already know things can't work between us. And yet there's still a part of me that wants to try. *That wants to be straight.*

"I think I'll hang out here for a while," I tell Vanessa.

"Can't get enough of Wanda World, huh?"

"Yeah, this bench is really calling my name right now."

After standing on my feet all day, it does feel good to lie back on the hard aluminum. But the relief's only temporary. As I listen to the sound of Vanessa's footsteps moving farther away, my loneliness comes rushing back, ready to swallow me whole.

"See you tomorrow, Luke."

"Yeah. See you then."

I'm not usually one to cry, but I pull my cap over my face.

Just to be safe.

Chapter

8

EMMETT

Stepping out onstage with my guitar, it's hard not to imagine what the amphitheater will look like when it's full. Two to three shows a day, five to six days a week. That's a lot of people to perform for. A lot of people to *fuck up* in front of.

But I'm not here to worry about the Jamboree. Tonight, I'm working on my song for the open mic. Which is perhaps even more terrifying. Writing a song is personal. I'll no longer have someone else's lyrics to hide behind.

What if my song isn't good enough?

What if no one cares what I have to say?

Part of me feels like this is already a lost cause. But it's not like Wanda Jean started out with her own amusement park and a string of multiplatinum hits. When she moved to Nashville, all she had was her guitar and a notebook full of songs. If she found the courage to put her own material out there, there's no reason I can't, too.

Grabbing a folding chair, I set myself up at the edge of the stage. "Good evening," I say. "My name is Emmett Maguire, and I wrote this song."

No, too stiff. And definitely not country enough.

"Hey, I'm Emmett. I hope y'all enjoy my song."

Playing the chords, I let my fingers warm up first. As the sound bounces around the empty amphitheater, I try adding the lyrics I have so far:

People believe in fairy tales
Spend their whole lives waiting for one
But knights in shining armor can be dull
Don't gotta marry a prince to have your fun

Yeah, sometimes at night I get lonely
Doesn't mean I don't like being alone
Cute boys are cute, but so what
Gonna find that happy ending on my own

So just turn around
With your boots
And those jeans
Ain't looking for no man of my dreams

I press down on the strings of my guitar, stopping their vibrations. *Jeans* and *dreams* aren't a perfect rhyme. But if you lay on a thick-enough accent, no one can tell. I try the chorus again. This time with a more exaggerated twang:

So just turn around
With your boots
And those jeans
Ain't looking for no—

I stop, looking up from my guitar to catch something in the top row of seats. No, not something. *Someone.* I squint, trying to get a better look at them. But they're wearing a hat, and it's too far away to make out their face.

They must've noticed me, because they quickly get up to leave. Only once they reach the exit, they pause, then turn back around and start heading toward the stage. *Toward me.* As they get closer, it finally dawns on me.

Holy shit.

I know those boots.

Did I just sing my Dream Cowboy into existence? No. That's impossible. But why is he here? And more importantly . . . *did he hear the lyrics I wrote about him?*

I feel light-headed. And not in a swoony way. I didn't think it could get more humiliating than running into him while dressed like a donkey.

I was wrong.

Dream Cowboy pauses halfway down the aisle. "Sorry, I wasn't meaning to eavesdrop."

"What?" I ask, even though I totally heard what he said.

He walks down another flight of steps. "I said I'm sorry for eavesdropping on you. I didn't know anyone else was in here."

"Oh. Yeah."

He puts his hands in his pockets. "Anyhow, I thought I'd let you know I got the job."

"The job? Oh, *the job*. Which restaurant?"

"Granny's Cupboard."

"No way, I eat there all the time! I haven't seen you, though."

Shit, does that make it sound like I've been looking for him? I mean, I totally have. But he doesn't need to know that.

"I work in the kitchen," he says. "As a dishwasher."

"Oh. Cool."

"Yeah." He takes his hands out of his pockets and then immediately shoves them back in. "I'm Luke, by the way."

"Emmett."

"I know. I heard you earlier. When you were pretending to introduce yourself?"

Heat races to my cheeks as I silently curse the acoustics of the amphitheater.

Luke smiles. "I almost didn't recognize you. Without the tail."

This cannot be stated emphatically enough: *I really hate my life right now.*

"You're a performer here, right?" he asks.

"Yes. But I only play a donkey for one song. I'm usually in my human suit. I mean, my human skin. I mean . . . I'm not usually dressed like that."

He bites his bottom lip, probably fighting back a laugh. "Got it."

"Our first show is next week," I say. "You've probably seen our posters around. Wanda's Good Time Jamboree? I don't mean for that to sound conceited. The thing about the posters, I mean. It's just that we're kind of a big attraction at the park. We're, like, the best show there is. Okay, wow. That sounded worse."

"No, it sounds cool," he says. "Maybe I'll check it out."

"Oh, I can give you my phone number!"

Why, Emmett?

Just . . . . why?

"What I meant," I try to explain, "is that I could get you into the show for free. If you texted me ahead of time."

He rubs the back of his neck and looks down at his boots. *The ones I wrote a fricking song about.* I'm coming on way too strong.

"Sorry," I say. "That was weird. You don't have to take my number."

"No. Um. It's nice of you to offer."

Luke meets me at the edge of the stage. But he can't bring himself to look at me. Not that I'm surprised. He takes his phone out and I give him my number, which I'm certain he's going to delete as soon as he leaves.

"I didn't realize what time it was," he says, slipping his phone back into his pocket. "I should go. But, um, thanks again for your help the other day. And good luck with the show. I'm sure you'll be great."

Yeah, I'm definitely never hearing from him. A wave of disappointment washes over me as I watch him turn around and walk away. Which doesn't make sense. Because according to my song, that's exactly what I wanted to happen.

Parking my car in Aunt Karen's driveway later, I try not to dwell on the myriad ways I've embarrassed myself in front of Dream Cowboy, whose real name is Luke. Thankfully, I'm quickly distracted by a spirited chorus of "Delta Dawn" coming from inside Aunt Karen's garage. And it's not only Tanya Tucker's voice I'm hearing. Aunt Karen is *really* going for it.

If I know my aunt, she's in her zone right now. She turned her garage into an artist's studio, though I haven't seen her spend much time in there since I arrived. Not with Grady coming over every night.

When I open the side door, I'm expecting Aunt Karen to be covered in clay, or paint, or thirty layers of wood glue. But she's not even wearing her artist smock. She's in her regular clothes, pressing down on a lever that looks like it's attached to a giant sandwich press.

When she finally notices me, she clutches her chest. "Emmett! You scared me. How long have you been standing there?"

"Um, just for a second."

I step into the garage. There's a large supply of padded envelopes and bubble wrap on a table off to the side. "I'm almost done in here," Aunt Karen says, turning down her music. "I made some sweet tea earlier. Why don't you go pour us some and I'll meet you inside?"

"What are you making?" I ask, stepping closer.

She glances uneasily at the press and lifts the lever back up. It's for T-shirts, not sandwiches. She peels a strip of plastic off the fabric and holds up the shirt for me to see. It's a drawing of Wanda Jean, winking and pointing her finger. Below her is a lyric from a song she wrote about her cheating ex-husband, Wyatt: *Darlin', even a wet blanket like you can't put this flame out.*

"Whoa, you designed that yourself?"

Aunt Karen folds the shirt and places it on the table. "Yep. I also have key chains, coffee mugs, and a dozen different tote bags." She gestures to all the merchandise in her garage. I check out some of the other quotes she has:

WWWJD: What Would Wanda Jean Do.

Baby, the only thing blue about me is my rhinestones.

Confidence is easy . . . just wear a bigger wig!

"These are cool," I say. "When'd you start making them?"

Aunt Karen piles her hair on top of her head, letting it fall back down before sighing heavily. "A while ago. I was going to send you some, but . . . I was too embarrassed, I guess."

"Embarrassed? Of what?"

"This is how my bills get paid these days, Emmett. No one wants to buy my sculptures; the things I pour my heart and soul into. But some cheaply made T-shirt? A set of Wanda Jean beer koozies?" She shakes her head. "People love spending money on that crap."

As she turns off the press and starts cleaning up the strips of plastic at her feet, my heart twists. I hate to think of Aunt Karen giving up on sculpting. My parents might not get her lifestyle, but I like that she's different.

I'm different, too. And Aunt Karen understands that. She doesn't think my dream of becoming a country music singer is irresponsible or too far-fetched. She knows that choosing to be an artist is a valid choice. But if she's still struggling to make it as an adult, what hope do I have?

After going inside and pouring ourselves some sweet tea, Aunt Karen and I head to her backyard, which is full of mismatched lawn furniture, overgrown plants, and enough DIY mason-jar candles to keep the local fire department on their toes. It's a little chaotic, but when you add it all together, it just works. Kind of like Aunt Karen.

"Okay," she says, taking a seat on a wicker sofa with sherbet-orange cushions. "Enough about my problems. Tell me how rehearsal went today."

"Better. But still not great."

She gives me a look. "Is it possible you're being too hard on yourself? Because Grady told me you're doing fine."

"No offense, but I'm pretty sure Grady's only saying that to be nice. He's not at rehearsals. He hasn't seen how many times they've had to stop and go over the blocking with me."

"Emmett." She crosses her arms, not buying it. "The man has eyes and ears all over the place. He'd know if the show was in trouble. Did you know he's personally in charge of Wanda Jean's appearances at the park?"

"He is?"

In the past two decades, Wanda Jean has become a bit of a recluse. She doesn't tour or do concerts anymore, and she hasn't put out new music in at least a dozen years. But Wanda World is her baby. And, occasionally, she'll pop in to surprise her fans.

"Unfortunately," Aunt Karen says, "it's very top secret. You know how rarely she goes out in public these days. Not that I haven't begged him for a hint. I mean, if I had a choice between meeting Jesus Christ and Wanda Jean . . . *Wait*, would that make a good T-shirt?" She takes a moment to consider it, then shakes her head. "Too religious. Anyhow, what were we talking about?"

"Grady."

She leans back into the cushion with a dreamy sigh. "Isn't he the best? I never planned to settle in one place for long. But now that I have Grady, well, I can't see myself leaving Jackson Hollow. That's why I ended up getting this." She traces her finger along the feather tattoo on her arm. "So I can still feel free, even if I'm tied to one place."

After pausing to take a sip of sweet tea, a mischievous smile spreads across her face. "Speaking of top secret, I've been dying to tell you something."

"Okay?"

"We're getting married."

"You and Grady? Oh my God! Congratulations!"

I give her a hug; she squeezes me so hard I almost pop.

"It's not official yet," she says. "But we've been talking about it. I don't like all the spectacle that comes with a traditional wedding. I mean, fuck the patriarchy, right? All I want is a small gathering as we stand barefoot somewhere in the sand." She laughs, covering her face. "I never thought I'd be the type of girl to dream up a beach wedding. But here we are!"

"Shut up, I will totally wear a Hawaiian shirt for you," I tease.

"You don't think I'm a sellout?"

"For wanting to get married?"

She shrugs. "It's pretty conventional."

"Who cares? You seem happy."

She squeals, letting it echo throughout her backyard. "I am!"

When we go back inside, instead of working on my song or practicing for the Jamboree like I should, I lie down on my bed and think about Aunt Karen. Even though no one's buying her sculptures and she's stuck making T-shirts, it's nice that she has Grady to look forward to at the end of the day. And maybe I'm a little jealous of that.

Taking out my phone, I play some Wanda Jean and open my texts. I have a bunch of messages from my friends from back home, asking how rehearsals are going and filling me in on the drama I've missed so far. But I don't answer them. Instead, I stare at my phone and wait. Just in case Dream Cowboy didn't delete my number after all.

Chapter
9

LUKE

I have no idea how long I've been sitting in our driveway. It feels like only a few minutes. But the pink sky in my rearview mirror tells me otherwise. I should've come home sooner. Or at least saved my slice of pecan pie for Gabe and Amelia. I'm sure they're hungry, waiting for me to fix supper. It's just . . .

I can't stop thinking about Donkey Boy.

I mean Emmett.

It's not my fault I was eavesdropping; we were in a public space. But hearing him practice his music . . . I don't know, it felt so personal. I really liked his voice. And he had that line about feeling lonely at night, but also not minding being alone. I felt like I could understand what he was saying. I think that's why I talked to him.

Emmett also sang about how he's not looking for a man of his dreams. Which, yeah, I'm not, either. Maybe that's why I was blushing so much when he gave me his number. Maybe that's why I panicked. When Cody and I first hooked up, I was drunk off my ass. I didn't have liquid courage this time. So to exchange numbers with Emmett, even under seemingly platonic circumstances, made my pulse race.

Emmett's a cute guy, though. And I'm sure he gets lots of numbers.

He was probably just being polite.

Heading inside, I find Amelia sprawled on the couch in the family room, with a bag of Twizzlers and her iPad.

"Where've you been?" she asks, not bothering to look up.

"Please tell me that's not your supper."

She shrugs, casually reaching for another Twizzler.

"Did you at least make sure Gabe got something to eat?"

Her eyes remain glued to whatever music video she's watching, and she's mouthing along to the lyrics as she continues to ignore me.

Just as I'm about to raise my voice and get ugly, a loud pop comes from the kitchen, like the sound of glass shattering.

Fuck. *Gabe.*

I'm expecting tears. Or worse: blood. But when I run in, it's Mama, not Gabe, who's standing in front of the fridge, with a collection of broken glass and pickle spears at her feet.

"Mama. What are you doing?"

"It's okay," she says. "I didn't drop it because I'm tired. I grabbed the jar by the lid, and it was loose."

"You shouldn't be downstairs," I say, grabbing the broom and dustpan from the closet.

"Gabe and Amelia were hungry. I was fixing them something to eat."

Heat creeps up my neck as I sweep clean the mess. I should've been here, taking care of my family. Not hanging around Wanda World, washing extra dishes and talking to Emmett.

"Honestly, Luke," Mama says. "I'm fine. If I wasn't feeling up to it, I would've stayed in bed. I know my limits."

As if to prove her point, Mama grabs a roll of paper towels and joins me on the floor. "Shame about the pickles," she says, sopping up their juice. "They were the only condiment we've got in this house."

"I've been meaning to go grocery shopping," I say.

When I look up at Mama, she's biting her bottom lip. "I didn't realize the cupboards were so empty," she says. "Do you need some money from Keith? I know we've been asking a lot of you lately. Once I get the okay to start working again—"

"It's fine, Mama. Let's just worry about supper for now."

As I empty the dustpan into the trash, Mama checks on the burgers she's got cooking on the stovetop. "We're all out of buns," she tells me. "So maybe you can toast some bread? And I guess we're gonna be topping them with mayo, Lord help us."

Mama wasn't kidding about our condiment situation. The ketchup bottle is squeezed dry, and there are only a few dollops of Dijon mustard left. But, actually, if we have a lemon and some olive oil, I might be able to save the day.

The lemon I find in the back of the crisper's withered, but it'll have to do. After combining the mustard and some mayo in a bowl, I drizzle in a little oil olive, add a few drops of lemon juice, and finish it off with a pinch of salt. After whisking everything together, I give it a taste. It's a bit acidic. Which I like, but Gabe and Amelia won't. So I open the cupboard and search for one final ingredient.

"Honey mustard aioli," I say, presenting it to Mama.

Mama grabs a Tater Tot off the baking tray she just pulled from the oven and dips it in. "Mm, that's good. Where'd you learn to make that?"

"Um . . . one of Nana's cookbooks."

Mama smiles. Which she wouldn't be doing if she knew I picked

☆ 71 ☆

it up from watching a prep cook at Granny's Cupboard.

Our meal may be a bit slapped together, but it's nice to have Mama sitting at the kitchen table with us. Even if she barely touches any of the food herself. And even if Amelia tries to spoil it by bringing her iPad.

"You know the rules, baby doll. No screens at the table."

"But I'm not even watching it," Amelia whines.

Gabe lifts the top slice of bread off his burger, making a face.

"We don't listen to music while we eat," Mama says. "Especially not country music."

"This is Maren Morris. She's country *and* pop."

Mama inhales sharply and Amelia pauses her iPad, sulking as she pushes a Tater Tot around her plate. "I don't get what's so bad about country music. Nana liked it."

"Your nana did like it," Mama says, suddenly looking tired again. "But it also broke her heart. Now, if you wanna listen to that kind of music, that's fine. Just not at the table. And not in front of me."

Except for the sound of Gabe scraping the aioli off his toast, the table stays silent.

"Why'd it break her heart?" Amelia asks.

I shoot her a look. She knows better than to push Mama on this. Besides, it's not like she doesn't already know the answer. If you type Nana's name into a search engine, you can read all about it online.

"Because she loved it," Mama says. "But then her career was over and she was sad she couldn't do it anymore."

That's an extremely simplified version. What Mama's leaving out is that Wanda Jean and Nana used to be best friends. And their manager—Wyatt, our grandfather—was Wanda Jean's husband first, before he left her to run off and marry Nana instead.

Thankfully, Amelia gives it a rest and Mama changes the subject by asking how my day was. I know I should tell her about Wanda World, but now's obviously not a good time.

"Work's fine," I say.

Mama smiles. "I'm sure they're glad to have you back this summer."

"I wanna new piece of toast," Gabe announces.

"We don't waste food," Mama tells him.

"But it smells funny."

"You didn't even try it," Amelia says.

"I don't like it. It's gay."

All the air is suddenly sucked out of the room, and I look down at my plate, hoping my face isn't turning beet red. Even if it's not, I'm sure everyone can hear my heart thumping away in my chest.

"Where'd you learn that word?" Mama asks.

Gabe shrugs, making a face like he knows he did something bad.

"I don't wanna hear you use it again. I'm serious, Gabriel."

There's an edge to Mama's voice. And, yeah, it hurts to know she'd be ashamed of me if she knew I was gay. But it's not like this is new information. So do what I always do: push my feelings back down and ignore them.

After we're done eating, I clean the kitchen by myself, which is a breeze compared to the restaurant. It's dark outside by the time I finish. And now that I finally have time to slow down and rest, I can't shut my brain off.

Did Emmett want my number so he could invite me to his show, or was it something more than that?

Were we flirting?

Mama's reaction to hearing Gabe use the word *gay* comes creeping back to me, so I shake Emmett from my thoughts and sit back down at the table to make a shopping list. I already know I won't have enough money to buy everything we need. I don't get my first paycheck from the restaurant until next week. And Wanda World pays less than the factory did. At the time, I was too excited about taking a job in a kitchen and getting away from Whizzer and Bulldog to care. But now, as I stare at my long shopping list, I see how selfish I've been.

Grabbing my keys from the counter, I decide to head to the Shop & Save. They're open all night and my money will stretch further there. Only once I'm back in my truck it's like I'm on autopilot. Instead of heading into town, I make a detour to the abandoned old diner off Highway 12.

Sitting in the parking lot, I cut my headlights and listen to the katydids as they call out to each other under the starry night sky. I like coming here when I need to think. It's like my own little corner of Jackson Hollow that nobody else seems to remember.

Before Wanda World, this strip of highway was probably the busiest spot in town. Which means my nana might've eaten here when she was my age. Before she moved to Nashville. Before she had her big falling-out with Wanda Jean and country music turned its back on her.

Mama doesn't usually talk about Nana, so it was strange having her come up at the table tonight. The few memories I do have of her are fuzzy. I mostly recall little details. Like the beaded rosary she kept on her nightstand, or the taste of watermelon that time she caught me sucking on a Jolly Rancher in church and made me spit it into her hand.

Just because I didn't know my nana doesn't mean I don't miss her, though. That's why I like using her cookbooks. That's why I like this diner. It makes me feel like we have a connection to each other.

I can't imagine Nana would like me working at Wanda World. But if I hadn't taken the job, I think I would've regretted it. Every chef has to get his start somewhere.

If I were the type of person to have big dreams, I'd want to open my own restaurant someday. Heck, it'd be cool to fix up this diner. I could cook *real* Southern food. A mixture of modern dishes and some of the classics from Nana's cookbooks.

A week ago, I would've dismissed that idea altogether. And while I still think it's too far out of reach, maybe there's a small part of me that wants to believe it wouldn't be impossible.

There are other things that seem out of reach for me.

Things that scare me even more.

Grabbing my phone, I pull up Emmett's info. I haven't been able to get him out of my head since I heard him practicing his song earlier tonight. I should delete his number, force myself to forget about him. That's what Mama would want me to do.

But what if I end up regretting it? If I hadn't quit the factory, I wouldn't be working in a kitchen right now. Maybe something good can come from this, too. I just have to find the courage to take that first step.

A warm evening breeze blows through my truck.

The katydids continue to chirp.

Hey, I text. It's Luke.

You still up?

Chapter 10

EMMETT

At the end of our final dress rehearsal this afternoon, Miss Trish had only one note for me—and it wasn't even critical. She said she could no longer see me concentrating on my steps. I finally had a smile on my face like I was enjoying myself.

I wish I could take the credit. But I was just imagining what the perfect first date with Luke would be. Would we hang out at the Frosty Freeze in town, laughing as we tried to lick the ice cream dripping down our cones? Would we enjoy the cool air-conditioning of a movie theater, blushing as we reached for popcorn at the same time? Or would we spend the evening at Wanda World, riding the Ferris wheel to the top, the entire park at our feet? I mean, if there's a better place for a first kiss than that, I can't think of it.

Not that I'm assuming there's going to be a kiss. Or that this is even a date. When Luke texted me again after rehearsal and asked me to meet him at the Old Gristmill, I assumed that was the name of a restaurant. I imagined crisp white tablecloths and dinner by candlelight. When I arrived at the address he sent me, however, I quickly discovered that the Old Gristmill is *literally an abandoned old gristmill*, complete with boarded-up windows and rotting wood.

It's not the type of place you invite someone for a first date.

It's the type of place you invite someone when you want to make sure no one's around to hear their screams as you harvest their organs.

I check my phone again. Luke's fifteen minutes late. I tried texting him when I first got here, but I'm in the middle of nowhere with no reception. I don't know how much longer I should wait. I could be practicing my song for the open mic or working on my demo tape.

I could be. But I don't *want* to be.

A few minutes later the sound of gravel crunching under tires fills me with hope, and a blue truck, dimpled with rust spots, pulls into the parking space at the top of the hill. I run a hand through my hair and double-check my breath.

Luke steps out of his truck, wearing jeans and a plain white T-shirt. I glance down, second-guessing my decision to wear a salmon-pink polo shirt. I mean, I love this shirt. But why did I dress like a preppy city boy when Luke looks like he could be on a billboard for today's hottest country music stars?

As he makes his way toward me, I bite the inside of my lip to keep from smiling too hard. His sandy blond hair is damp, like he recently got out of the shower. *Great.* Now all I can think about is the lucky bar of soap that got to glide over every last inch of his glistening body.

"Sorry," he says, joining me down by the mill. "I got off work late."

"That's okay. I just got here."

Lies. I was ten minutes early.

I try not to objectify him, but it's impossible. I admire his forearms. How tan his skin is. The way the sleeves of his T-shirt hug his biceps. *Fuck. I'm staring.* In an attempt to focus my gaze elsewhere, I lock eyes with him.

"I'm sorry, what?" I say, mesmerized by two irises that can only be described as golden-honey-dreamboat brown.

His lips stretch into a smirk. "I didn't say anything."

"Oh. Sorry. I thought you asked me a question."

"Nope."

An awkward silence descends upon us. Well, an awkward silence *and* a swarm of gnats. Which, honestly, is a welcome distraction at this point.

"You wanna take a walk?" Luke asks, swatting the gnats away.

"Um . . . okay. Where?"

"Along the water."

I look down at my pristine Top-Siders.

"Don't worry." He kicks off his boots. "We'll leave them here."

Luke leads me down to the creek, which is wider and rockier than I expected. Lake Michigan's the third largest lake in the United States, so it's not like I don't know how to swim. But when it comes to bodies of water, I guess I'm more used to Oak Street Beach and the Chicago Riverwalk.

"We have to go across," Luke says, rolling up his jeans. *Damn.* It's like those boring costume dramas my parents watch. The ones where some man with excellent posture and a stuffy cravat is scandalized by a woman showing off her ankles. I get it now. It's sexy.

In front of us, a line of rocks dots its way across the stream. Some of them are submerged, slick with the cool, clear water that rushes by. Luke doesn't hesitate in crossing. As I try to follow him, I take my first step into the creek and gasp.

He turns around. "You okay?"

"Cold," I say, wincing as I try to keep my balance.

Luke continues on with a chuckle. I'm glad to have his back to me again. This way, when I slip and fall, I won't have to die from embarrassment. I can just float down the creek and let the water carry me off to a more natural death.

By some small miracle, we both make it across safely. There's a clearing on this side of the shore, and the wet sand feels good as it squishes between my toes. Even the gristmill looks less menacing now.

"It's nice down here," I say.

"You've never been before?"

"No."

"Ah, I should've guessed. Are you a part-timer, then? Or seasonal?"

My heart pounds, like I've been caught in a lie. "I'm not sure what you're asking."

A smile sneaks across his face. And I swear, his eyes twinkle as the sunlight reflects off the creek. "Sorry, that's what we call the out-of-towners who work at Wanda World. Part-timers commute in from bigger towns. Seasonal people are only here for the summer."

"Oh, yeah. I'm from Chicago. Well, actually, Oak Park. A suburb. But I'm staying with my aunt for the summer. So I guess that makes me seasonal."

"What part of town does your aunt live in?"

"The regular part?"

He lifts one eyebrow. And even though it's not mathematically possible, the look on his face is 10 percent cocky and 100 percent cute.

"I'm guessing she's in the newer part of town," he says. "The part that wouldn't exist if Wanda World wasn't here."

There's a hint of judgment in his voice, like the newer part of town is bad. Aunt Karen's house isn't much. But it is in the neighborhood where all the fast-food chains are, not to mention the only Starbucks within a fifty-mile radius.

"Come on," Luke says. "I want to show you something."

Following a path that takes us farther into the woods, I attempt to climb over a fallen tree trunk and end up with a crotch full of bark. But when we come back out, we're standing on a giant boulder jutting over the creek. The water's calmer here. Probably deeper, too.

"This," Luke says, gesturing to the view in front of us, "is the real Jackson Hollow."

A breeze rolls through, rustling the leaves in the trees. I can see the gristmill in the distance. And beyond that, the deep purple peaks of the Great Smoky Mountains. It's beautiful. And Luke's right, as cool as it is to work at Wanda World, at the end of the day it's a business. But this place? This is where Wanda Jean grew up. All those songs she wrote about her childhood, about falling in love for the first time . . . they all happened right here.

Goose bumps run down my forearms. Not from the wind. From the sudden realization that Wanda Jean might've written a lyric about this very spot.

"No freaking way," I say.

I start humming, waiting until I get to the chorus of the song: *"Because that's what happens in a small town. People like talkin'. Gossip's a thrill. Good thing only the trees could see us, when you kissed me by the mill."*

Luke's eyebrows knit together.

"It's a Wanda Jean lyric! Do you realize what that means? She could've been standing in the same exact spot we're in now!"

His expression doesn't change.

"Sorry, I'm kind of a fan." Well, that's an understatement. But I don't want to scare him too much yet. "I'm sure it's a lot less impressive when you live here," I say. "You're probably used to all this stuff by now, huh?"

He takes a seat on the boulder. "Yeah, I don't listen to her music."

I almost choke. "Are you serious? But you live in Jackson Hollow! How can you grow up in the birthplace of Wanda Jean Stubbs and not have an appreciation for her? That's like being a fish in the ocean and saying you don't enjoy going for a swim."

"Um . . . I'm not sure that analogy works."

"Hold up. I need to understand this better." I take a seat next to him. "If you're not a fan of Wanda Jean, who do you listen to?"

"No one. I don't like country music."

Oh my God. He's serious.

"Wow," I say. "I can't believe you don't have any taste."

Luke's jaw tightens, and I start to think I've pushed him too far, but then he leans back on his palms and gives me another half smirk. "Okay, I'll bite. What's so great about country music? Enlighten me."

"Um . . . *everything*."

"Hmm. Real specific answer. Thank you. You've converted me."

His sarcasm catches me off guard. I give his shoulder a playful shove—which, damn, feels good.

"I'm not done yet," I say, trying to collect my thoughts. There are a million reasons why I love country music: Each song tells a story. Sometimes it's fun and campy—and sometimes it hits upon something so real and so true, you're certain whoever wrote it was able to peer into your soul and put everything you were feeling into words.

But my favorite thing about country music is its ability to take me somewhere else.

"This is going to sound silly," I say. "But I need you to close your eyes."

Luke gives me a funny look.

"Come on, just do it."

He closes his eyes. And when I'm certain he's not peeking, I do the same.

"Okay, here's what I see when I listen to a good country song: Mud-splattered boots on a back porch. Red paint chipping on the side of a barn. A hot summer day and a cooler full of pop. Sparklers on the Fourth of July."

I crack one eye open, just to make sure he's not cheating.

He's not. There's a hint of a smile on his face, as though he can see it, too.

I take a deep breath and steel myself for what I want to say next: "I see two boys. Sitting on a boulder. Next to a pool of water."

Luke's eyes flutter open. If he's startled, he hides it well.

"I don't get it," he says. "What's any of that got to do with country music?"

"It transports me."

"It transports you here? To the swimming hole?"

"Well, maybe not here specifically. But to a simpler, happy place."

"Oh, I see how it is." He shakes his head. "You think we're a bunch of hicks. Should I be spitting my dip into an empty Big Gulp? Does that fulfill your little fantasy, too?"

"No. That's not what I meant. It's just . . ."

I pause. It doesn't matter how many times I come out; the fear of being rejected never fully goes away. And yet something tells me I can be honest with Luke. I'm still not sure what his orientation is, but he seems decent enough.

"I'm gay," I tell him.

His face softens; I try not to think about how badly I want to kiss him.

"I'm comfortable with it now," I say. "But it wasn't always easy. Growing up, part of me felt like I didn't fit in. And I assumed that was how my life was always going to be. But when I listened to country music . . . I could imagine I was living in a small town, kind of like this one. It gave me a home."

Luke picks up a loose rock and chucks it into the water. "I hate to break it to you, but not everyone in this town's exactly welcoming of gay people."

"You seem to be okay with me."

The tops of his ears turn pink. He opens his mouth to say something but quickly changes his mind.

"I'm not naive," I say. "I realize it's an idealized version of life in a small town. But I can still believe in the possibility of it, right? That's why I want to be a country singer. So I can perform the gayest country songs possible and help normalize it."

Luke looks at me again, and for a second, I think he's finally going to open up. Maybe he'll tell me he's gay. Maybe—if I'm lucky—he'll say he also feels something between us.

He scoops up another rock, bouncing it in his hand. "Well, you tried your best. But I'm sorry, I still don't like country music. In fact, the only reason I'm working at Wanda World this summer is because my ex-girlfriend got me the job."

"Oh," I say.

Because how else can I respond? I poured my heart out about being gay. About loving country music. And all I found out about him in return is that he hates country music and dates girls. I guess it was silly of me to get my hopes up.

Luke tosses the rock and it hits the water with a plop. As it makes its way to the bottom of the swimming hole, my heart sinks with it.

Chapter

11

LUKE

What the actual fuck is my problem?

Here's this cute boy, in a cute pink shirt, talking openly and honestly about being gay, and I choose *this* moment to bring up having an ex-girlfriend?

I could've told him the truth. For a second, I thought I was going to. But there was something about the way he was looking at me. Like he could tell what I was thinking. Like he already knew.

I panicked.

"It'll be getting dark soon," Emmett says. "Maybe we should head back?"

He sounds disappointed. Or maybe that's just me. I don't know what I thought tonight was going to be—a date, a hookup, two people hanging out together?—but whatever outcome I was hoping for, Emmett gave me the perfect opportunity to open up to him, and I chickened out.

I hate being a coward. It makes me want to overcompensate by doing something courageous. Like at last year's homecoming party, when Jason McCall called that sophomore kid a fag and I crushed an empty beer can against my forehead.

Okay, so that wasn't exactly courageous. But it did get Jason to stop, if only because it took all the attention off that poor kid and put it on me.

"We can't leave yet," I say, standing back up. "We haven't gone swimming."

"Um . . ." Emmett looks up at me. "Are you serious?"

I lift my shirt off over my head. "Dead serious."

Emmett looks away, like he's trying not to check me out. But his eyes keep finding their way back to me. Before I can lose my nerve, I unbutton my jeans and lose those, too. Although I'm wearing underwear, I couldn't feel any more exposed if I were standing here naked.

"C'mon," I say, trying to psych myself up. "It'll be fun."

Three steps—that's all I get before I reach the edge of the boulder and I'm suddenly flying through the air. The calm surface of the water below comes rushing up, and I break through it with a loud *whoosh*, plunging into the depths of the swimming hole. It's cold but invigorating. Every cell in my body is jolted into feeling alive.

In a matter of seconds, I'm back above the water and taking in a fresh gulp of air. But the feeling doesn't go away. It ripples through me.

Emmett's standing at the edge of the boulder, his mouth gaping open. "I can't believe you did that."

"It's not that cold," I lie. "You'll get used to it."

"No way. I'm not getting wet."

"I thought you wanted to live out your small-town fantasy?"

He peers over the edge, looking entirely unconvinced. After a little more waffling, he takes off his shirt, folding it up neatly before moving on to his shorts. It wasn't my intention to get Emmett half naked. But now that he is, I'm not complaining. He's definitely got that nerdy-cute musician thing going on.

Hugging an arm across his chest, Emmett looks down at the water.

"I'll give you a countdown," I tell him.

"Are there fish?" he asks.

I'm not usually one to giggle, but that sets me off.

"Are you . . . afraid?"

"No. Do the countdown."

I only get to "two" before he takes a running leap. His shriek echoes off the boulders around us as he cannonballs into the water. Air bubbles come up first. Then Emmett, reemerging with a dramatic gasp.

"Are you fucking kidding me? It's freezing!"

"Isn't Chicago on one of the Great Lakes?" I tease. "Or do you only swim in heated pools?"

"Shut up. Look at my teeth. They're chattering!"

Looking at Emmett's mouth, I suddenly want to kiss him. But how do I know he wouldn't tell someone about me? Mama's always saying you can't trust strangers. Of course, Mama would also say two boys shouldn't be kissing in the first place.

"Calm down, Rose," I say, pushing the thought out of my head. "You're not gonna die from hypothermia."

"Wait, was that a *Titanic* reference?"

"Um, maybe?"

"Oh my God, I hate you even more."

I slap water across his face and we both laugh. Despite wanting to seem tough, my body starts to shiver as well. We only last another minute before climbing out to grab our clothes. If it were earlier in the day, we could lie out and wait for the sun to dry us. But the boulder's covered in shade now, and the woods are getting dark.

"Here," I say, handing Emmett my T-shirt. "Use this. Yours is too nice."

He hesitates but pats himself dry with it. When I pull my shirt back down over my head, the drops of water that were on Emmett's skin mix with mine. It's strangely exciting. Like a striptease in reverse, where the act of putting your clothes on is hotter than taking them off.

By the time we get back to the gristmill, the sun has almost set. Behind the mountains, the sky looks like melted orange sherbet, with streaks of purple and pink running through it. Emmett might have an idealized version of what it's like to live in a small town. But that doesn't mean he's completely wrong. We do have our moments where life's better here.

"So," Emmett says. "Were you planning to head back home, or . . ."

I let his question hang in the air, unsure of my answer. There's something thrilling about hanging out with Emmett. It's like I can be myself around him. Kind of like I was with Cody. Except no one's drunk this time.

I'm sure he'd be cool with me telling him I'm gay. How could he *not* be? But what if I let my guard down around him and can't put it back up later? It's too dangerous. I may not like Wanda Jean. But that song of hers was right: People in this town love to gossip. There's no telling what rumors could be started about me. Still, I don't want this night to be over yet. I think back to when I first texted Emmett.

"Actually," I say, "there's something else I want to show you."

I offer to drive us there. But as soon as I turn in the parking lot, where overgrown weeds push their way up through the cracks in the asphalt, I second-guess myself. Cody was the only person who knew I was gay. But this place . . . the abandoned old diner, the secret dream I have for it . . . I've never shared that with anyone before.

"Wow," Emmett says. "Taking me to all the hot spots tonight, huh?"

"I knew you'd be impressed," I reply, trying to ignore the funny feeling in my stomach.

Emmett exits my truck. I follow him, still nervous. The diner's been shut down for a few decades now, and the inside's been torn apart and vandalized. But as we peer through the windows, I can still imagine what it used to look like. The row of shiny red stools at the front counter. The hungry customers who sat hunched over baskets of burgers and fries. The refrigerated display case, where slices of key lime and banana cream pie rotated under fluorescent lights.

"Very postapocalyptic," Emmett says. "But seriously. Is there some sort of significance to this place? Did Wanda Jean once work here?"

"I doubt it. If she had, it'd be a museum or five-star hotel by now."

"Hey, that sounds cynical."

"Am I wrong?"

He scrunches his nose. "Probably not."

We take a seat on the front steps. Now that it's dusk, the katydids have started their nightly symphony again. Maybe bringing Emmett here was a mistake. But when my head hits my pillow tonight, I don't want to feel regret. I want to feel like I did when I jumped into the water: fearless and alive. If I can't bring myself to tell him I'm gay, then maybe I can share something else.

"I'd like to have my own restaurant someday," I tell him. "I thought it'd be cool to fix this place up."

Before he has a chance to respond, I add: "It's silly."

"Why is that silly?"

"I can think of a million reasons," I say. "And they're all connected to money. I'd want to do it right, you know? Go to culinary school first. Earn my stripes working under some asshole chef at a fancy restaurant in New York City. Do a culinary tour of all the countries I can't afford to go to. Then, when I was done, I'd come back home and make the best Southern food anyone has ever tasted."

Emmett smiles. "Again, why's that silly?"

"It's not realistic."

"I want to make a living singing country music. Do you think that sounds realistic? No. But I'm not going to let it stop me from trying."

"Yeah, well, not everyone gets the luxury of trying."

I shouldn't make assumptions about Emmett. Even if he does wear nice polo shirts.

"Sorry," I say. "I didn't mean it like that."

"No, you're right." He nods, thinking it over. "I can always depend on my parents to bail me out. But that only makes me want to try all the harder. If I'm given an opportunity, the worst thing I could do is waste it, right? And I'm sorry, but I'm not backing down on what I said. You shouldn't give up on your dreams so easily, either."

He pushes a stray curl out of his face. He's cute when he's impassioned.

"I heard you practicing your song," I say. "You're good."

"Are you trying to change the subject?"

"No. I'm only saying it's different for me."

"How?"

"You want to be an artist," I tell him. "And you've got the talent for it. I'm just a dishwasher who likes to cook."

He gives me a look.

"What? It's a fact."

"That's not a fact. That's bullshit."

How would he know? We've only hung out for, what, a few hours? Even my friends from school don't know me that well.

"No offense," I say. "But why do you care so much?"

He shrugs. "It sounds like someone should."

I roll my eyes. But on the inside, a warmth spreads throughout my chest. Like my defenses are melting away.

"Let's start with this," Emmett says. "Why do you want to be a chef?"

"I don't know. Because I like to cook?"

"Come on. You can do better than that."

"Okay, fine. Give me a second."

I picture myself in our kitchen at home. Thumbing through the musty pages of one of Nana's cookbooks until I find a recipe to try. Not every dish has been a success. My spoon bread collapsed in on itself and I don't think grits have any business being made into a souf- flé. But Mama said my black bottom pie was as good as Nana's. And Amelia and Gabe are always begging me to make them hush puppies now.

"I like it when people enjoy my food," I say. "It makes me happy."

"Okay," Emmett says. "What else?"

I picture myself in a different kitchen. This one's fully stocked. With pots and saucepans on the stove, and the occasional plume of steam billowing up. I have my own set of knives—expensive ones, the kind that come in their own roll-up case. And as I stand there in my chef's coat, with a stack of clean white plates next to me, I can hear the buzz from the dining room, where hungry customers are waiting to eat.

"I like the possibility of creating something," I say. "Maybe there's a dish I'm known for. Or a classic I've found a way to make my own. I just think it'd be really cool if someone came to a restaurant because they wanted to taste *my* food."

Emmett smiles. "See? You're not a dishwasher. You're an artist!"

He's being smug.

Smug, but cute.

"You don't believe me, do you?"

"No," I say. "I don't."

"Okay, think of it this way. When I write a song, I'm creating something that was never there before. And when I'm done, I turn it over to my audience. You do the same thing when you're cooking. You can follow someone else's recipe, but it's always going to be different. Because it was made by you."

I want to tell him he's wrong. But that warm, happy feeling is only growing more intense. Part of me *does* want to believe what he's saying.

"Which is why you shouldn't give up yet," Emmett says. "Think of all the hungry people you'd be denying your art to."

I like how Emmett isn't afraid to say things like that.

I like how he goes after what he wants.

"You have to promise me," he says, fixing his eyes directly on mine.

I bite back a smile. "Yeah. Okay."

"No, you actually have to say the words out loud."

It feels silly, but Emmett doesn't seem embarrassed.

"I won't give up," I say. "I promise."

The words have a heavier weight than I was expecting them to. I guess I've never taken my cooking this seriously before.

"Okay then," Emmett says. "Now tell me more about your restaurant. Have you picked a name yet? I know you're not big on country music, but Wanda Jean really is your biggest selling point. Think of how many tourists would go to your restaurant if they thought it was associated with her."

"I wanna name it after my nana—I mean, my grandma," I say.

"Oh. Cool. What's your grandma's name?"

I feel myself bristle. I shouldn't have said that. But if I'm going to name my restaurant after anyone, it's sure as hell not Wanda Jean. Emmett must notice the change in my body language because the excitement fades from his face.

"We don't have to talk about your restaurant," he says. "Not if you don't want to."

I don't like talking about my nana with anyone. But Emmett's a good listener. And he did get excited about my cooking. So maybe I should trust him with this, too.

"Her name was Verna," I tell him.

His face lights back up. "Oh, that's the name of another country singer from Jackson Hollow. Verna Rose. She wasn't as famous as Wanda Jean, but a lot people still remember her. Wanda Jean and Verna were best friends. Until Verna ran away with their manager, who was also Wanda's husband. It became this huge scandal and basically ruined Verna's career. That's why they call her the Lost Rose of Country Music."

"Yeah," I say. "I know."

A silence falls between us. I can see Emmett slowly trying to work it out in his head. His expression goes from confused to astonished to doubtful. "When you say *you know* . . . is that because you're from Jackson Hollow and it'd be general knowledge to anyone who lives here? Or do you know because . . ."

I close my eyes, focusing on the sound of the katydids. "I know because Verna Rose was my grandmother."

When I open my eyes, Emmett's staring at me.

"What . . ." He pauses, searching for his words. "What's your last name?"

"Barnes."

"But that would mean . . . that would make . . . *Wyatt Barnes was your grandfather?*"

"Only on paper," I tell him.

I can already feel him looking at me differently. Unfortunately, Wyatt's last name isn't the only thing I inherited. We don't keep any pictures of him in our house. But it's not like they don't exist online. There's no denying I favor him.

"Holy shit," Emmett says, shaking his head. "I don't know what to say right now."

"It's better if you don't say anything," I tell him. "I don't like to talk about it."

"Why not?"

"Because my grandfather wasn't a good person. I know people blame my grandma for stealing him away from Wanda Jean. But everyone seems to forget that he ditched my grandma soon after and took all their money. He was supposed to be this great manager and all, but when people think about him now, they only remember him for being a womanizer and a drunk."

"But none of that's your fault," Emmett says. "I mean, you know you have nothing to be ashamed about, right?"

"Just promise me you won't tell anyone."

"Of course not," he says. "You can trust me, Luke."

He rests his hand on my knee. When I look up at him, I expect to find pity in his eyes, but there's none. Maybe it's foolish, but I think I do trust him. His hand hasn't moved. And part of me really wants to tell him I'm gay. But I still don't know how to say those words out loud. So I try something else.

"Can I kiss you?" I ask.

I'm not sure which one of us is more shocked. But I'm glad I said it. I'm tired of hiding from the things I want. If I want to be a chef and have my own restaurant someday, I should. If I want to kiss a boy, I should.

Emmett still looks startled.

"Or not," I say, panicking.

He leans forward and presses his lips against mine. It's a sweet, gentle kiss. Not like when Cody and I were together, drunk and fumbling in the front seat of my truck. Cody and I kissed like we were starving. Emmett kisses like he's savoring.

"Was that okay?" he asks, pulling away.

"Yeah," I say, a little breathless. "It was."

I lean in to kiss him some more. And it's like jumping into the swimming hole all over again. A jolt to the system, but the very best kind.

Chapter
12
EMMETT

Luke's lips should come with a warning label. *Caution: May impair your ability to drive or operate heavy machinery. Use with care.* That's the only way to explain the fuzziness happening in my brain right now. The blurred vision. The inability to do anything but smile.

Honestly, I feel kind of drunk.

Which is a problem.

"Listen up, y'all," Miss Trish says, talking over the pre-show buzz. She's wearing a pink sequin jacket that shimmers under the fluorescent lights in the dressing room, and her blond hair is teased to the heavens for our opening night performance.

"The Lord sure did bless me with a strong cast this year," she says, looking directly at Cassidy and Jameson. "And when y'all are big stars, you'd best not forget about us."

Jameson smirks, puffing his chest out.

Cassidy preens demurely.

Jessie and Avery roll their eyes.

"Every season I say I'm not gonna cry," Miss Trish continues. "And every season, y'all ruin my makeup!" She dabs carefully at the corners of her eyes. "Okay, go out there and make me proud. It's y'all's show now."

Everyone hollers and claps. I try to mimic their excitement, but I'm already back to thinking about Luke. *I can't believe I kissed the grandson of Wyatt Barnes and Verna Rose.* Not that his family changes how I feel about him. I liked him before I knew. But it's not as if I can ignore this new piece of information, either. I mean, he's related to country music royalty. Or, if not royalty, at least crucial footnotes.

Having absolutely no chill, I invited Luke to tonight's show. But he still maintains that country music's "not his thing." Which . . . *ugh.* But whatever, I'm willing to overlook it if it means I get to kiss him again.

"Emmett! Are you listening to me?"

I snap out of it to see Cassidy standing in front of me. Her stage makeup is flawless. Her curls are luxurious and buoyant. And her cleavage is prominently on display, yet still modest enough for a family show.

"I'm sorry . . . what?"

She groans. "Can we review our steps, please? For 'Calamity Joe'?"

Cassidy is lead vocal for that song. And at the end of the number, she does an intricate rope trick to lasso Jessie and me in our donkey costume.

"Oh, right." I try to clear all thoughts of Luke from my head. "Um . . . left turn, right turn. Two steps back. Spin. Whinny. Spin."

Her eyes almost pop straight out of her skull. "Are you kidding me right now? It's two steps *forward*! If you mess up, I'll be lassoing nothing but air, and it's going to make *me* look like the idiot. Not you."

"Yeah, I got it. Don't worry, it's easier for me to remember when I'm onstage."

"Don't worry? *Don't worry?* Oh my God, you have no idea how important tonight's performance is, do you? This is show business. Not some high school musical you invite your parents to."

"I know the right order, Cassidy. I swear."

I hate how whiny I sound. Like a little kid.

She closes her eyes and takes a deep breath. "I'm sorry. I didn't mean to yell." When she opens her eyes again, she's back to being perky, megawatt-smile Cassidy. "Have a great show, Emmett. We're all going to have a great show, okay?"

On her way out, she gives her curls one final fluff and performs a quick sign of the cross. If I didn't know any better, I'd say Cassidy was nervous.

"Don't worry about her," Avery says from the next mirror over.

"Yeah," Jessie agrees, leaning against the makeup table. "You know those steps inside and out by now."

Hardly. I managed to get through our final dress rehearsal without making a mistake. But that was before Luke and I made out. Will I really be able to concentrate on what steps I should be taking when I can be thinking about Luke instead?

"Maybe Cassidy's right," I say. "She's always so confident during rehearsals. So if she's freaking out right now, it must be because of me."

Avery and Jessie exchange a look.

"Oh God. Does *everyone* think I'm going to make them look bad?"

"This isn't about you," Jessie says.

"We didn't know if we should tell you or not," Avery says. "We didn't want to make you more nervous before the show. This being your first performance and all. . . ."

Okay, now I'm definitely freaking out. *What the hell are they talking about?*

Jessie bites her bottom lip. "Grady told Cassidy that Wanda Jean's making an appearance at the end of the show tonight."

I immediately break into a laugh. Because how absurd is that? *That I would see Wanda Jean in person? That I would be on the same fricking stage as her?* I mean, she's been known to make the occasional appearance around the park. Or pop into a show and surprise the audience every once in a while. But if Wanda Jean were making an appearance at one of our performances, Grady would've told Aunt Karen. *I'd* be the first cast member to know.

"Cassidy has to be wrong," I say.

"I don't think she is," Avery says. "I saw two security guards backstage already."

A bead of sweat breaks through the layer of foundation on my forehead. "But that means if we're onstage doing our thing . . . and Wanda Jean is in the wings, waiting to come out . . . then theoretically . . ."

"She could see us performing," Jessie says.

"That's why Cassidy's freaking out," Avery says. "That's why we're *all* freaking out."

My mouth goes dry. All thoughts of steps and spins fly out of my head. All thoughts of Luke fly out. Above us, there's a crackle of static. Our stage manager's voice comes on over the dressing room speaker: "This is your five-minute call to places. Five minutes, y'all."

If there's one thing I don't have time for, it's the luxury of panic. As soon as I step onstage, my adrenaline kicks in, and I don't stop moving. If I'm not stomping my boots, then I'm moving scenery or running backstage for a quick costume change. It's kind of a relief not to be able to think about how terrifying this is.

Once I make it through the first couple of songs, I actually start to enjoy myself. And the audience is certainly having a good time. After every song, I'm pretty sure I can hear Aunt Karen hollering louder than anybody else. She told me she was going to print up a T-shirt that read "Emmett's #1 Fan." I have no doubt she followed through with it.

Halfway through the show we have our big line-dance number. It's our most complex choreography by far. Even Jessie and Avery take time to review the steps before every rehearsal. If there were a song I was going to majorly fuck up, it'd be this one. But somehow, for the first time ever, I'm killing it. I'm so conditioned at this point, I don't even have to think about it. My body just knows what to do.

As we belt our final note, I slap my boot heel extra hard before stomping it back down. Except I must be getting too cocky, because I raise my *right* heel, instead of my left like everyone else.

Fuck.

Thankfully, the audience gives us our biggest applause yet. I'd say it makes me feel better about messing up, but there's no time to dwell on it. I run offstage, where I have sixty seconds to get into my half of the donkey costume.

"Did you see that?" I whisper to Jessie as we change in the wings.

"See what?"

"I ended on the wrong foot!"

Her eyes peek out through the gaping mouth of the donkey. "Big deal. Everyone messes up once per show. Now that it's happened, you don't have to worry anymore."

One of the dressers rushes over and attaches the two halves of our costume together. The smell of stale sweat fills my nostrils.

"Trust me," Jessie says from inside the suit. "We've got this."

The music for "Calamity Joe" starts up and Jessie leads us back onto the stage, where we immediately receive another round of applause. As Cassidy sings about what a stubborn old mule we are, I hear muffled laughter and the occasional scream of a delighted child through our stifling, fifty-pound costume. The audience is eating this up. They even clap along at the chorus:

> Stronger than a whirlin' tor-nader
> Meaner than an alli-gader
> Stubborn ol' Calamity Joe
> I can't help but love you so!

Toward the end of the song, the tempo picks up and Cassidy lets out a yodel, which is her cue to start her rope tricks. With my hands firmly on Jessie's hips, we begin our final steps for the big finish.

Left turn, right turn.

Two steps forward.

Spin. Whinny. Spin.

Since I'm in the back and have more ground to cover, I always get dizzy at this part. But that's why I have Jessie to hang on to. All I have to do is follow her lead until we stop spinning and wait for Cassidy to lasso us.

"*Stubborn ol' Calamity Joe,*" Cassidy sings.

I listen for the last line of the song, but all I hear is an "*oof.*" The next thing I know, there's the sound of fabric ripping. Which is followed by a thud. Which is followed by bright, blinding stage lights.

It takes my eyes a second to adjust. I look down and see Jessie. Or rather, the front half of a donkey costume with Jessie's legs sticking out.

I look over at Cassidy, whose face is stricken with panic as she holds the other end of the rope Jessie's feet are tangled up in.

I look out at the audience, who are all sitting up straight and waiting to see what the hell will happen now.

Nobody moves. The lights don't fade to black. We're all waiting for Cassidy to finish the song. But she's just standing there, completely frozen. After a silent eternity, I decide there's only one thing to do. I throw my arms in the air, breathe from my diaphragm, and belt out the last line: *"You can't help but love me so!"*

There's another beat of silence. And then, as if on cue, the audience laughs. I immediately run over and help Jessie to her feet, the audience breaking into applause as she stands back up. They become so enthusiastic, in fact, that we have no choice but to take a bow. I brace myself for the daggers undoubtedly shooting out of Cassidy's eyes. But when I look back over, she's still too shocked to move. The lights finally start to fade and Jessie and I run offstage together.

"I'm sorry," I say. "Was that my fault?"

"No. Cassidy threw the rope too early. I tripped over it."

We don't have much time to get out of our costume, but before I can unbutton the first strap to my overalls, a voice echoes across the amphitheater and stops me cold: "My goodness! That ol' donkey always was a wily little rascal!"

I'd recognize that voice anywhere. Its rich Southern twang. The way it sounds like a cold pat of butter melting on a fresh biscuit.

A chill runs through me, and I turn around. Wanda Jean is

walking out from the opposite side of the curtains. She's holding a bedazzled microphone and strutting across the stage in an orange jumpsuit dripping with sparkly fringe. When she waves to the crowd, they absolutely lose it.

I'm about to lose it, too. Though not from excitement.

I can't believe she saw us fuck up.

"Y'all are too kind," Wanda Jean says. "But let's hear it again for our performers. I count my blessings every day to have such a talented bunch."

As the audience claps, one of the dressers nudges me and helps me out of my costume. But I don't dare take my eyes off the stage. After all the time I've spent listening to her music, and studying her lyrics, and taping posters of her onto my bedroom walls . . . I can't believe I'm standing this close to her.

"Speaking of blessings," Wanda Jean says, walking toward center stage. "I have the greatest fans in the world. Y'all are so special to me. It wouldn't be right if I came out here and didn't perform a song for y'all."

The audience roars as though they each won a million dollars. Except this is way better than money. Because Wanda Jean *never* performs in public anymore. I look over at Jessie. Our mouths are both gaping open.

"This here's one of my favorites. I hope y'all enjoy it."

The music starts and my eyes instantly fill with tears. She's going to do "In My Rainbow." A song about acceptance and being true to yourself. A song that basically saved me from a lot of anguish when I first figured out I was gay. And as I stand in the wings and listen to her sing it now, it's like I'm hearing the lyrics for the first time.

They say that roses are red
And violets should be blue
The grass is better when it's greener
And the beauty of a sunrise
Comes from its orange and yellow hue

But what about the silver lining in a cloud?
Or winter's first glistening flake of snow?
Beauty lies in every color
When you look beyond the rainbow

Yes, tulips and daffodils are nice
But flowers need the soil to grow
You can be any color you want
And still be in my rainbow

When the song is over, Wanda Jean thanks her fans and quickly exits the stage. As the crowd cheers her off with a standing ovation and chants of her name, I'm still trying to process what happened. Did I really just watch my biggest hero, performing one of my favorite songs, in the greatest place on earth? Whatever this moment is, I'm not ready for it to be over. I want to stand here in the wings and soak it all in.

"Hey," Jessie whispers, waving her hand in my face. "Snap out of it."

"That was amazing," I say.

"Yeah, I know. But we have to get back onstage now."

Oh. Right. We still have a finale to perform.

"Where's your cowboy hat?" Jessie asks.

My cowboy hat. The thing that goes on my head. The thing Jessie and all our other castmates are currently wearing. *Fuck.*

I run backstage to the storage rack. And just as I grab my hat and turn around, my feet stop moving. Because standing before me in all her sparkling rhinestone glory, flanked by two refrigerator-sized security guards, is Miss Wanda Jean Stubbs.

And she's looking directly at me.

"Well, hey there, sugar."

Okay, so *this* is what it feels like to have a spiritual experience. To stand in the presence of something greater than yourself.

"We screwed up," I say, blurting out the first thing that comes to me.

She laughs. "You did great out there, kid. And you sure have a lot of grit. That's important. Never lose that."

My body quivers. There's so much I want to tell her: How much her music means to me. How it changed my life. How she's the reason I'm pursuing my dreams in the first place. But before I can get out so much as a "thank you," her security guards whisk her away.

The music starts back up.

If I don't leave now, I'll miss my entrance.

But I stand there anyway, watching Wanda Jean be escorted away. And I swear—before she goes, she looks over her shoulder and shoots me a wink. If I couldn't hear the rhinestone beads on her fringe swishing and clacking together, I'd be convinced I made the whole thing up.

Chapter

13

LUKE

Corn bread's not a complicated recipe. Especially if you cheat and use a boxed mix. Some people would call that Northern corn bread. It's sweeter and has a more cakelike density, which Gabe and Amelia like better anyhow. But tonight, I'm not taking any shortcuts. I pulled out our cast-iron skillet and made my batter from scratch. I even asked the guys at work to sneak me some bacon grease. This is going to be real corn bread. The Southern kind.

The timer on the oven goes off. But before I can get to it, my phone buzzes. Emmett's sending me a string of texts.

I'm out of control. I've contacted everyone in my phone.

It's just . . . SHE SAID I HAD GRIT!!!

Even my dad pretended to be impressed.

Ever since our kiss, Emmett's been messaging me nonstop. Not that I'm complaining. It's nice to have someone to talk to again. Someone who knows who I really am. It's just—Emmett's like a machine on his phone. I can barely keep up.

OMG. My dentist just texted back.

She sent me the dancing lady emoji.

I shake my head and smile, only half aware the oven's beeping.

It's a really big deal, I text back. *You should be telling everyone.*

Thank you for getting it. Even though you hate country music.

I didn't say I hate it. I said I don't listen to it.

The hate was implied.

You're never gonna let this go, are you?

Definitely not.

"Um, hello?" Amelia storms into the kitchen, shooting me a look as she stomps over to the oven and turns off the timer. "And Mama and Daddy think *I'm* the one who needs a limit on her screen time."

"I was gonna get that," I say, setting my phone back down. Picking up my wooden spoon, I lift the lid of the pot of collard greens I've got going on the stovetop. A cloud of steam billows out and I'm hit with a pungent odor. Dang, I still don't understand how something that tastes so good can smell so bad.

"Ew." Amelia peers into the pot like it's a cauldron full of dismembered body parts. "What's that?"

"You know what collards are, Amelia."

"Yeah. I know I don't like them."

"Well, maybe you'll like mine."

"Maybe I'll vomit."

I'm in too good a mood to let her get to me. "Why don't you go set the dining room table," I say, giving the greens another stir. "Use Mama's good napkins. The cloth ones."

"Why can't we eat in the kitchen?"

"The dining room's nicer."

"So?"

"So I'm the cook. I decide."

Amelia puffs out her cheeks like a blowfish. I hand her the silverware and send her on her way. Turning the heat off on the greens,

I chop some parsley for my main dish: cowboy casserole. It's not the most glamorous of meals. But I found it in Nana's cookbook and it fits our budget. I'm even using real potatoes instead of Tater Tots. If money weren't an issue, I would've fixed us fried pork chops, or blackened catfish, or—*oh shit.*

I forgot the timer was for my corn bread. Grabbing the oven mitt, I pull the skillet from the oven and set it on top of the stove. It's a little darker around the edges than I'd like, but the middle's a perfect golden brown. I smile, thinking about how Emmett said I was more than just a dishwasher who likes to cook.

As Keith heads upstairs to escort Mama down from her bedroom, I help Amelia finish setting up the dining room. Until tonight, this table's mostly been home to old church bulletins, Gabe's half-finished Lego projects, and a box of Christmas ornaments that never made it back down to the basement.

Moving a stack of junk mail, I spot an envelope with a red "Past Due" notice stamped on top. The envelope's already open, so I take a peek inside. My stomach drops. I don't know much about owning a house, but I'm pretty sure you're supposed to keep up with your property taxes. *Do Mama and Keith know this is still here? Do we not have the money to pay it?*

"My goodness," Mama says.

I drop the pile of mail on the sideboard cabinet and turn around to see Mama surveying the food we set out. "This looks too good to be true," she says.

"I helped," Amelia says.

"Begrudgingly," I add.

She sticks out her tongue.

"I wanna help," Gabe whines, showing up to the table with the Legos I just cleared away. He hasn't played with them in months, so of course he can't eat without them now.

"Don't worry," I tell him. "There are plenty of dishes y'all can wash later."

As the rest of us take our seats, Keith stifles a yawn. He works four overnights a week, ten-hour shifts each night. On his days off, he switches his sleep schedule back to match ours so he can spend more time with us, making his circadian rhythm more of a circadian clusterfuck.

"This looks nice, Luke," he says. "What's the special occasion?"

I kissed a boy and promised him I'd take my cooking more serious.

"No occasion," I say. "I thought we could start having family suppers more often. That way I can get more practice cooking."

Mama smiles. "That's a lovely idea. But you're already a great cook."

"Well, I could get even better. If I wanna cook professionally someday, I'll need to be good enough to get into culinary school."

The table is silent. I've never talked about wanting to be a chef before. Not until my conversation with Emmett.

"Isn't cooking school for rich folk?" Amelia asks.

Mama and Keith look at each other. I wait for one of them to tell Amelia she's wrong. That I could get a scholarship or find some other way to support myself. But their lips stay pressed tight.

"It was just an idea," I say. "We should eat before everything gets cold."

"It's good to have dreams," Mama says. "But let's focus on one thing at time for now, starting with this delicious-smelling meal."

She stretches her arms out. "Amelia, will you say grace?"

As I grab Gabe's sticky hand, I try not to let my disappointment show. I should've expected this reaction. They're just being realistic. Swallowing back my emotions, I close my eyes as Amelia leads the prayer.

"Dear Lord. We thank you for putting food on our table."

Buzz.

"We thank you for watching over our family."

Buzz.

"And we thank you for reminding us you're not supposed to bring your phone to the table, because it's not fair to those of us who've been told repeatedly that they can't use their iPad during supper. Amen."

Buzz.

Everyone's looking at me. I take my phone out and turn the vibrate setting to silent. But first, there are more texts from Emmett.

Hey, what are you doing after work tomorrow?

I have a break between shows if you want to hang out.

How do you feel about Ferris wheels?

"Sorry," I say, returning my phone to my pocket.

"Who was that?" Mama asks.

"No one."

Amelia studies me. "Then why were you smiling?"

"I wasn't smiling."

"Was it the same person you were texting in the kitchen?" she asks.

"Amelia, leave your brother alone."

"It's just some guys from work," I say, grabbing the bowl of collards and spooning a large helping onto her plate before she can protest. "We're gonna hang out after our shift tomorrow night." I look at Mama and Keith. "If that's okay?"

Technically, that's not a fib. Emmett's a guy, and we do work at the same place. I just left out the part about quitting the factory to work at Wanda World. There's no point in upsetting Mama right now. She's got better things to worry about. Even though she's loading up her plate with food, she won't have more than a few nibbles.

"Of course that's okay," Keith says.

"What happened to your friends from school?" Mama asks.

Her question catches me off guard. I'm not close to any of the guys. Sure, we hang out in between classes, or play video games at each other's houses on the weekends. But they only know the Luke I'm pretending to be.

"I saw Vanessa the other day," I say.

As soon as the words are out of my mouth, I regret saying them. I promised myself I wasn't going to use Vanessa as a shield anymore.

Mama's face lights up. "How is she?"

"She's good."

"I always liked that girl," Mama says. "I know it's not my business, but I'm glad y'all are hanging out again. Honestly, I still don't understand why you broke up. You're too handsome not to have a girlfriend."

My face goes warm. Mama probably thinks I'm embarrassed. And I guess I am. But not for the reason she thinks.

"Vanessa's working at Wanda World this summer," I say, testing Mama out.

The corners of her mouth droop. The change in her eyes is less subtle. They go from bright and hopeful to sad and faraway. "Well,"

Mama says. "I suppose we all gotta make money somehow."

Good Lord, Mama, she's working at Wanda World. Not robbing banks.

I guess it's good I haven't come clean about my job yet.

"Speaking of work," Keith says, deftly changing the subject. "I've got some news."

He looks over at Mama and she perks back up.

"I wasn't gonna say anything yet," Keith continues, "because it's not official. But it looks like the plant is cutting the third line. I can go back to working day shifts."

"Yay!" Gabe shouts, clapping.

Even Amelia smiles.

I can understand why Gabe and Amelia might think this is good news; they'll get to see their daddy more. But I don't know what Mama and Keith are so happy about. Do they seriously not remember that past-due bill I just found?

"I thought you started working the night shift because you could get more hours that way," I say.

Keith nods. "I did. But our union reps are working out a deal to keep us on full-time. There's just a lot of paperwork to get through first."

I want to be as optimistic as everyone else. But if Mama's not working, and we're already behind on our bills, I don't see how I can be. Money's always been tight for my family, and I've always done my best to chip in. But now that I'm at Wanda World, I'm not even making as much. I never should've left the factory. It was wrong of me to put my own interests first.

"Hey," Keith says, looking at me. "You've got nothing to worry about. This family always finds a way to make things work, don't it?"

Well, he's got a point there. It's not like we haven't had unpaid bills before. Mama always said Nana raised her on a hope and a prayer. Same thing happened to Mama after my father left. Maybe I just need to find a way to help out more. I could ask Rodney for a raise. Or sweet-talk him into breaking his no-overtime rule.

"Luke," Mama says, interrupting my thoughts. "Did you make this corn bread from scratch? This tastes just as good as what you'd get at a restaurant."

I look over to see that she's eating it. And not just a bite—she's finished almost an entire slice already. As Gabe concentrates on the cheesy top layer of my casserole and Amelia takes a bite of collards without making a face, the tension in my shoulders melts away.

Maybe Mama's getting better.

Maybe my family will be okay.

Maybe, if I work hard enough, I'll really be a chef someday.

Chapter

14

LUKE

Although Keith and Gabe gave me a break from washing dishes last night, today I'm back to scraping half-eaten meals off people's plates. It's hotter than an armpit, too, and I'm trying not to pass out every time I lift the dishwasher hood. I don't get how the cooks do it. They spend their entire shift in front of the stovetop—boiling, frying, and sautéing—with only a quart container of ice water to keep them cool.

"Hey," César shouts. "Where are those mixed greens I asked for?"

I look up and see he's talking to me.

"Come on, güero! Quit daydreaming. We've got hungry customers here."

If there's one thing this kitchen doesn't have an urgent need for, it's more mixed greens. No one looks at our menu of Southern home-style cooking and thinks: *Dang, a salad would really hit the spot.* Even the vegetarians are smart enough to order the mac 'n' cheese.

I'm starting to think César sent me into the walk-in cooler because he felt sorry for me. And if that's the case, I'm grateful. I take my sweet-ass time in there, relishing the cold air as it hits my face, my arms, the back of my neck.

While cooling off, I check my phone to see if Emmett has texted.

We have plans to hang out again after my shift. When I don't find any new messages, I'm surprised how disappointed I feel. Emmett's cute. And easy to talk to. But he's also a *huge* Wanda Jean fan. And very much out. I don't know if it's smart, spending so much time with him. Then again, he's only here for the summer. Which means we can have our fun now, and before things have a chance to get any more serious, he'll be gone.

When I finally leave the walk-in and bring the bag of mixed greens to César, I watch him in action for a minute. I can't believe how fast his knife moves. The blade hardly even makes a sound as it hits the cutting board. He's like a machine. If I tried to move that fast, I wouldn't have all my fingertips still.

César points to the end of the counter. "Set it there, güero."

I return to my station with a smile. I like how the cooks don't treat me any different because I'm the dishwasher. And it's cool that I have a nickname already. Later, when my shift is over and I run into Vanessa by the lockers, I ask her what it means.

"Is that, like, the same as calling me 'buddy' or 'dude'?"

She laughs. "Not exactly. They're calling you 'blondie.'"

I must get a hurt look on my face, because she quickly adds, "Relax. It's not an insult. It's more like a friendly tease. They're not calling you 'pendejo,' right?"

"What's 'pendejo' mean?"

"It's like saying someone's a dumbass. Or if you want to get literal, a pubic hair."

"For real?"

"Well, that's the Latin root of the word."

"Okay. I'll definitely take 'blondie' over that."

She smiles, pulling her long dark hair into a ponytail. "Hey, are you doing anything right now? I'm pretty sure I could murder some-one for a root beer float."

"Oh. I can't. I gotta go home and, um . . . take care of some stuff."

I'm the worst liar in the world. She probably thinks I'm trying to avoid her.

"Tomorrow night?" I ask.

"I'm not working tomorrow." She closes her locker and stuffs her dirty apron in the hamper. "It's fine. I'll ask one of the servers. Have a good night, Luke."

Fuck. I wish I didn't have to mislead Vanessa. I should've told her the truth when we broke up. But how do you tell someone you were only dating them because you wanted to believe you were straight?

Besides, once I tell one person I'm gay, there's a good chance more people will find out. Gossip spreads like wildfire in this town. I can't risk it getting back to my family. Mama needs stability right now so she can focus on getting better, instead of worrying about her son being a sin.

It's better to keep this part of myself a secret. Which is why, when Emmett and I hang out together later, I make him sneak into a fenced-off area that appears to be for broken or retired park equipment.

"I can't tell if this place is funny weird," Emmett says, "or *weird* weird."

Next to us, Zoltar the fortune-teller watches us from his glass box. Except half his face is missing and some of his mechanisms are exposed, so he's more like Zoltar the Terminator.

"I thought some privacy might be nice," I say, stopping in front of an abandoned Viking ship built for two.

Emmett smirks as we take a seat in it. "Well, I didn't want to be too forward, but I only have forty-five minutes before I have to be back at the theater. So if you want to fool around, we should definitely start now."

Emmett moves in to kiss me. But after a few minutes of making out, his leg ends up on my lap and the seat belt buckle starts digging into my ass.

"Is this okay?" he asks, pulling me in closer.

"Yeah," I say. "I think so."

"Ouch. Fuck."

He rubs his elbow, which he just slammed against the hard plastic seat. It's a *very* small ship, not easy to get comfortable in. I think it used to be one of the kiddie rides here. Though what Norse water vessels have to do with country music is beyond me.

"Maybe we should wait," I suggest, repositioning myself and hoping it's not too obvious how turned on I am already.

"Good call. We can just talk for a while."

A silence falls over us. Somewhere nearby, the games at the penny arcade whistle and ding. As we continue to sit there, not saying anything, I start to feel claustrophobic. I don't have any experience with crushes, or talking to guys I'm interested in. Have Emmett and I run out of things to say to each other already?

"Hey," Emmett says. "You want to grab something to eat? I wouldn't say no to a plate of Super Nachos right now."

I picture us sitting down together at one of the red picnic tables, as park-goers pass by with pink and blue puffs of cotton candy. Maybe Emmett would get some cheese sauce on the corner of his mouth and I'd laugh. Maybe our knees would touch under the table. It sounds romantic. But to do that out in the open? *In public?*

"Ooh," Emmett says. "Or how good does a cold root beer sound?"

My pulse quickens. Vanessa was craving a root beer float. What if she didn't go home? We might run into her.

"I'm not really hungry," I say.

"Well, I'm starving. I skipped lunch because I've been trying to work on an original song for this open mic I'm planning to do. I should probably eat something before my next show. Do you mind tagging along?"

"Actually . . ."

I could make up an excuse. Tell him I can't be around food after washing dishes all day. Or pretend I have to go home and check on Amelia and Gabe. But if I really want to be myself around Emmett, I shouldn't be lying to him already.

"Actually . . . ," I try again. "I'm not out to anyone yet. And, uh, I'm worried about running into my ex-girlfriend, since she works here, too."

"Oh." He sounds disappointed. I'm sure he's used to being with guys who are out like him.

"Sorry," I say. "I should've told you sooner."

"Oh my God, no. You don't have to apologize for that."

He smiles, and it seems genuine. Like maybe this isn't a big deal.

"You don't have to answer this if you don't want to," he says. "But do you know how you identify yet? Are you gay? Bi? Still questioning?"

For the longest time, that was a question I tried not to think about. Or if I did, I willed the answer to be "straight." But I think I've always known. I just kept my answer hidden from everyone. Including myself.

"I'm pretty sure I'm gay," I tell him. "Or, at least, *mostly* gay? I don't know. I'm definitely attracted to guys. And while I think part of me can still be attracted to girls, the attraction's not the same. Which is why I don't think I'm bi. Like, if I walked into a room full of super-attractive naked people, my eyes would go right to all the guys."

"A room full of super-attractive naked people, huh?" he teases, raising his eyebrows. "You walk into those often?"

"Shut up. You know what I mean. What I'm trying to say is . . . I think I'm mostly gay. And maybe a tiny bit not. If that makes any sense. Or maybe I *am* bi. I don't know."

"If it helps, I don't think anyone is one hundred percent anything."

"What about you?" I ask.

"Oh. Well, I just happen to be, like, ninety-nine percent gay. But there's still that one percent of me that would totally make out with someone who wasn't a guy under the right circumstances."

It's strange how sure of himself he is. He doesn't come off as cocky. But I also get the sense he isn't bothered by what people think of him. Not in the way I am.

"Have you been out for a while?" I ask.

"Well, I doubt it was ever much of a secret. My aunt was the first person I told. Then my parents. Then I joined the Gay-Straight Alliance in sixth grade, started wearing a pride pin on my backpack, and did my year-end social studies project on the history of Stonewall. Which I got an A-plus on, by the way."

He pauses, running his finger along the edge of the boat. "That's not to say it was always easy. I was bullied a lot in middle school. And I'm still bullied now sometimes. But after a while, you get better at tuning that stuff out. Especially if you surround yourself with good people."

He looks at me and smiles. I want to believe what he's saying. But it's probably different for him, having grown up in Chicago. We have plenty of good people here in Jackson Hollow. But we also have people like Whizzer and Bulldog. Or some of the guys from school. Or even my mama, who's a good person but also puts her faith in a Bible that condemns her own son for being something he never chose to be.

"I guess that makes you braver than me," I say.

It comes out sounding more bitter and hurt than I mean it to.

"You know it's not a contest, right?" he says. "No one wins for being first."

"Yeah," I say. "I know."

He puts his hand on my knee. "I'm serious, Luke. You can come out whenever you're ready. You shouldn't feel pressured to tell people."

Rationally, I know he's right. But things aren't so black-and-white in the real world. When Emmett gives my knee a squeeze, I feel like standing up and hollering loud enough for all the park to hear that I have a crush on him. But when he takes his hand away, and I return home later tonight, I know I'll go back to lying about who I really am.

"Am I the first guy you've been with?" Emmett asks.

"I was seeing someone last summer. But not for long."

"What happened?"

"He left for college. And like most people who leave Jackson Hollow, I doubt he's ever coming back."

Emmett bites down on his lip, hiding another smirk. "I'd say I'm sorry to hear that, but I'm glad he left. Otherwise, I'd be sitting here alone."

My cheeks instantly grow warm. I'm not used to having a guy flirt so openly with me. It's kind of nice.

"I'm sure you could find some other lonely townie," I tease.

"Not one I like as much as you."

He leans in close, until our lips are almost touching again.

"Was this guy a better kisser than me?" he asks.

"Like you said, it's not a contest."

"Sorry, but this one is."

Emmett closes his eyes and kisses me again. And suddenly it doesn't matter that we're in a boat. Or that I have to keep this part of my life a secret from everyone. All that fades away until it's just Emmett and me.

I may not be big on theme parks.

But I'd buy an endless number of tickets to stay on this ride.

Chapter

15

EMMETT

I've never been all that great in the kitchen. My specialties include instant ramen, microwave popcorn, and mixing two kinds of cereal together in unexpected combinations: Corn Pops and Cocoa Puffs. Fruity Pebbles and Frosted Flakes. Cap'n Crunch and an off-brand version called Lieutenant Munch.

Tonight Aunt Karen put me in charge of making a salad, which I thought I could handle. But so far, I've been too distracted to even open the bag of prewashed spinach. I still can't get over the fact that this cute Southern boy likes me. Not only is Luke cute, he's also modest—something I'm rarely accused of being. And while outwardly he presents as the strong, silent type, I can tell there's a real depth to him. He likes to think things over. He doesn't rush into his decisions. Not like I do.

Oh, and he's a good kisser.

Such a good kisser.

Of course, Luke's also a distraction. The open mic's getting closer, and I basically have to give the performance of my life there, because I'm not sure when I'll get another chance like this. Talent scouts aren't scrolling through my YouTube channel. They're here, at the Rusty Spur. I should be spending all my free time with my guitar, not Luke.

But on the other hand, Luke's not the type of guy I'd meet back home, either. I mean, I still can't believe my lips have touched someone who shares the same freaking DNA as Verna Rose and Wyatt Barnes.

I promised Luke I wouldn't tell anyone about his grandparents. And I haven't. But ever since our first kiss, the words have been bubbling up inside me, waiting to spill out. I practically have to clamp a hand over my mouth anytime I'm around Jessie and Avery. I considered texting some of my friends back home, people Luke would never meet. But a promise is a promise. I don't want to lose his trust.

Luke's trust is the only reason tonight's happening. After a week of meeting in abandoned parking lots and secluded sections of the park, I told him it'd be nice if we were able to hang out together in public. I was thinking we could grab dinner somewhere, do something that felt more like a date. But Luke was worried about being spotted by someone he knew, so I suggested he come over here. He wasn't sure at first, and I didn't want to push. But I promised I'd introduce him as a "work friend," and he eventually agreed.

"Emmett," Aunt Karen says, walking in from the patio with a platter of grilled corn. "They're going to be here soon. You'd better get moving on that salad."

"Yeah, sorry." I rip the bag of spinach open and pour it into a wooden bowl. Next I start washing the tomatoes, but I must be standing at the sink too long, because Aunt Karen nudges me in the arm.

"Thinking about anyone in particular?"

"What?" I turn the water off. "No."

She raises an eyebrow. "You sure about that? That's a very nice shirt you've got on."

I wore my favorite button-down tonight. It has a pattern of pink cowboy boots on it. I know I'm overdressed again. But I can't help it. I want to make a good impression.

"I told you," I say. "Luke's just a friend from the park."

"Who said anything about Luke? I didn't bring him up. You brought him up. Hmm, that's interesting. I'll try not to read into it."

She knows. Of course she does.

"Emmett." She grabs the tomatoes from me and sets them on the cutting board. "You can tell me anything. You *know* that."

"I know. It's just . . ." I lean against the counter and sigh. There's no point in lying to her now. "I promised Luke I wouldn't tell anyone. He's not out yet and I want to respect that."

Aunt Karen lets out a squeal, then thinks better of it. "I'm sorry I made you spill the beans. But honestly, it's better this way. Your face is too sweet and innocent to sell me a lie. I would've teased you relentlessly during dinner. Now that I know, I won't."

"You promise you won't say anything?"

"Of course not."

"Not even to Grady?"

She wrinkles her nose. "I don't like lying to him. But, yes, I'll keep this information to myself. And don't worry, when it comes to things I'm not supposed to know about, I've gotten very good at keeping quiet."

"Um . . . okay?"

She brings her thumbnail up to her mouth and chews on it. "Wanna know one of my secrets? This way we can be even."

"Uh . . . ," I say.

"Come on, before our *men* get here."

☆ 124 ☆

Aunt Karen drags me out of the kitchen and down the hallway to her other spare bedroom, the one she turned into a home office.

"Okay, before I show you this," she says, stopping in front of her desk, "I need you to know I wasn't snooping. I was looking for my shipping labels. Since Grady sleeps over so much, I told him he could use this space as well. But I never imagined he'd be keeping such *sensitive material* here."

My mind immediately goes to Wanda Jean. Is it her park schedule? Her home address? A catalogue of all the songs she's written over the years but never released?

Aunt Karen opens a drawer. From under a stack of manila files, she pulls out a folder. It's colorful and glossy, with a picture of a heterosexual white couple on an equally white sandy beach. Across the top, over an unnaturally blue ocean, it reads: "Villa Delphine Luxury Resort and Spa."

"Grady's surprising you with a vacation?" I ask.

"A *beach* vacation, Emmett."

It takes a second, but then I remember what Aunt Karen said: If she ever got married, she'd want to do it barefoot in the sand.

My mouth drops open. "Does this mean . . ."

She nods. "I think so."

"Seriously?" I give her the biggest hug possible. "I'm so excited for you! When is it? *Where* is it?"

She hides the folder back in the drawer. "I don't know yet. And I don't want to know. I didn't peek inside. I figured I should let part of it be a surprise."

The doorbell rings. Aunt Karen lets out a nervous yelp.

"That's Luke," I say. "Remember to act normal."

"Emmett, you don't have to worry about me."

As it turns out, she's right. *I'm* the one I need to worry about. When I open the door and see Luke—dressed in a blue-and-white gingham shirt, holding a ceramic bowl covered in tinfoil—I just stand there with my mouth ajar, unable to speak.

"Come on in," Aunt Karen says, shooting me a look.

I try to pull myself together. But my head's tingling as if I stood up too fast. How is it possible he gets cuter every time I see him?

"Thank you, ma'am," Luke says.

Aunt Karen places a hand over her chest. "Okay, I know I'm supposed to say you can call me Karen. But honestly, I love it when a polite young man such as yourself refers to me as ma'am. It makes me feel so respected." She points to the bowl. "Ooh, is that for us?"

Luke blushes. "I hope y'all like banana pudding."

"Well, bless your heart." Aunt Karen takes the bowl from him. "Oh, and I don't mean that pejoratively. I've lived here long enough to know when someone says 'bless your heart,' they're usually calling you a dumbass. But this one's sincere. *I love banana pudding.*"

Thank God Aunt Karen's talking as much as she is. I don't know why I've clammed up. Maybe it's because Luke looks extra handsome right now. Or maybe it's because this is the first time I've brought a boyfriend home. Not that this is my home. And introducing someone to Aunt Karen is different than introducing them to Mom and Dad. But still, I—

Wait. *Boyfriend?*

Luke's not my boyfriend. He's just this guy I can't stop thinking about. This guy I want to hang out with every single day, even if it means having less time to work on my music. This guy I could kiss for hours and hours and never grow bored.

Fuck. I think I *want* Luke to be my boyfriend.

And it doesn't feel weird.

Aunt Karen leads us into the kitchen. After putting the banana pudding into the fridge, she checks her phone. "Looks like Grady got tied up at the office. Why don't you boys go hang out on the patio while I finish this salad? Or you could give Luke a tour of the house. Just don't expect much."

I opt for the tour. But only because I have an ulterior motive. As soon as I bring Luke into the garage, I close the door behind us and practically knock him down flat as I start making out with him.

"Whoa," he says once we eventually separate. "What was that for?"

That was for me realizing I want him to be my boyfriend. But I can't tell Luke that. If he doesn't want people to know he's gay, he's probably not ready for anything more serious than what we already have. So instead I say, "That was for showing up tonight. I know you were kind of worried. Is everything going okay so far?"

"Yeah." He nods, relaxing his shoulders a bit. "So far so good."

Putting his hand on the back of my neck, he pulls me in for another kiss. I totally get why people close their eyes when they do this now. (I mean, besides not wanting to look creepy.) My whole world tilts when I'm kissing Luke. It's like being on a roller coaster. You know it's going to be fun and exciting. But just before you hit the first big drop, you have to squeeze your eyes shut because the thrill of it is too much to take.

When we stop kissing and I open my eyes again, I see Luke's focused not on me, but on something behind me.

"What's all that?" he asks.

I turn around. "Oh. My aunt sells that stuff."

He walks past the T-shirt press and over to the table of Wanda Jean merchandise. "She makes money doing this?"

"Yeah. People will buy pretty much anything related to Wanda Jean."

He picks up a pair of pot holders. One has a drawing of flirtatious-looking Wanda Jean. The other says: *If you can't stand the heat . . . best not touch my biscuits.*

Luke puts them back down with a frown.

"Sorry," I say. "I forgot she had all this stuff out here."

"Why are you apologizing?"

"Well, I mean . . . I can understand if you hate Wanda Jean."

He inhales sharply. "I don't hate her. I just think it's unfair the world only got to hear her side of the story."

Having your best friend run away with your husband is the kind of story you could write a country song about—which is exactly what Wanda Jean did. She released an entire album about the scandal. And while Wanda soared to superstardom, Verna went home to Jackson Hollow and slowly faded into obscurity.

"I know it's not fair to blame Wanda Jean for what happened to my grandma," Luke says. "After all, my grandma stole *her* husband. But that doesn't mean she was a bad person. Maybe she just made one bad mistake. And maybe she had her reasons for doing it. My mama always says the truth is more complicated than the tabloids made it out to be."

"Did you know your grandma well?" I ask.

Luke studies a jacket with Wanda's name bedazzled on the back, mulling over his answer. "She lived with us, but she died when I was five. I have a few memories of her. And I know she loved me. But I also know she hardly ever left the house. I think she was pretty unhappy, actually. I don't ever remember hearing her sing."

How's that even possible? She was good enough to land a recording contract and perform at the Grand Ole Opry. And then she just . . . stopped?

"You've at least heard recordings, though," I say. "Right?"

"A few. But that's not the same, I don't think. I would've liked to hear her sing in person."

"Yeah. I'm sorry. That really sucks."

He shrugs. "At least I got to know her. That's more than I can say for my grandfather. But even with Wyatt, I hate that everyone knows him as a villain. He was an asshole for leaving my grandma. And for leaving Wanda Jean. But, like, if he was a drunk, maybe he had a reason for trying to cover up his pain. I know he grew up extremely poor. The kind of poor where you're lucky if your clothes aren't made from potato sacks. And despite where he came from, he went on to be this big music manager in Nashville."

I nod, because I don't know how else to respond. Luke has a point. And although I still believe Wanda Jean had a right to tell her side of the story, it does make me wonder what Verna and Wyatt would've said if they were given the chance, too.

"Do people really remember my nana?" Luke asks. And the way he calls her "nana," it leaves this little twist in my heart.

"Yeah. Have you never looked your grandma up online?"

"Only a bit. I was afraid it'd be a bunch of people trashing her."

"Well, it's the internet, so no one's safe. Even Wanda Jean has her haters and trolls. But your grandma definitely has fans, too. The songs she released may not have been as popular but, Luke, she was really good."

His eyebrows push together, like he's deep in thought. "Would people buy a T-shirt of her?"

"Yeah, probably. Why?"

He shakes his head. "Just wondering."

I want to ask him more about his grandma, but I can see talking about her makes him uncomfortable. So I leave it for now. When we go back inside, Luke and I help Aunt Karen bring everything out to the patio.

"Oh, Luke," Aunt Karen says, handing him a set of steak knives and a mason jar of her homemade BBQ sauce. "I forgot to have Emmett warn you ahead of time, I keep a vegetarian household. I hope you're okay with grilled tempeh?"

"Um . . ." He looks at the steak knives and BBQ sauce.

"It's a meat alternative. Made from fermented soybeans."

Without missing a beat, he smiles. "Sounds delicious, ma'am."

It's almost dusk by the time Grady arrives and we finally start dinner. But it doesn't matter. It's still the perfect night to eat out in the backyard. And either Luke's an expert liar, or he's really enjoying the tempeh.

"It has kind a nutty flavor," he says. "Almost like mushrooms."

"Yes!" Aunt Karen gives Grady a look. "See, some people like it."

"I never said I didn't like it. I said I'd still prefer a real steak."

"Well, I'd prefer leaving a smaller carbon footprint and not ingesting toxic chemicals."

"And that's one of the many things I adore about you," Grady says, shooting her a wink.

I was a little worried about tonight. There are so many secrets at this table that—statistically speaking—at least one of them was bound to come out. Grady thinks Aunt Karen doesn't know he's planning to propose. Aunt Karen and I don't want Grady to know we already saw the folder. Aunt Karen and Grady aren't supposed to know Luke and I are together. And I'm afraid Luke will find out I already told Aunt Karen.

And then there's the biggest secret of them all. The one I still can't believe myself: that we're having dinner with the grandson of Wyatt Barnes and Verna Rose.

Thankfully, we make it all the way to dessert without any disasters. And when Aunt Karen brings out Luke's banana pudding and we all take our first spoonful, silence falls over the table.

"Oh my God," Aunt Karen says. "You made this?"

"It's not my recipe," Luke says. "I found it in an old cookbook we had lying around my house. I just tweaked the ingredients a bit."

"It's so good," Grady says with his mouth full.

Aunt Karen closes her eyes as she savors her next bite. "I'm sorry, but from here on out, you're coming over for dinner every Sunday night. And you're always in charge of dessert. I'm not joking."

Luke's smiling, but only because he thinks no one's looking at him. I'm looking, though. And what I see is someone I desperately want to be my boyfriend.

"Luke's going to be a chef," I announce.

The smile drops from his face, and my stomach quickly follows. Fuck. Was I not supposed to tell anyone? Was that supposed to be a secret, too?

Luke clears his throat. "I mean . . . I'd *like* to be a chef someday."

"Oh, honey." Aunt Karen helps herself to another spoonful. "You already are."

Luke looks over at me. This time, he's beaming.

Chapter

16

LUKE

As a stepdad, Keith's imparted some solid wisdom to me over the years: Always treat your mama with respect. Shave against the grain for a closer cut. And don't worry about what your youth pastor said. Everyone does it. Just be sure you're not doing it *too* much.

One of the lessons he's passed on from his time at the auto plant is that the bigger your job title, the less work you actually have to do. This appears to be the case as I knock on the door to Rodney's office. He minimizes the game of solitaire he has going on his computer and grabs a spreadsheet from his desk.

"Luke. What can I do for you?"

I was nervous about coming in here today. But now that I'm spending time with Emmett and not home as much, I need to do more to protect my family. That past-due bill's still sitting on the sideboard cabinet, and I looked up what happens when you don't pay your property taxes. The government can sell your house in order to pay your debt.

I push my shoulders back, standing up straight.

"Sir, I was wondering if I could start picking up some shifts as a line cook."

"No overtime."

"It wouldn't be overtime. I was hoping I could be promoted?"

That was supposed to be a statement. Not a question.

"Remind me," Rodney says, looking up from his spreadsheet. "You got any previous experience working in a kitchen?"

"I cook quite a bit, sir. Just the other night I made corn bread from scratch. And collard greens. My mama said it was the best she's had in years. Now, my mama's gonna be biased. But my siblings are picky eaters, sir, and even they—"

He puts his hand up. "Restaurant experience, son."

"Not yet. Though I'm eager to learn."

Rodney smiles. But it's the type that doesn't reach his eyes—a bullshit smile.

"I admire people who want to move up in this world," he says. "Look, I get it. I wasn't always a manager. But what I need right now is a steady dishwasher. And you're doing such a good job in that position that I can't afford to lose you there. So let's revisit this at the end of the summer. We'll see where we're at then, m'kay?"

I'll be heading back to school then, and Rodney knows that. Unfortunately, I still need this paycheck, no matter how small it is. So I swallow my pride and continue to kiss ass. "Yes, sir. Thank you."

He cocks his finger like it's a pistol. "Shut the door on your way out."

Leaving Rodney's office, I pass by César. He's holding a clipboard and signing off on a stack of invoices. "¿Que pasó, güero? You look like someone shot your dog."

"Oh. Yeah. It's nothing."

César nods and returns to his paperwork.

I stop. The guys in the kitchen have been good to me. Better than

Rodney. And if Emmett were here, he'd want me to speak up. "I asked Rodney if I could start working the line," I say. "I wanna learn how to be a cook. But he said no."

"Rodney's a pendejo."

Yes, he most certainly is a pubic hair.

César taps his pen against the clipboard, studying me. "I can teach you how to cook, if you really want to learn. But you'd have to start with the boring jobs—chopping vegetables, making stock, cleaning out the pantry."

"Prep work," I say, a little too eagerly. "I can do that."

"You'd have to get here early. Before Rodney. And I can't pay you. This would only be for the experience."

"Yes. Of course."

César gives me a smile. A real one. "Órale, a trabajar, güero. You're one of us now."

Arriving home from work that evening, I'm greeted with one of the best food smells in the world: freshly baked dough topped with something cheesy.

"Daddy left us money for supper," Amelia explains, pointing to the coffee table, where three large pizza boxes are piled on top of one another.

My first thought is that we could've bought a more economical amount of groceries with that money. My second is that Amelia and Gabe should be using plates so they don't get crumbs all over the couch. And my third is that I'm starving and I hope at least one of those pizzas has mushrooms and pepperoni.

I'm in luck. I happily cram down a few slices as I sit with Amelia and Gabe, watching some mindless reality show where straight people are stranded on a tropical island to compete for love. Or maybe they're competing for money. I don't know. I'm only half paying attention because Emmett keeps rapid-fire texting me.

I have a proposition for you.

That sounds dirty. It's not.

Have you ever been to the Rusty Spur?

Again, not dirty. It's a music venue.

Anyhow they have an open mic night there.

I'm going to perform.

He hasn't said what his proposition is, but I think I can guess. He wants me to go. And the thing is, I *do* want to see him perform. He keeps dropping hints about getting me into his show at the park. And every time, I feel bad for giving him another excuse for why I can't go.

It's not because I don't like country music.

It's because I don't trust myself when I'm around him.

Sometimes it scares me how much I like Emmett. I've only known him for a couple of weeks, but he makes me doubt myself less. I feel like I can finally let my guard down with him. Which is exactly why it's a terrible idea for us to be in public together. What if I forget myself and mess up? My family's got enough to worry about without that getting back to them.

My song isn't ready yet, Emmett texts.

I'm kind of freaking out about it.

But I thought maybe you'd like to go?

In case you're into watching live train wrecks.

Emmett couldn't be a train wreck if he tried. He's so confident in everything he does. I can already see him standing onstage with his guitar. And his perfectly tousled hair. And that infectious smile he gets whenever country music is mentioned.

Can I have some time to think about it? I text.

Of course.

I look over at Amelia and Gabe, who are still glued to the TV. Would anything really change if my family knew I was gay? Part of me thinks it wouldn't. But then another part of me thinks about Mama. About the cross she wears around her neck. About her reaction when Gabe used that word. She was disgusted when two men kissed on TV. How'd she feel if she knew her own son was doing that kind of thing?

Better get ready for the next show, Emmett texts.

Oh, and my aunt is insisting you come for dinner again next weekend.

I'm supposed to tell you she likes pecan pie.

I text him back a thumbs-up. I liked his aunt. And Emmett was right: even if his aunt and her boyfriend didn't know the truth about us, it was nice to spend a few hours together where we didn't have to hide from the rest of the world.

"I want a Popsicle," Gabe whines.

"We ate them all," Amelia says.

"Nuh-uh. I didn't get any."

"Okay. *I* ate them all."

"Hey," I say, stopping whatever fight's about to break out. "I made you each your own cup of banana pudding yesterday. But first y'all have to bring me your dirty laundry."

Once they return, I pile everything into the laundry basket and head downstairs to the basement. Standing at the bottom of the steps,

I flick the light switch on and wait a second. I'm not saying I believe in ghosts. But if they did exist, they'd be hanging out somewhere down here.

I start with a load of whites, making sure all my work shirts are accounted for. The restaurant provides us with an unlimited supply of aprons, but we're responsible for keeping our uniforms clean. The only upside of Mama being on bed rest is that I don't need to worry about her going through my laundry. If she saw the monogram for Wanda World stitched into my shirts, she'd have questions.

After starting the washing machine, I linger for a bit. As great as it is that César's going to start teaching me in the kitchen, that won't make Rodney budge on giving me more hours or a raise. My paycheck from Wanda World is barely enough to cover groceries and gas. I still don't know how we're going to keep up with our bills while Mama's not working. Which is why, ever since yesterday, I've been thinking about what Emmett said in his aunt's garage: that people would buy a T-shirt of my nana.

The only thing I know about mass-producing T-shirts is that you probably need lots of cash up front. But what if I could find another way to make us money? What if we have something more valuable than cheaply made clothing? Something that wouldn't cost anything to produce?

Walking to the far end of the basement, I stop in front of the large shelving unit Keith organized a while back. I start taking down boxes and go through them one by one. I'm not exactly sure what I'm looking for, but I hope I'll know it when I see it.

It's not the accessories to Amelia's old dollhouse.

Or the last five years of our tax returns.

Or all the bad macaroni art I made in grade school.

I don't know why Mama kept all this crap but nothing of Nana's. I'm down to the top shelf now. And just as I'm ready to give up and put everything back, I spot a box labeled "Verna's Stuff."

Bingo.

My nose wrinkles at the musty smell coming from inside. Most of her stuff appears to be junk. There's a set of spongy pink hair curlers. A set of chipped turquoise serving bowls. And wrapped in old newspaper, a set of cherubic angel figurines with their hands pressed together in prayer.

When I pull out an old butter cookie tin, however, something rattles inside. I pry the lid off to discover a bunch of makeup. Powder brushes with their bristles stained pink. Tubes of bright red lipstick that have long since cracked.

At the bottom of the tin, there's a yellowed piece of paper folded into a square. I open it and a plain silver locket slides out. It's not expensive looking. And there aren't any photos inside—just an engraving.

One side reads: *I'm falling in love.*

The other: *With the sweetest Rose.*

The timer on the washing machine buzzes and my heart nearly leaps out of my chest. I fold the locket back up in the paper and slip them in my pocket. After putting everything back exactly where I found it, I throw the clothes into the dryer and take another look around the basement before heading back upstairs.

If there is a ghost down here, I'm pretty sure someone once gave her this locket. I just hope she isn't still attached to it.

Chapter 17

EMMETT

After our final show of the day, the general chaos that usually reigns over the dressing room is strangely subdued. No one's making plans for the evening or ignoring the stage manager as she tells us to hurry up and put our costumes away. Even Cassidy's not running around, subtly fishing for compliments about herself by telling everyone else what a great job they did.

"What's with the mood in here?" I ask Avery.

"Everyone's focused."

"On what?"

He stops applying his makeup remover and gives me the side-eye. "On the open mic?"

"But that's not until next week."

"Oh, I see. So your song is perfect and ready to go, then?"

"Well . . ." I haven't looked at it much since Luke and I started hanging out.

"Avery and I are practicing tonight," Jessie says, zipping her cowgirl costume into its garment bag. "If you want to join us?"

"I thought it was just going to be the two of us?" Avery says.

Jessie gives him a funny look. His cheeks flush red. "Of course you can join us," he quickly adds. "The more the merrier."

Avery wipes off his makeup remover with a towel, but an awkwardness lingers in the air. Does he not like me anymore? Does he think I'm his competition now?

"I'd better take a rain check," I say. "I already have plans."

I should really work on my song with them. But Luke texted earlier and said he has something important he needs to talk to me about. I don't want to get ahead of myself, but maybe he's ready to have the So Are We Boyfriends Now? talk as well.

"Suit yourself," Jessie says, walking her garment bag over to the costume rack. "Hey, Aves, wanna splurge on a turkey drumstick first? I'm starving."

A smile tugs at the corners of his mouth. "Yeah, that sounds great."

Oh. Okay. So maybe there's a different reason he didn't want me there. Maybe he's worried I'd be the third wheel.

After cleaning myself up, I check my phone. Luke's shift is almost over. We're supposed to meet at our regular spot tonight, but that's all the way on the other side of the park. Would it really be so bad if I just met him at the restaurant? I get that Luke's not ready to be out yet, but does that seriously mean we can't be seen together at all? I want us to be able to share a turkey drumstick like Avery and Jessie can. I mean, it's not like I'm going to bat my eyelashes and make kissing noises. Everyone would assume we're friends. Unless . . . what if Luke's ashamed of me? Is that why he makes me meet him in secluded areas of the park?

A heaviness tugs at my heart. Maybe Luke's not ready to be boyfriends. Maybe he's only using me as a hookup. If that's the case, I should've taken Avery and Jessie up on their offer. Luke's hot, and I don't think I'll ever get tired of kissing him. But a hot guy's not worth sacrificing my career for. There has to be something more in it for me. I thought I was starting to find that with Luke. There are so many things I like about him: The way he gets shy about his cooking. The way he smiles at me when I go on a tangent about music. How polite and kind he is.

I take a breath, calming myself. Luke's a good guy. He wouldn't be using me. Maybe I'm making this into a bigger deal than it needs to be. Maybe we both are. Luke was worried about coming over to Aunt Karen's, and that turned out fine. So now I just need to prove that it's okay for us to be together in public, too.

When I arrive at the restaurant, the dining room has the same lawless energy as my school's cafeteria on a Rally Day. Except instead of the football team acting unruly, it's small children who are throwing food and pounding their fists on tables.

"Welcome to Granny's Cupboard," someone says behind me. "Where you're guaranteed to leave with a full belly and an even fuller heart."

I spin around. "Um, hi. I'm just waiting for a friend. He works here."

The server—a girl with tan brown skin, who's wearing a tacky floral dress and a name tag that reads "Vanessa"—drops her bubbly persona. "Oh. Who's your friend?"

"Luke. The dishwasher? I'm early. I was going to wait until his shift is over."

She takes a look around the dining room. "Yeah, so here's the thing. Our boss is kind of a dick. It's better if I grab you a table. You don't need to order anything. In fact, how does a sweet tea sound? On the house."

"Really? That's nice of you."

She shrugs. "It's not coming out of my paycheck."

After leading me over to a booth near the back, she hands me a laminated menu that's thick as a magazine. I barely get past the first page before she returns with my tea and a plate of biscuits. "I stole those off another table," she says, nodding toward the biscuits. "Check for bite marks first."

"Um, thanks."

"Don't mention it." She takes out her notepad and pen, pretending to write my order down. "So you must be a *very* close friend of Luke's."

My chest tightens.

Fuck. Did I blow his cover?

"My friends would never pay full admission just to visit me at Wanda World," she says.

"Oh. Right." I start breathing again. "I'm an employee here, too. That's how I know Luke. I perform in the Jamboree."

"The Jamboree, huh? I hear that's supposed to be good."

"I like to think so," I say. And then, because I'm apparently a nonstop publicity machine, I add: "I could get you a free pass. If you wanted to see it, I mean."

A man in an offensively yellow tie passes by us, and Vanessa stands a little straighter. "Okay, so that'll be the meat loaf platter with an extra side of gravy."

As soon as the man's out of earshot, she shoots me a wink. "I'll tell Luke you're here."

After taking a sip of sweet tea, I swirl my straw around the ice cubes and sigh. That was close. *Too close.* I shouldn't have shown up here. It's just . . . I didn't realize how hard it would be to keep Luke a secret. My friends back home would die if they knew about him. I was the only one in our group who didn't want to bring a date to prom. And now I can't even tell them I'm seeing someone.

My phone vibrates. I get excited when I see Luke's name. But then I read his texts, and my heart starts racing for a very different reason.

What are you doing here?

You need to leave.

NOW.

Sliding out of the booth, I knock my glass of tea over. *Fuck.* I grab a napkin and sheepishly try to clean it up, but it's like trying to stop Niagara Falls. I give up, running outside in a panic.

My phone buzzes. Out back.

By the dumpster.

I hurry around to the other side of the restaurant. My heart leaps into my throat as the rear door flies open and Luke steps out, still dressed in his dishwashing uniform. He takes off his apron and throws it back inside before shutting the door behind him.

"We can't be here," he says, immediately walking past me.

I follow him, too afraid to say anything. We head back into the main part of the park, where it's easier to blend in with the crowd and the loud, colorful rides spinning above our heads. But more people also means more ears listening in.

"Luke," I say, pointing to a photo booth. "In there?"

He looks skeptical, but steps inside with me. "I'm sorry," I say, pulling the curtain shut behind us. "I don't know what I was thinking."

That's a lie. I was thinking I was tired of sneaking around. Tired of feeling like I'm something Luke has to be embarrassed about. I know that's probably not true. But it sure seems like it sometimes.

Luke inhales sharply. "You can't do that, Emmett. You can't visit me at work."

Shame creeps over me. "I know. I'm sorry."

Even though it's dark in the photo booth, we're standing close enough that I can read the disappointment all over his face.

"In my defense," I say, "it's not like I went in there and introduced myself as the guy you're fooling around with. I only said I was your friend. I swear, I would never do anything that might out you. You have to believe me."

His face softens. "I do believe you. And I'm sorry I freaked out. But that server you talked to? Vanessa? That's my ex-girlfriend."

"Oh my God." I clamp my hand over my mouth. "Luke, I'm so sorry."

He smiles, which makes me feel a tiny bit better. "You don't have to keep apologizing," he says, taking my hand back down. "I'm asking a lot of you."

Is he, though? Luke's risking having his entire world flipped upside down to be with me. What am I risking being with him? Less time working on my music? Not being able to brag to my friends that I'm dating someone? No way that's comparable.

"That reminds me . . . ," Luke says, taking a seat on the little bench in the booth. "There's something I need to talk to you about."

I sit next to him. As my knee presses into his, my stomach flutters. Luke pulls a square of paper from his pocket. For a second, I think maybe he *does* want to be boyfriends and he's written down what he wants to say to me. Which is incredibly adorable. But then he unfolds the paper to reveal a silver locket. He holds it out to me and . . . I don't know what to think. Did he buy me jewelry? Or is this a joke?

I go with the latter: "Thanks, but I'm more of diamond necklace kind of guy."

"Just open it."

I open the locket and read the inscription:

I'm falling in love.

With the sweetest Rose.

The locket suddenly feels weightier in my palm. "Was this your grandma's?"

"Yeah. Do you think it could be worth something?"

"Well, um. I don't know anything about appraising silver."

"I mean does it have any sentimental value," he says. "Would someone spend money on it if they knew it belonged to Verna Rose?"

He has an intense look in his eyes, like he needs the answer to be yes.

"Probably," I say. "But you'd have to prove it really belonged to her. I mean, anyone can take a locket and have this engraved on there."

"That's why I need your help. You know literally everything there is to know about country music. I was hoping you could figure out a way to prove it was hers."

I don't know *everything*.

Only, like, 99 percent of the things.

"It would help if you had a picture of her wearing it," I suggest.

He shakes his head. "I've tried looking for photo albums. But I don't think my mama kept any of them."

"I could try searching for photos online," I say. "We might get lucky that way. But, um, doesn't this hold any sentimental value for you?"

He takes the locket back and snaps it shut. "I'm guessing my grandfather gave it to her. So, no. And it's not like I'm trying to make a quick buck off my dead nana. My family could really use the money."

His jaw tightens. Like I hit a nerve.

"Sorry," I say. "I didn't know that."

"Yeah, well, I don't go around spilling my business to strangers."

I must have a hurt look on my face, because he quickly adds: "I didn't mean it like that. I just meant we didn't know each other until a couple of weeks ago. And I don't tell my friends about this stuff, either. So you shouldn't feel bad."

"You don't have to tell me about it if you don't want to," I say. "But I hope you know you can trust me. Despite the fact that I showed up at your restaurant today."

I want Luke to be able to open up to me. Keeping our relationship hidden is hard enough. We shouldn't be keeping secrets from each other on top of that.

"It's just . . ." He pauses. "I hate people feeling sorry for me. My life's not like one of your sad country songs."

"Luke, I would never think that."

He looks down at the locket, winding its chain around his finger before speaking again. "My mama's got multiple sclerosis. She had a flare-up recently, so she isn't working right now. And I'm not sure my stepdad can support us alone. We have a hard enough time paying our bills as it is. With more hospital expenses . . . I think we're falling further behind. So, yeah, I'd like to bring in some money for my family if I could."

"That sounds like a lot," I say, choosing my words carefully. "And I'm sorry you have to deal with that. Which isn't the same as me feeling sorry for you." Luke nods, but his head stays bowed. "Is your mom going to be okay? How serious is it?"

"She gets infusions to help slow the disease. And it's not progressive yet. So that's good. But this last relapse scared me. I don't want her to get worse."

"I can only imagine how tough that must be for you and your family," I say. "But I'm glad you told me. And of course I want to help you any way I can."

He places the locket back in the yellowed paper. "I wish my mama had kept more of my nana's stuff. Then I'd have more to sell."

"Is that your grandmother's writing?" I ask, pointing to the faded cursive on the paper.

Luke looks at it. "I don't know . . . probably?"

"Can I see?"

He hands me the paper. I take my phone out and turn the flashlight on. The cursive is squished together and hard to read. But what's on the page is clearly written in stanzas. I try not to get too excited on the off chance I'm wrong—though I don't think I am.

"Luke, do you know what this is?"

He shrugs. "Some kinda letter?"

"No. It's a song."

He leans in closer and takes another look. "One of my nana's?"

"I don't know. It's not one I'm familiar with. Your grandma only released one album. But she wrote her own music, so theoretically, she could have a whole collection of songs she never recorded."

He pupils dart back and forth, like his mind's racing ahead of mine. "Could *those* be worth something?"

"I guess. Though we'd still have to prove they were hers. If we could get them authenticated somehow . . . then, yeah, maybe you could sell them to a collector. We'd probably need documented samples of her handwriting. And her signature."

"No . . . what about selling her actual songs?"

"What do you mean?"

"Like, if she was a good songwriter, wouldn't other musicians want to buy them? We wouldn't even have to prove they were hers. We could pretend that you wrote them."

A spark goes off in my chest. Like someone lit a match inside me.

"First we'd have to set the lyrics to music," I tell him. "Then, if we really wanted to do this right, we'd have to rent a recording studio and cut a proper demo. It'd be a lot of work. And we'd need a music publisher to take us on. Or someone who's well connected in the industry."

"But it's possible, right?"

Yes, it's possible. But I've wanted to be a country singer since I heard my first Wanda Jean song. And the furthest I've gotten so far is performing at Wanda World. What if I'm not good enough to pull off something like this?

"Just start with the first part," Luke says, folding the piece of paper into my hand. "Set the lyrics to music."

I look at his face, already knowing I won't be able to say no. Not that I *want* to turn down singing a song written by Verna Rose. It's just . . . I hope I can give it the justice it deserves.

"Okay," I say. "I'll do it."

Luke leans in and gives me a kiss, and all my worries from earlier melt away. If I could only capture the happiness I feel when we're together in private like this, then maybe it would help me feel less bad that we have to ignore each other in public.

"Can I ask for something in return?" I say.

He leans in again, like he thinks I'm about to ask for another kiss. "Name it."

"Can we take our picture together in this booth?"

"Emmett . . ." He sits back. "That's not a good idea."

"Hold on," I say. "I get that taking a selfie is too dangerous. Someone might see it on my phone. But this would be a physical copy. I'd keep it tucked away someplace safe. It would never leave my bedroom, I swear."

He frowns, like he's about to say no.

"It's okay," I tell him, trying not to sound disappointed. "We don't have to."

I shouldn't be asking him to take a risk.

"Wait." He grabs my hand. "I want to."

"Really?"

"Yes."

He sounds like he's trying to convince himself more than me. But I slide a few bills into the machine before he can change his mind.

The first flash goes off and Luke stiffens next to me. For the next photo, I make a funny face, which gets him to at least crack a smile. But I'm still not satisfied. So I tickle him until we're both laughing for the third flash. And then, right before we get to the final photo, Luke pulls me in for a deep kiss.

Afterward, two sets of photos print out. One for each of us. Maybe we didn't have the "boyfriend" talk tonight. And maybe we still have to keep our relationship a secret—which, yeah, isn't exactly ideal. But this strip of photos is a good reminder for me that I just have to give Luke a little more time. He'll get there eventually.

Chapter

18

LUKE

A lot can change in a week. You can go from thinking there's only one way to slice a carrot to mastering the difference between a julienne and a bâtonnet. You can learn how and why you should devein shrimp. (How: run a paring knife down the back, pull the vein out with the tip, rinse. Why: it's not really their vein, it's their digestive tract.) And, perhaps most importantly, you can discover firsthand why it's important to always be paying attention in the kitchen. If you lose focus for a second—daydreaming about a certain musician, for example—you might end up with nine fingers instead of ten.

"What did I tell you?" César says, approaching my station with the first aid kit. "Your hand should be like a claw when you dice. If you're going to slice something, a knuckle is better than a fingertip."

"Yes, chef," I reply, applying pressure to the white dish towel I wrapped around my finger.

"Let's have a look."

I brace myself for a geyser of blood to start gushing everywhere. But when César unwraps the dish towel, there's only a small sliver of red. "Sharper knives mean cleaner cuts," he tells me. "Lucky for you, this one's more of a boo-boo."

The other cooks snicker. But it feels more like a rite of passage.

They've been really helpful this past week. Paulo even gave me a break from some of the dishwashing so I could get more practice prepping the line.

César hands me a blue bandage for my finger. "Your shift ended five minutes ago, güero. Go home. One of the other guys can finish."

"Yes, chef. Thank you, chef."

Normally, I don't like to leave a job half done. But I know better than to argue with the chef. I also know better than to keep Vanessa waiting. She's been itching to get a start on her styling career ever since she turned down that internship. But since she doesn't have clients, or access to a professional photo studio, she has to "DIY this bitch." I don't really know what that means. But she asked me to drive her to some thrift store over in Rayburn, and I said yes.

"Okay, how about Vintage by Vanessa?" she asks, applying her mascara in the passenger side of my truck.

"For what?"

"For my brand. Keep up!"

"Oh. Do you *wear* vintage clothes?"

"How d'you think I made it through sophomore year without having to repeat an outfit? I may look expensive, Luke, but I can shop on a budget when I need to."

Something tells me shopping on a budget has a different meaning for Vanessa than it does for me. She lives in a nice house, drives a nice car, and, yes, wears a lot of nice clothes. But it's not like she flaunts it. And she's always been generous with her friends. She paid for most everything when we were dating, no matter how much I protested.

"Vintage by Vanessa's great," I tell her. "But people will love whatever you call it. You're very persuasive."

She looks over at me with a smile. "Thanks. I like this new Luke, by the way."

"New Luke? What happened to the old one?"

She shrugs. "You're in a better mood these days."

I focus my attention back on the road, willing myself to stop blushing. She's right, of course. And part of me is bursting to tell her about Emmett. But what am I supposed to say? *Hey, sorry I was such a mediocre boyfriend. But I'm happy to report I'm not defective. I can* actually *be* with someone.

How could I tell her that without hurting her feelings? Besides, I don't want to saddle her with keeping my secret.

When we get to Rayburn, I'm reminded of all the trips I made here last summer to visit Cody. It's weird to think he was the first guy I kissed, the first guy I slept with. And now we don't really mean anything to each other.

Is that what's going to happen with Emmett?

Will he forget about me when he goes home?

I thought Emmett only being here for the summer was a good thing—less time for things to get complicated. But now I'm starting to see the flip side. What if I get too attached? What if I don't *want* him to leave?

I push Emmett out of my mind. I'm with Vanessa right now. And I want to be a good friend to her. Which is why, when she hands me her phone and asks me to film her in the parking lot of the Bargain Bucket, I say yes.

"Hey, y'all. It's your girl, Vanessa. Right now I'm at one of my favorite places to shop, the Bargain Bucket in Rayburn, Tennessee. You can find a lot of quality brands here without having to pay designer prices. Because, let's face it, you don't *need* a million bucks to *look* like a million bucks. Today I'll show you how to style yourself on budget. So come on, y'all. Let's see what we can find!"

She twirls, striking a pose at the end. "Okay, cut."

I stop recording, surprised by how easily she slips in and out of performance mode.

"Was the twirl too much? It felt like too much."

"No," I say, smiling as I watch it back on her phone. "This is great."

She raises an eyebrow. "What, you thought it wouldn't be?"

Inside the store, Vanessa searches through the racks of clothes. I take photos of her in different outfits and we shoot a few more videos where she dispenses advice like: "The key is to mix and match. A vintage dress pairs perfectly with a modern cardigan." And: "If your friend tells you shoulder pads are making a comeback, find a new friend."

As Vanessa disappears into the dressing room to change again, my phone buzzes.

My voice cracked onstage tonight.

Like, in the middle of a song.

Fuck me. How can I not be done with puberty yet?

I shake my head and text back, I don't mean to downplay what was obviously a traumatic situation, but I bet it was also kind of cute.

No. Luke. This is not a good omen for the open mic.

Emmett's open mic is at the end of this week. I still haven't said if I'm going or not. I want to be there for him, but Jackson Hollow's a very small town. If I go, there's a good chance I'll run into someone I know. And if anyone sees me talking to Emmett, it won't take long for the rumors to start. *Who's that boy Luke was with? The one who was wearing that fancy pink shirt? Did y'all notice the way Luke smiled at him?*

Is that really worth the risk? Especially since Emmett's going back to Chicago once summer's over, where he'll probably get himself a real boyfriend.

Maybe it's better to keep things more casual, like Cody and I did. We enjoyed each other's company, but we never acted like we wanted anything more than that. Which was probably for the best. Plus this way, when Emmett eventually leaves me, like Cody did, I won't care as much.

This isn't my subtle way of trying to pressure you, Emmett texts.

I'll understand if you can't go.

It might be a disaster anyhow.

"Okay, I'm ready."

I look up. Vanessa's in enormous sunglasses and a fuzzy purple coat.

"Everything okay?" she asks.

"Um. Yeah." I slide my phone back into my pocket. "My mama wants me to pick up a few groceries on the way home."

Vanessa takes off her sunglasses. "How's your mama doing? I've been thinking about her. She was always so sweet to me."

"She's better," I say. "Her doctor still wants her to take it easy, but she's finally off bed rest."

The concern in Vanessa's face melts away. "That's great, Luke."

I feel bad for lying about who was texting me. But it's nice Vanessa cares so much. I'm not used to having friends I can be open with.

After posing for a few more shots, Vanessa leads me over to the men's section. "Okay," she says, flipping through a rack of colorful dress shirts. "Now we need to find a few things for you to try on."

"No. Absolutely not." I'm all for helping Vanessa out. But I prefer to stay behind the scenes. Not in front of the camera.

"C'mon. You're in the demographic I'm trying to reach."

"What demographic is that?" I ask.

"Clueless country boys who don't know how to dress."

"Very funny."

"No, really, I've thought this through. Building an online platform's a good start. But I need real-life experience, too. This town may not be swimming in movie stars and red-carpet events. But what it does have a lot of is wannabe musicians. And while I hate to generalize, guys often need more help in the fashion department."

I cross my arms. "It's not happening."

She ignores me, holding two different shirts up to my chest. "I wasn't going to play this card, but you leave me no choice. I got you the job at Wanda World. Technically, you owe me one." She hands me a teal button-down, which I accept with a groan. But when we move to the rack of pants, I draw the line.

"What's wrong with white jeans?" she asks.

"I don't wear them."

"Okay. And is there a reason for that?"

"Yeah. They're too . . . white."

She rolls her eyes. "Do they threaten your masculinity, Luke? Are you less of a man if you put these on?"

It's not that *I* think that. I just worry everyone else will. But I don't know how to explain that to Vanessa. So I take the jeans, too, and make my way to the dressing rooms.

"I look ridiculous," I say after I've changed, pulling the curtain aside.

"Hush your mouth. I'm not done yet." Vanessa turns me to face the mirror and cuffs the sleeves of the shirt. "There. That's better."

"Are you serious? That's it? That's what you expect people to pay you for?"

She lightly punches my arm. "Rude. And also: inaccurate. My job is to push people out of their comfort zone. To show them it's okay to take risks." She straightens the collar of the shirt and takes a step back to study me. "Bright colors look good on you. But if you really hate it, we can try something else."

I check myself out in the mirror again. Maybe the clothes aren't the problem. Maybe *I'm* the problem. There's no way I could wear something like this and not be paranoid everyone was staring at me. It's not a step outside of my comfort zone. It's a leap.

"I don't hate it," I say. "I just don't think it's me."

"Okay, fair enough. Wait here."

When Vanessa returns, she hands me a pair of black jeans and a retro polo shirt that looks like it should be worn by someone named Skippy or Chip.

"No judgment until you try them on," she tells me.

I close the curtain again. The shirt's a muted yellow with bold navy stripes. And while I don't have the same relationship with religion my mama does, Lord help me if these jeans aren't tight. Still, if I saw this outfit on someone else, I might say it looked good.

"How's it going in there?" Vanessa asks.

"Um . . ."

"Stop fussing. What are you so afraid of?"

I'm afraid people will notice me. I'm afraid putting any amount of effort into the way I dress will tip everyone off that I'm not who I pretend to be. I'm afraid if I wear these clothes, and spend more time with Emmett, and keep working to be a chef . . . eventually, everything around me will come crashing down.

"I'm coming in," Vanessa says.

She opens the curtain and looks startled for a second, like she hates it.

"What?" I ask.

"No, it's nothing. You look really, um . . ."

"I knew it," I say. "I can't wear this."

"Good God, Luke. You can be so infuriating. You look hot, okay? Will you stop being so modest for once and own it?"

My face burns up. I put my hands in my pockets, then immediately take them back out.

"Now will you please let me take some pictures of you?" Vanessa asks.

I don't put up a fight. And when I look at the photos on her phone afterward, I can *almost* admit they aren't half bad.

"You're really good at this," I tell her.

She smiles. "I certainly got you out of your comfort zone."

Back in the dressing room, I remember what Vanessa said about taking risks. If I hang out with Emmett in public, there's a risk someone might see us. If I become attached to him, there's a risk he'll go home at the end of the summer and forget about me.

But what's the alternative? Not spending time with Emmett? Closing myself off from him? I'm not sure that's any better.

I take out my phone and pull up my old texts from Cody. We had fun together, and I don't regret spending time with him. But I don't think we ever really *knew* each other. Not in the way Emmett seems to already know me. Maybe I don't want Emmett to be another Cody. Maybe I want him to be something more. Which means I should probably stop comparing the two. If I want to give my relationship with Emmett—or whatever it is we have together—a real chance, I need to put Cody behind me completely.

I delete Cody's messages.

Followed by his number.

"By the way," Vanessa says through the curtain. "I'm buying you that outfit."

"I can't let you do that," I say.

"Yes, you can. Just promise me you'll wear it somewhere."

I look at my texts from Emmett.

The ones about the open mic.

"Okay," I tell Vanessa. "I will."

Chapter
19
EMMETT

Procrastination has always been a key part of my creative process. It's hard to stare at a blank page and fill it with words that don't sound like garbage. Especially when your phone is sitting right there, ready to distract you with hours of mindless scrolling.

Tonight, however, as I sit on the wicker furniture in Aunt Karen's backyard, my attention is being pulled elsewhere. I can't stop staring at the pictures of Luke and me in the photo booth. The third frame is my favorite—the one where he's laughing. I want to make him laugh like that all the time. But I can't, not in public.

I get why Luke has to be careful. And it's not like he hasn't opened up. That first time we hung out together, down by the gristmill, he was so guarded and reserved. But now, when it's just the two of us, he's different. It's like he's stopped looking over his shoulder, because he's too busy looking at me.

Which is why these past few days have been so hard. Outside of a few quick moments in between lunch breaks and shows, we haven't spent much time together. Luke's been heading into the restaurant early every morning, and I've been coming straight home at night to work on my song for the open mic.

Well, I've been working on my song for the open mic *and* on Verna's lyrics.

Okay, fine. Mostly just Verna's lyrics.

I know her song shouldn't be my priority. But Luke's trusting me with it. I have to make sure it doesn't suck. Besides, hers is easier to work on. I didn't have a lot of confidence in my songwriting skills to begin with. Once I started working on Verna's lyrics, however, I couldn't help comparing the two. Her lyrics are clever. They tell a good story. Everything I write feels immature and clichéd. "Dream Cowboy" is just a silly song I came up with back when I thought I didn't want a boyfriend. It's not even accurate anymore!

Accurate or not, though, it's all I have at this point. I tuck the strip of photos back into my songwriting notebook and grab my guitar. The open mic is tomorrow night. I need to *focus*. But when my fingers start moving, I find myself strumming the opening chords to Verna's song again. I add her lyrics, pleased with how good they sound over my composition.

When I get to the end of the song, I'm startled by someone clapping. Aunt Karen's standing on the patio, which is lit up with twinkle lights. "So," she says, dabbing at the corner of her eye. "You're planning to make everyone at the open mic cry, then, huh?"

"Why?" I ask. "What's wrong?"

She shakes her head, picking up a pitcher of sweet tea and walking over to me.

"Nothing's wrong. It's a really good song, that's all."

"Oh, thanks. But that's not for the open mic. It's just . . . something else I'm working on."

"Well, I'm a fan," she says, refilling my glass.

I strum the opening chords again, getting a sinking feeling in my gut.

"Did you like this song better than the other one I played for you?"

"The one about the cowboy?"

I nod. She pauses, drumming her fingers against the side of the pitcher. "They're both good songs. They just have different sounds. I think you should perform whichever one you're most confident about."

Hmm. Sounds like a diplomatic way of saying she doesn't want to choose for me. Probably because she doesn't want to be the one to tell me "Dream Cowboy" sucks major ass compared to Verna's song.

"I hate to interrupt a work session," Aunt Karen continues. "But I just got off the phone with your mom. She says you're ignoring her texts again."

I lean back in my chair and groan.

"They miss you," Aunt Karen says. "I know that may seem like a nuisance. But the way you feel about music . . . well, that's how they feel about you. It wouldn't kill you to call them back and at least pretend to be homesick."

"Wow, thanks for the guilt trip."

She smiles and turns to head back inside. "I can't always be the Fun Aunt, Emmett."

I haven't purposefully been ignoring Mom and Dad. I've just been busy with everything else. And they shouldn't take it personally. I've abandoned pretty much everyone back in Oak Park. I'm sure my friends think I'm a jerk for not keeping up with our group chats. But I only have three months here. I need to be efficient.

Still, I guess I owe it to my parents. They didn't *have* to let me leave for the summer. And even though I'm the opposite of homesick—I'd stay here forever if I could—I'd be lying if I said I didn't miss them a bit.

"Derek!" Mom shouts, answering my FaceTime call. "I've got him on the iPad."

"Just a sec," Dad calls from somewhere off-screen.

"What are you doing that can't wait?"

"Nothing. Relax."

Dad enters the frame, his hand buried deep in a bag of pretzels.

"Seriously?" Mom asks. "We ate an hour ago."

"What? I have a fast metabolism."

"Since when?"

"Um, hello . . . ," I say. "It's me. Your son calling. Maybe you can discuss Dad's metabolism another time?"

Mom and Dad settle down next to each other on the couch. I haven't been gone a full month yet and they appear to be one passive-aggressive comment away from a meltdown. I knew I should've pushed harder for them to get a dog.

"How's the show going?" Mom asks. "You've given me bragging rights at the office. Everyone else's kids are doing band or theater camp this summer."

"Any more Wanda Jean sightings?" Dad asks.

Okay, so maybe I'm glad I called. Mom and Dad might not get what country music is all about, but that's never stopped them from acting excited because they know it's important to me.

"The show's going well," I say. "And no more Wanda Jean sightings yet. But something else cool is happening. There's an open mic night at this music venue in town. Talent scouts come to it."

"That's nice," Mom says.

Nice? Nice is your grandma coming to your high school band concert and telling you you're talented. We're talking about industry professionals here, who will actually be on hand to see me perform. It's *freaking amazing*.

"Sometimes," I say, filling in the blanks for them, "if someone's really good, a scout might offer them a recording contract."

I wait for Mom and Dad to say something, but Dad just reaches for another pretzel.

"I'm going to perform in the show," I tell them. "I could be one of those people who is offered a contract."

Still nothing. If Dad wasn't busy chomping away, I'd think the screen froze.

"Well," Mom finally says. "Just be sure you don't get your hopes up too much."

Unbelievable. It takes everything I have not to roll my eyes. Mom's words shouldn't come as a surprise. She's always been a pessimist—or, as she prefers, a "realist." But knowing that doesn't help soften the blow.

"I'm not saying it *will* happen," I say, trying not to sound as annoyed as I feel. "I'm just saying it *could*."

"Do music venues usually let minors perform?" Mom asks.

"I'd think you'd at least need to be eighteen years old," Dad says. "Did your aunt put this idea in your head?"

"Forget it," I mutter.

"Emmett," Mom says. "We only want to make sure you're being careful."

Dad nods. "Yeah. And we never said it couldn't happen. This

business is tough. But if anyone's going to prove us wrong, I'm sure it's you."

Um . . . *thanks*?

I shouldn't complain. It's not as if my parents don't support me. They have good, steady jobs, which have paid for a lot of music lessons over the years. But we have very different ideas of what my future looks like. They see my music as hobby, something to pursue in my free time while I'm busy with my "real" job. I'm glad my parents love their careers, but I'm not like them. I don't have a choice—I have to do my music. It's the only thing I'm passionate about.

And, yeah, my chances of catching a scout's attention are slim. But is that really a reason not to try?

"I know you don't want to hear this," Mom says. "But don't forget you have to come home once summer is over. A music career can wait. Senior year can't."

"Yes, I'm fully aware," I say, feeling the weight of her words press down on me.

I know my parents think they're looking out for me, but their pessimism only fuels me to try all the harder. I have to show them I can do this. I have to show everyone. I don't want to go back home and be the kid who spent his summer working at a theme park. I want to go back home and be the kid who got discovered by a talent scout and is now one step closer to making his dreams come true.

After saying goodbye to my parents, I look over at my songwriting notebook, where the photos of Luke and me are tucked away. Mom's right about one thing: my time here is limited. I need to make the most of it.

I leave the photos where they are and pick up my guitar again.

"Dream Cowboy" might not be as good as Verna's song. But I have twenty-four hours to get it to where it needs to be. And I can't let anything—or anyone—get in my way. No matter how much I want to be spending time with him right now.

Chapter 20

EMMETT

If there's one good thing to be said for the bathrooms at the Rusty Spur, it's that they certainly don't lack for reading material. The stalls are covered in names, and phone numbers, and loopy half circles that look like boobs. Then again . . . they could be butts. Or maybe they're testicles? The point is: There's a lot of graffiti. Under an alarmingly misshapen penis, someone even had the audacity to write: "Kenny Rogers sucks."

The man performed "The Gambler," one of country music's greatest songs, and opened a successful chain of fast-food chicken restaurants, and *this* is the thanks he gets?

If there's a second good thing to be said for the bathrooms at the Rusty Spur, it's that they make for a great hiding spot. I mean, there's a reason they don't call this place the Clean, Recently Sanitized Spur—no one's going to come in here and linger any longer than needed. Which is good. Because now that I'm in this stall, I'm never leaving.

My phone lights up with a text. I'm so jittery, I almost drop it in the toilet.

I'm here.

Ready to be proven wrong about country music.

Oh God. I shouldn't have invited Luke. It's not that I don't want him to see me perform—I've only dropped a million hints about it. But it would've been better if he'd come to the Jamboree. I can do that show in my sleep by now. But this? The open mic? There's too much riding on it already.

What if my song sucks? What if the talent scout doesn't show up? What if they do show up, and they decide I don't have any talent worth scouting?

The door to the bathroom creaks open. "Emmett? You still in here?"

It's Jessie. If I don't respond, she'll go away.

"I wanted to check if you're okay. Sometimes they run out of toilet paper."

"There's plenty of toilet paper!" I shout.

Because why *wouldn't* I announce that?

Jessie's footsteps echo across the linoleum floor until her shiny silver cowboy boots stop in front of my stall. "You're sitting on the toilet fully clothed, aren't you?"

I pull the door open with my shoe. Jessie's wearing a red bandana knotted in her hair and an old Shania Twain concert T-shirt with the sleeves cut off.

"How are you not freaking out right now?" I ask.

She shrugs. "After you give one of the worst performances of your life on live TV, the stakes for an open mic feel a lot less intense. Besides, I come from a family of performers. My mom's a concert pianist. And by the time he was my age, my yé ye was a highly acclaimed erhu player in Beijing."

"So you're not at all worried about performing in front of the A&R scout?"

Jessie bites her bottom lip. "I grew up listening to a steady diet of Mozart, Chinese folk songs, and Faith Hill. Music's in my blood. So, yeah, of course I want to do well. But the only thing I have any control over is my performance. What the talent scout thinks of me . . . there's nothing I can do about that. I know I belong in country music. It's part of who I am. Which is why I plan to get up on that stage and perform my ass off tonight."

Jessie's right. I *know* she is. But after she leaves, I take a moment to stand in front of the bathroom mirror and study myself. The reflection staring back at me only makes me doubt myself all over again. To be a male country singer, you can't just slap on an oversized belt buckle and your best pair of cowboy boots. You have to really think about and cultivate your style. Is your signature look going to be plaid button-downs or plain white T-shirts? Do you wear a traditional cowboy hat or go for the more modern baseball cap? Can you pull off wearing distressed jeans? One of those military dog tag necklaces? What about a sleeve of tattoos?

I tried to keep it somewhat simple tonight by wearing a vintage black Western shirt with gold stitching. But as soon as I walked into the café, it became painfully obvious that I'm always going to look like the suburban kid who's trying to fit in. It's not even about the clothes. It's about the person wearing them. I don't look like a good old country boy, the kind who's strong enough to lift fifty-pound bales of hale all day yet tender enough to wrap you in his arms at night. No, I look like I'm about to ask if you want whipped cream on top of your nonfat skim milk latte.

It's not fair that your image can matter more than your talent. I mean, I get it. It's a business. The agents and managers and producers and CEOs know what type of artist sells the best. And if the formula ain't broke, why bother fixing it? But what about those of us who don't fit the mold? Don't we deserve our shot, too?

The bathroom door opens again. Jessie's head pops in.

"Emmett. We found him."

My thoughts immediately go to Luke. No one's supposed to know he's here.

"The A&R scout," she clarifies.

If I wasn't on edge before, I most definitely am now. But I didn't take all those music lessons, post all those YouTube videos, and bust my ass in the Jamboree for the past few weeks to hide in the bathroom when I have my first real chance at being discovered. I'm far too ambitious for that.

Pushing my nerves back down, I follow Jessie out into the café and upstairs to a small loft area overlooking the rest of the venue. The Rusty Spur isn't as big as the amphitheater at Wanda World. But it's not as small as the coffee shops I'm used to performing at back home, either. Peering over the railing, I see the tables are quickly filling up below.

"Where is he?" I ask.

Avery points to a row of tables lining the far wall. "Over there. The one who's sitting by himself."

The guy he's pointing to is holding a beer in one hand and scrolling through his phone with the other. He's younger than I expected. But I guess I don't know what a talent scout is supposed to look like.

"How do we know *this* guy's the one?" I ask.

Avery shrugs. "He has nice shoes."

"Seriously? That's all we're going off of?"

"What? You see a lot of guys wearing brown oxfords in this town?"

"Hey." Jessie waves her phone. "We should head back down."

As they turn to leave, I hang back to look for Luke. We already agreed we wouldn't talk to each other tonight—just to be safe. But I'd still like to know where he's sitting. That way I can at least direct my smile toward him when I'm looking out into the bright lights.

I scan the back of the room where Luke said he'd be, but don't see him there. In fact, I don't see him anywhere. Maybe he ran into someone he knew and had to leave? Or maybe he changed his mind. I check my phone. No texts.

Searching the rest of the crowd, I spot Aunt Karen and Grady sitting close to the front. My breathing stops when I see the third person at their table. *Shit.* Did Aunt Karen corner Luke and force him to sit with them?

He doesn't appear to be there under duress. Also: damn, he looks good. I mean, he always does. But he's wearing this cool retro shirt that makes him look . . . I don't know, dapper? Super-fucking-hot? My vision starts to get dark, and I grab on to the railing, suddenly feeling light-headed. *Am I about to pass out?*

No. Wait, that's just the houselights dimming. The buzz of the audience quiets as the stage lights come up and the host comes out to start the show. I hurry back downstairs and join Jessie and Avery at a table off to the side.

Thankfully, the three of us arrived early enough to sign up for the best performance slots. You never want to be first, because it takes the audience a few songs to warm up. And you never want to go last, because everyone's paying their tabs by then. So we're right in the middle. Which gives us time to check out our competition.

A burly guy with an impressive beard is the first to take the stage. After tuning his guitar, he uses a handkerchief to nervously wipe the sweat from his brow. I'm expecting his voice to be equally shaky. But when he sings, the sound that comes out of him is pure country. He has this deep, raspy tone that conjures up images of dusty red sunsets and dark amber whiskey.

My heart sinks. It'd be wrong to actively root against my fellow performers. But that doesn't mean I can't secretly hope no one's better than me.

The next couple of performers are also good. Someone even plays a dulcimer. I mean . . . *a freaking dulcimer?* How am I supposed to compete with that? I look over at the scout. He's still absorbed in his phone, but every once in a while I notice one of his expensive shoes tapping along to the beat.

The closer we get to my performance slot, the less sure of myself I become. A month ago, back when I was performing at coffee shops and posting YouTube videos from my bedroom, I was so certain I'd make it in this industry someday. But now that I'm here, now that I see all these other performers who are just as talented as me, if not more so . . . I'm not sure what I have to offer that they don't.

These people are the real deal.

I'm just a kid from Oak Park.

Cassidy takes the stage next. She's wearing a fringed suede vest and dark denim jeans that fit her like a second skin. With her wavy blond hair and glossy pink lips, she looks like a rodeo girl competing in the Miss America Pageant. Which is to say, she looks perfect. I glance at the scout. He's definitely not scrolling through his phone anymore.

"Hey, y'all," Cassidy says, smiling at the crowd. "What a fun audience! Y'all sure know how to make a girl feel welcome. I'm Cassidy, by the way. Cassidy St. Clare."

"That's not even her real name," Jessie whispers. "It's Cassie Jankowski."

Avery snickers. "Yeah, and I didn't realize they said *y'all* so much in Wisconsin."

Heat rushes to my cheeks.

Is that what everyone's going to think of me?

Cassidy begins her song. On a technical level, she's in tune and her phrasing is on point. But still, there's something off about her performance. I remember what Jessie said before: Cassidy's great at doing an impersonation, but when it comes to her own material, she's hollow and stiff.

You say you have to take things slow
And it's true, I'm not the only fish in your sea
But don't let me be the one that got away
'Cause, boy, you ain't never gonna find another girl like me

I hate to say it, but Jessie's right. Cassidy's like one of those animatronic opossums at Wanda World. There's no feeling or emotion behind her words. She might as well be singing out items from a grocery list.

Apple of my daddy's eye
Sweeter than that last sip of tea
It's time you realized what's in front of you
'Cause, boy, you ain't never gonna find another girl like me

At the end of Cassidy's song, Avery, Jessie, and I head backstage to a cramped green room. Jameson's already seated on the couch back there. And *shit*, he's also wearing a Western shirt. Of course it looks more authentic on him.

"'Sup, Jessie," he says, standing.

She gives him a polite smile, then grabs her guitar to start warming up.

"You nervous about performing?" he asks.

"Not really. I just need to focus right now."

Jameson nods. "Yeah. I get it. There's a lot riding on tonight. But hey, at least you and Avery have a leg up on the competition, right?"

Jessie stops strumming long enough to shoot him some serious side-eye.

"Because . . . um, you both stand out. And record labels are, like, looking for that sort of thing." Jameson's face turns pink as he stumbles over his words. "Sorry, that came out wrong. I just meant that straight white men are canceled now, you know?"

"Straight white men aren't canceled," Jessie tells him. "*Assholes* are canceled."

"Have you listened to the radio lately?" Avery asks. "Straight white men are thriving. Hell, they don't even need to be good."

Jameson folds his arms over his chest, pouting. "Well, *some* of them are good."

"I don't have time for this," Jessie says. "I'm up next."

Avery and I wish Jessie good luck. Not that she seems to need it. She carries herself with confidence as she goes to wait in the wings.

Jameson curls his mouth into a frown. "Guess I ruined my chances for Jesse James version 2.0, huh?" He grabs his guitar case and leaves the green room.

"Jesse James?" I ask Avery.

"That was their showmance name last summer. Like the outlaw?"

"Um. Okay."

Avery laughs. "Yeah, Jessie hated it when people called them that." He looks down at his guitar, fiddling with the tuning keys. "She deserves someone better than him."

"Someone like you?"

Avery looks back up at me, surprised.

"Sorry," I say. "I know it's not my business. But you two spend a lot of time together."

He shakes his head. "Nah, I don't think she likes me like that."

"Have you asked?"

Avery's a sizable guy. But his voice sounds tiny, defeated. "She said this was her year of saying no to everything, remember?"

"Maybe she'd make an exception for you."

"I doubt it."

Before we can argue the point further, Jessie gets called to the stage. Avery and I move to the wings to watch. I see Jessie perform in the Jamboree every day, but now that she's standing under the spotlight, I'm reminded of why she was so good on *Make Me a Star*. She has a great stage presence. And her voice is this perfect blend of twangy country and bubbly pop. Her talents are definitely wasted in the front half of our donkey suit.

After she finishes, she exits on the opposite side of the stage.

I grip my guitar so tightly I'm surprised I don't get splinters.

"Try and have fun out there," Avery says, giving my shoulder a pat. "That's all you can do at this point."

I want to believe him. But as I stand behind the curtain and wait for my name to be called, doubt fills my body like cement. My Dream Cowboy song still feels too amateurish. Everyone's going to see right through me.

"All right, y'all," the host says. "Next up, we have Emmett Maguire."

As the audience claps, I plaster a smile across my face and walk out there with as much confidence as I can muster. The stage lights are too bright, and the stool wobbles when I sit on it. But I try not to let that fluster me. I perform in front of audiences every night for the Jamboree. Why should tonight be any different?

After positioning my guitar, I do a quick scan of the room.

Aunt Karen is recording me on her phone.

Luke's biting back a smile.

The A&R scout just stifled a yawn.

Okay, so maybe tonight *is* different. The last thing I want to do is disappoint any of those people. Pushing a curl out of my face, I lean into the microphone. "Hey, I'm Emmett. This song is something I've been working on. I hope you like it."

My tongue feels too heavy. My throat's too thick. I check my posture and breathing, waiting for my performer instincts to kick in.

Come on. Everyone's waiting.

I start playing the intro, letting the familiarity of the chords wash over me. But my pulse is still racing too quickly.

Just pretend you're practicing in your bedroom. Pretend everyone is naked. Wait . . . don't pretend Luke's naked. That's too distracting. Try not to think about Luke. He's never seen you perform before. Oh God, what if I choke and he thinks I'm always this terrible?

Shit. I missed my opening line.

Relax. No one noticed. Just play the intro again.

As I repeat the notes I've already played, I feel every last eyeball on me—the audience knows something is up. I make the mistake of looking over at the scout. His chair's empty.

It's okay. Maybe he's at the bar.

Or maybe he's in the bathroom, writing "Emmett Maguire sucks more balls than Kenny Rogers" on the stall.

Reaching the end of the intro for a second time, I open my mouth. But no words come out. My fingers stop moving. My mouth clamps shut.

Why are you stopping? You have to play something.

Except I can't. The strings of my guitar send out their last vibrations, until the only sound left is the pounding of my heart.

21

LUKE

I've always been comfortable with silence. In fact, I usually prefer it to meaningless chitchat or too much background noise. I don't listen to podcasts, or play the radio when I drive. And I hate loud parties where you have to shout to be heard. That might make me sound like a grump. But there's something to be said for shutting out distractions. For being in the moment.

Except this moment.

This moment sucks.

The audience has gone completely still. No one's reaching for their drink or sneaking a peek at their phone. Even the clink of ice cubes over at the bar has stopped. We're all just sitting here, waiting for Emmett to do something.

Did he forget his lyrics? Have a sudden brain aneurysm?

Each passing second stretches out painfully. Tonight's super important for Emmett. I hate to watch him suffer like this. I feel like I should do something. *Say something.* But I can't. From the way my pulse is racing, you'd think I was up on that stage.

Next to me, his aunt finally breaks the silence.

"You've got this, Em!"

Emmett snaps out of it. Without missing a beat, he leans into the microphone. "That's my aunt, everyone."

People laugh, and it's like the audience has taken a collective sigh of relief. Emmett turns to look at me. We lock eyes, and I get the feeling he's trying to tell me something. But I don't know what.

"There's actually this other song I've been working on," he says, strumming his guitar again. "It's a little more old-fashioned. Classic country, I guess you could say. But I think you might like it better."

The chords he's playing this time are different.

They're softer. More tender.

"Anyhow . . . This is called 'Empty Rooms.'"

As he plays the intro, it finally hits me: That's what was written on the paper I found the locket in. I asked Emmett to set my nana's lyrics to music, but I didn't think he'd be performing it for people already. If he had warned me ahead of time, I'm not sure I would've come. Because what if the song's not any good? What if people hear it and they decide my nana's music was better off sitting in our basement?

Suddenly the room's too hot. I can feel the damp sweat collecting under the collar of my new shirt. I look around to see if anyone else has recognized the title. But of course they haven't. It's never been recorded before.

Dear Postmaster General,
From Paris, Texas, to Paris, France,
Your postmen have a long ways to go
And when December rolls around
They even make a stop at the North Pole

Well, today I'm writing to let you know
You can cross me off your delivery route
My mailbox is empty; no one sends love letters
Since the day my baby ran out

The hairs on the back of my neck prick up. Everything else around me fades away. Is this song about Wyatt leaving my nana?

Empty rooms in an empty home
Empty nights spent waitin' by the telephone
My baby promised we'd never be apart
But the only thing I live with now is a broken
And empty heart

Yeah, it has to be about that. But the way Emmett sings it, you can almost believe it happened to him. His voice is good, real clear. But there's also a layer of sadness to it. I read this article once about my nana. It said you could hear the teardrop in her voice. At the time I didn't know what that meant. But now that I hear Emmett sing the words she wrote, I think I do.

Dear Sears and Roebuck,
From shiny new dishwashers to fine silk robes
I'd turn the pages of your catalog with a smile
Checkin' off the things my baby and I would buy
To decorate our house in style

Well, today I'm writing to let you know
You can cross me off your delivery route
My bed is empty; no one lays their head next to mine
Since the day my baby ran out

I picture how empty our house must've looked without any of our furniture. Without Gabe's toys scattered around every room. Without Amelia's soccer cleats hanging from the banister on the stairs. Nana must've felt so alone. Did she know she was pregnant yet? Did she hold out hope that Wyatt would return?

Empty rooms in an empty home
Empty nights spent waitin' by the telephone
My baby promised we'd never be apart
But the only thing I live with now is a broken
And empty heart

My eyes grow wet. I don't want to cry. Especially not in public. Without saying anything to Emmett's aunt or her boyfriend, I scoot my chair back. I keep my head down as I make my way through the packed house, hoping it's too dark for Emmett to see me.

Outside, the temperature's dropped. Cooler winds blow down from the mountains this time of night, cutting away at the summer heat. I take in the fresh air—one large gulp of it—and push back my tears.

I don't know what happened in there. It's not like I didn't know how sad my nana's story was. But I guess I'm used to getting someone else's version of it. The version my mama tells me. The version Wanda

Jean has in her songs. The versions random strangers come up with online. This was my first time hearing the story in Nana's own words. I wasn't expecting to be so bothered by it.

If I'm going to get emotional, though, the parking lot of the Rusty Spur's not the place for it. There are too many tourists milling about this part of town. Heading off to Doolittle's Steakhouse for the all-you-can-eat buffet. Stopping by the Magic Kettle, then tossing handfuls of kettle corn to the geese as they stroll along the river walk. Or, if they've had enough liquid courage, visiting one of the many tattoo shops where they can fulfill their lifelong dream of having Wanda Jean's face permanently inked on their body.

Moving to the privacy of my truck, I take a minute to try to straighten myself out, but it's no use. I can't get my nana out of my head. It's like her music opened up something inside me, and now I can't shake it loose.

Did she ever get over Wyatt?

Or did she spend the rest of her life feeling empty inside?

Maybe I'm not only sad for my nana. Maybe I'm also sad for myself. I'm not saying I'm in love with Emmett—I'm not sure I'd know what that felt like. But I do know Emmett's not sticking around for long. If I never come out, and never leave Jackson Hollow, and never find anyone else . . . am I destined to end up alone like Nana did?

I think the worst part about my nana is that no one knew what she was going through. Her song was tucked away in a cookie tin. She never got to share it with anyone. Maybe she didn't want to, though. Maybe it was easier to write her feelings down and hide them away so she'd never have to think about them.

I've tried to hide my feelings, too. And right now, part of me just wants to stick my keys in the ignition and drive off. But I'm tired of living that way. So I take a deep breath instead and exit my truck.

By the time I make it back into the Rusty Spur, a new performer's onstage. I scan the crowd, looking for Emmett. But it's impossible to see over everyone. As I push my way through the cluster of people standing in back, a familiar voice stops me cold.

"Holy balls! Look who it is."

My body tenses.

"Hey, Whizzer," I say, turning around.

He's holding a Bud Light, which he takes a long pull from. "Shit, Lucille. I didn't know you liked country music."

Somebody tries to shush him. Whizzer flips them off.

"I . . ." My brain searches for the right answer. "Yeah, country music's okay, I guess."

"You guess? C'mon, now. Country music speaks to my soul."

Hold up, is Whizzer being *sincere?*

He gives my shoulder a punch. "So what the hell happened to you? Too much of a princess to work at the factory? Didn't like getting grease under your pretty little fingernails? Let me guess, you wanted to stay home so you had more time to wax your lady bits?"

Okay, there's the Whizzer I know.

"Actually," I tell him, "I got a job working in a kitchen."

He looks surprised, like he didn't think I'd have the guts to do it.

"Fuck. Lucille, that's great! Let me buy you a beer."

Coming here tonight, I was worried about running into someone I know. And while I wouldn't say I'm exactly relaxed around Whizzer right now, it's also not as bad as I thought it'd be. It was nice of him to offer to buy me a drink. Even if it doesn't erase all the homophobic jokes he made when we worked together.

"Maybe some other time," I tell him.

Just because I appreciate his offer doesn't mean I'm obligated to take him up on it. Leaving Whizzer behind, I make my way past the bar and end up by a door covered in posters for upcoming shows. The door swings open and a performer comes out with his guitar case. In the back hallway behind him, I catch sight of Emmett pacing nervously.

I stop the door with my boot and step through.

"Luke?" Emmett says, looking up at me.

He takes a step toward me, then stops.

"I'm so sorry. I swear, I wasn't planning to use your grandma's song. It's just . . . well, I knew mine sucked. And hers didn't. So I made a split-second decision. I should've asked for your permission first. But I panicked. The lights were so bright up there, and all I had to eat today was a bowl of cereal and some half-melted M&M's I found in my car before the show. Not that that's an excuse for what I did, but . . ."

As Emmett rambles through his apology, I walk over to him, take his face into my hands, and pull him in for a kiss. He's surprised but relaxes into it. Kissing Emmett always makes my stomach feel like a swirl of colors—like when you rinse out a set of watercolors and all the reds, and greens, and blues, and yellows mix together before circling down the drain.

"You left early," he says, when we finally separate. "I thought you were mad."

"I wasn't mad."

He looks at me, and I worry he can tell I've been crying. I know I shouldn't have to act tough around Emmett. But I can't help it.

"Thank you for putting my nana's words to music," I tell him.

"Did you . . . did you like it?"

The look on his face is so earnest it makes me want to kiss him all over again.

"Be honest," he says. "I can take it."

I've always kept my romantic life separate from my family life. And I have to admit, it's weird to watch the two cross paths like this. But if anyone's going to perform one of my nana's songs, I want it to be Emmett.

"I liked it," I say.

Relief floods his face, but only for a second.

"There's something else I have to talk to you about," he says, biting his lip. "And I'm not just bringing this up because you said you liked my song. I've been thinking about it for a while. But, um . . . I've never done this before, so I'm not sure how to do it. What I'm trying to say is . . ."

He pauses.

"I think we should be boyfriends, Luke."

I don't know why, but my immediate reaction is to laugh.

"It doesn't have to change anything," he says. "I don't care if no one else knows we're together. But *I* have to know. I don't want you to be some guy I'm fooling around with. I've fooled around with plenty of guys before. Okay, not plenty. But enough to know this feels different."

My heart starts racing. I don't know if it's out of fear or excitement. Maybe both. I've only been with one other guy. So I don't have a lot to compare it to. But what I do know is I've never wanted to be with anyone as much as I want to be with Emmett.

"Okay," I say.

"Really?" he asks.

"Yes. Really."

He smiles. And it's the kind of smile you could frame and hang in a museum. Like the gay *Mona Lisa*. The swirl of colors returns to my stomach. And as Emmett leans in to kiss me again, all I can think is: *I'm kissing my boyfriend.*

Chapter

22

EMMETT

Virginity can be a tricky thing. Lose it too early and people might think you're easy. Lose it too late and you could be labeled a prude. Lose it in the back hallway of a place called the Rusty Spur . . . and, well, you might become a cautionary tale in the lyrics of a country song.

Luke and I should slow down. Someone could walk in on us back here. But I can't think rationally right now. It's like we're standing at the edge of a cliff and I'm not afraid to fall. I just want to be with him—my boyfriend, officially.

Unfortunately, whoever keeps texting me is doing their best to ruin the moment.

"Maybe you should answer that," Luke says, kissing my neck.

"Maybe I have better things to do."

The buzzing doesn't let up. When I finally take out my phone, I have a bunch of missed calls from Aunt Karen. I read the most recent text she sent: **Some man is asking for you. He seems kind of important.**

She ended her text with a long string of nail polish emojis. Which is confusing. Plus my head is still dizzy from making out with Luke. But once I finally process what's happening, my whole world shifts.

"Is everything okay?" Luke asks.

I grab on to a fistful of fabric from his nice shirt.

"Emmett. What is it?"

I show him my phone, afraid if I say anything out loud, I'll jinx it.

"The talent scout?"

I nod.

"What are you waiting for? Get out there!"

I'm too stunned to move. *Finally, my potential has been discovered!* It feels conceited to think that. But I doubt modesty has ever landed anyone a recording contract. If you're going to make it in this industry, you have to believe in yourself. Full stop. And then you have to find someone else who believes in you just as much. Someone with connections and experience and power.

Luke practically has to push me down the hallway. When we get back into the café, the stage is empty and people are standing about. I look for Aunt Karen but almost get trampled by a group of women who are trying to get a line dance started for the Miranda Lambert song that's playing on the jukebox.

Squeezing my way through the crowd, I keep my eyes focused on everyone's feet. I'm looking for brown oxfords. No, wait—they were tan. And shiny. Like they had been recently polished. But were the toes pointed or rounded? Did they have those little dots? What's that called . . . broguing? *Jesus, Emmett. Just look for the person who's not wearing cowboy boots.*

"There he is! That's my nephew!"

I look up. Aunt Karen's waving me over. She and Grady are talking to someone, but there are too many people blocking my view for me to get a good look at them. As I make my way over, I glance back down at the floor. My excitement deflates like an untied balloon.

Boots.

Not oxfords.

"Emmett!" Aunt Karen pulls me in for a hug and squeezes me so tight she almost spills her drink on me. "You were amazing! Honestly, you were the best one onstage tonight. And I'm not just saying that because I'm your aunt. Well, okay, I *am* saying that because I'm your aunt. But look . . ." She releases me from her grip. "We have an unbiased opinion. This is Mr. Merrick. He thinks you were great, too!"

The man standing in front of me is a lot older than the A&R scout Jessie and Avery pointed out. He has a goatee, and salt-and-pepper hair that's pulled into a ponytail. I can't quite get a read on his style. He's wearing a blazer, which seems professional enough. But then jeans and a T-shirt underneath. Could this guy really work for a record label? Or is he just some random dude who liked my song enough to tell me so?

"Orrin Merrick," the man says, extending his hand.

I give him the firmest handshake I can, just in case. "Emmett Maguire."

"Your aunt's right, Emmett. You were very good up there."

Part of me thinks he's wrong. If I were good, I wouldn't have frozen in front of everyone. I would've been more prepared and performed my own song. But now's not the time to listen to my inner critic. Now's the time to sell myself.

"Thanks," I tell him. "That was my first time performing that song in front of an audience."

"Well, you couldn't tell. Do you write all your own music?"

"Yes. I do."

I don't realize it's a lie until the words are out of my mouth. Those were Verna's lyrics. Not mine. And although I was the one who set them to music, it feels wrong to take any of the credit. But I don't correct myself. Instead, I check to see if Luke heard. Except Luke's not here. I thought he was following me, but he must have hung back.

My shoulders sink. He should be a part of this.

"Do you have a demo ready to go?"

My attention snaps back to Orrin. Did he just *ask me for a demo*? I've waited for this moment for so long. Now that it's finally happening, I don't know how to process it. Is hysterical crying still considered unprofessional?

"I . . . um . . . yes, I have a demo."

Another lie. I have a collection of recordings. And they're not nearly good enough.

He pulls out a business card. "Great. Why don't you send it to me? I can't make any promises. But if I like what I hear, maybe we can set up a meeting."

I take the card and study it: *Orrin Merrick, Foothill Records.* I've never heard of his label before, but it looks official enough. I mean, it's on thick card stock and the logo's printed in color. So it's not like he made this on some janky-ass printer.

"Okay," I say, somehow managing to sound way more collected than I am. "I'll do that."

Orrin smiles at Aunt Karen and Grady. "It was nice chatting with y'all. Now if you folks will excuse me, I've got an early meeting with some clients in Nashville tomorrow." He points to me. "I'm looking forward to hearing that demo, young man."

As he walks away, I finally let my jaw drop. *He has a meeting with clients in Nashville? He's looking forward to hearing my demo?* Aunt

Karen and Grady are quick to congratulate me. Avery and Jessie come rushing over, too, demanding a word-for-word recap. It's great to celebrate with them, but I can't stop looking for Luke. He's the one I want to share this with the most.

When I finally have a chance to break away from everyone, Luke's waiting for me by the back hallway again. Except we're no longer alone. Musicians are collecting their guitars and congratulating each other on their performances.

"So?" he asks. "What happened?"

"He asked for a demo."

"Like, *for real*?"

"Yes. For real."

"Oh my God. Emmett. That's amazing!"

Luke looks so happy for me, and it's taking everything I have not to grab him by the face and pull him in for another kiss.

"Come back to my aunt's house," I say.

"Tonight? It's kinda late."

"You can spend the night."

"Your aunt won't think that's weird?"

"Of course not. Why would she—"

Shit. He doesn't know I already told Aunt Karen about us. I should've told him as soon as it happened. But I was worried about dinner going well and not scaring him away. The longer I wait now, the worse it's going to get.

"My aunt knows we're dating," I say. "I told her."

His body tenses. His eyes search my face, like he's trying to figure out how I could break his trust after promising not to.

"She'd already figured it out," I tell him. "And I knew if I tried to deny it, it would only make things worse. So I told her. Fuck. I'm so sorry, Luke. I know this probably doesn't make it any better, but my aunt was the first person I came out to. And she didn't say anything to my parents until I was ready to tell them myself. You can trust her, I promise."

He takes a breath. Then a second one.

"Okay," he finally says.

I don't know if that's a good okay, or a bad one.

"Are you mad?" I ask.

"No. If you thought telling her was the best thing to do in that situation . . . then, okay. I trust you."

"You do?"

"Yeah. I do."

It physically hurts, not being able to kiss him right now. Thankfully, as soon as we're back home, there's nothing *but* kissing. Aunt Karen's room is at the opposite end of the hallway, and I want to be respectful. But this is the first time Luke and I can make out someplace and not have to worry about being walked in on. It's hard to believe we've been together for almost a month now and we still haven't seen each other naked.

It's a situation we're doing our best to remedy.

Shoes and socks are the first to go. Luke pulls me in for another kiss, then rips open my shirt. (Who knew snap buttons could be so hot!) I feel like I should find a hanger for his shirt, seeing how nice it is. But Luke just tosses it onto the floor.

Pushing me onto the bed, he starts to crawl on top of me. Which is incredibly hot, except I'm also distracted by what's hanging from his neck.

"Your grandma's locket," I say, touching it.

He blushes. "Oh, yeah."

"I thought you wanted to sell it?"

"I do. I just, um, started wearing it for now."

"That's sweet."

His face goes red. Sitting back up, he tries to take the necklace off. But his fingers struggle with the tiny clasp.

"You can leave it on," I tell him.

"Emmett. I'm not having sex with my grandmother's jewelry on."

Oh. Right. He turns his back to me and I unhook it for him. Strangely enough, it feels more intimate than anything else we've done so far.

"Better?" I ask, handing it to him.

He sets the locket on the nightstand and turns around to kiss me again. And as we fall back into bed, it finally hits me: *He said we're going to have sex.* I mean, I want to. But I haven't planned for this moment yet. I always thought I'd lose my virginity later, after high school. I've never had time for boyfriends. Or even a one-night stand. My music always came first.

My heart beats wildly as we get down to our underwear. I really want to do this, but I can't quite shut off the overachiever part of my brain. The part that likes to be prepared. "How do we know who does what?" I ask. "Should we, like, figure out the logistics first?"

He looks at me. "Yeah. We can do that. Or we can go with the flow."

"I just mean . . . I didn't plan ahead. I don't have any protection."

"Don't worry." He kisses my shoulder. "I got us covered."

"You do?"

"Hold on, I should double-check the expiration date." He stops and grabs his jeans from the floor. Pulling a condom out of his wallet, he reads the foil package and flashes me a smile. "Yeah, we're good to go."

"*I've never had sex before.*"

I didn't mean to blurt it out. It just happened.

He laughs.

"Oh my God. You can't do that, Luke! You can't laugh!"

"I'm sorry. I'm not laughing at you, I swear. It's just . . . I can't believe there's finally something you haven't already done before me."

"Not everything has to be a contest," I tell him. "Also, wait—you've done this before? *With a guy?*"

Now it's his turn to be embarrassed. His cheeks go pink. "Yeah. Does that surprise you?"

No, I guess not. But it does make me more nervous. What if I'm not any good? What if it hurts too much? What if I do something wrong and embarrass myself?

"Hey," Luke says. "We can wait if you're not ready. It's not a big deal."

I look at him, allowing myself to get lost in those soft brown eyes. Back at the Rusty Spur, Luke said he trusted me. And I know I trust him, too. So maybe it's a good thing that he's already done this. Maybe I can stop trying to control the outcome of everything for once and let Luke take the lead.

"I want this," I say, pulling him back into me.

Sex with Luke isn't magical. Or rather, I should say sex with Luke isn't *only* magical. Because, yes, there are some moments where I'm like, *Holy shit, why haven't I been doing this sooner?* But there's also some awkwardness. And a few moments where I feel a little uncomfortable. Especially since this is my first time. But in the end, once it's over, none of that matters. Because even the less magical parts add up to something good.

Afterward, as we lie tangled up in one another, it doesn't take long for Luke's breathing to grow heavy. But I'm too excited to sleep. So many good things happened tonight: Luke and I became boyfriends. Luke and I had sex. A freaking scout gave me his freaking business card.

Thinking about Orrin, a small jolt of panic rushes through me. He wants me to send him my demo. The demo that's been rejected by every label I've sent it to. The demo with songs that are nowhere near as good as Verna's. The demo I was supposed to be working on this summer but didn't, because I let myself get distracted.

Although this past month with Luke has been amazing, I've often stopped putting my music first. Tonight was the perfect example: I choked onstage and almost blew my shot at the open mic. And now that Orrin wants to potentially meet with me, shouldn't my focus be back on my career? The thing I've spent so much time working toward?

I hate to admit it, but what Luke and I have is temporary. We both know I'm going back home at the end of summer. Sure, we could try the long-distance thing. But for how long? As much as I love the Jamboree, I don't want to come back and work at Wanda World again next summer. I want to sign with a label. And go on tour. And be famous enough to have my own amusement park someday.

I've been in Jackson Hollow for almost a month now. And trying to find a balance between my music and Luke is tough. If I were forced to choose between the two of them right this second, I'd choose Luke. How could I not? But what if Orrin wants to meet with me and offers me a contract? Would I really be able to turn that down?

My mind won't stop racing. I sit up slowly, careful not to wake Luke. Back home in the suburbs, it's usually pretty quiet at night. But there's something different about the silence here in Jackson Hollow. The house is completely still. Over at the window, the shades are still open a crack, allowing moonlight to spill in and illuminate the locket on the nightstand. I pick it up and read the inscription again.

All those years ago, Wyatt was falling in love with Verna.

And now, I think I'm falling in love with Luke.

That scares me a bit. I've never been in love before. Sure, I love my family. And country music. And Wanda Jean. But being in love with a guy? Being in love *with Luke*? That's new. And it's not just my career I might be sacrificing in choosing to be with him. There's also the matter of my feelings. My heart. What if I get too attached? When I go back home in a few months, those other things will still be there for me. Luke won't.

Maybe that's another reason to put my music first. But when I lie back down and Luke wraps his arms around me, pulling me closer to him . . . it feels like I'm making the right choice. A recording contract would still be great, of course. But this moment right here? I wouldn't trade it for anything in the world.

Chapter

23

LUKE

I'm not always a morning person. So when I wake up in a strange bed and find two eyes staring back at me from under a curtain of curly dark hair, it takes me a second to remember where I am.

"Sorry," Emmett says. "I was being creepy and watching you sleep."

As the events of last night slowly return to me, a smile stretches across my face. There's no point in trying to play it cool. That may not have been my first time having sex. But it *was* my first time that didn't involve a six-pack of beer and the back of my truck. Waking up next to Emmett is a million times better.

"Hi," I say, my face still half buried in the pillow.

Emmett blushes. "Hi."

We stare at each other for a while. I like studying Emmett's face. His long eyelashes. His dimples. That smile.

"So," Emmett says. "Last night."

"Yeah. Last night."

"Should we talk about it?"

"Which part?"

"Deciding to be boyfriends? Deciding to . . ." He drops his voice to a whisper. ". . . *have sex?*"

I try not to laugh at how cute he is. "Are you having regrets?"

His eyes go cartoonishly wide. "No! Are you?"

"No."

"Okay. Good."

"What about the part where you killed it at the open mic and talked to a talent scout?" I ask. "You didn't forget about that, did you?"

"Are you kidding me? I've only wanted this for, like, my entire life. And that's not an exaggeration. I sent my first demo to a recording studio when I was twelve. It was terrible! But I've sent plenty of less terrible demos since then, and no one's ever responded."

He pauses, and the smile vanishes from his face. "You know what, I don't want to jinx it. This guy might not even listen to it."

"Emmett. He wouldn't have asked for it if he didn't want to hear it."

"We don't know that!"

"Are you serious?"

"Look, I'm just trying to manage my expectations in case nothing happens."

"Fine. But I want you to promise me something, okay?"

"What?"

I try to say it with a straight face, but my smirk gives me away: "That you won't forget about me when you get famous."

"Shut up."

"I'm serious. When you go to the Grammy Awards and collect your trophy for Hottest Dude in Country Music, I expect to be acknowledged in your acceptance speech. I slept with you *before* you were somebody. Don't forget that."

"First of all, there's no award called 'Hottest Dude in Country Music.' Second, who says I'm good enough to win a Grammy?"

"C'mon, you don't think you are?"

"I mean, I *want* to believe I could be good enough someday. But there's more to it than that. It's a popularity contest, just like anything else. And when it comes to male country singers, the straight ones are a lot more popular."

"So your first hit song isn't going to be about how you lost your virginity to a cute dishwasher from Jackson Hollow?"

"Oh my God." He grabs his pillow and hits me with it. I try to wrestle it away from him, but he retaliates by tickling me. Before things can get too hot and heavy again, there's a knock on the door. We both freeze.

"Emmett?"

"Uh . . . yeah?"

"I made pancakes. In case anyone's interested in breakfast."

"Okay. Thanks, Aunt Karen."

He puts his pillow over his face, muffling his laugh. When he sits up, I see his curls are even more ridiculous in the morning. I try not to smile too much, but it's impossible. I can't believe I have a boyfriend. I can't believe I get to see what he looks like at the beginning of the day, before anybody else does.

"You want pancakes?" Emmett asks.

I do. But I'm not sure about having breakfast with his aunt. It was one thing to sit with her at the café last night. But now that I've spent the night in her guest room, she's going to know Emmett and I had sex. That shouldn't embarrass me, but it does.

"I should probably head home," I say.

Emmett sighs. "Yeah. I need to work on which songs I'm sending to the scout."

We go back to staring at one another. Neither of us wants to be the first to move. I'm sure he's itching to work on his demo. Just as I'm sure my mama's about ready to send out a search party. But for the next couple of minutes, the only thing that matters is this.

Arriving home later that morning, I make sure to open our front door as quiet as I can. It always sticks in the door frame, announcing your entrance with a rattle. I don't know why I'm being so secretive, though. I texted Keith last night and told him I was going to a party in Rayburn, then crashing with some of the guys from school.

Entering our foyer, my nostrils sting as I catch a whiff of something acidic and lemony. Keith's not home from his shift yet, and Gabe or Amelia wouldn't do housework without being bribed. Which leaves one option: Mama's in one of her cleaning moods.

"That you, Luke?"

I look down at my new shirt, which is wrinkled from sitting on Emmett's floor all night. "Vanessa picked it out for me," I say.

Mama stands, clearing a loose strand of hair out of her face with the back of her glove. "Is that so?" She sounds pleased. Like she's been praying for this moment since Vanessa and I broke up a few months ago. "And how *is* Vanessa these days?"

"She's fine, Mama."

"Is that who you were hanging out with last night?"

"No," I say, a tad too defensive. "It was just a bunch of people from school."

Mama can't help herself. She's grinning like I just won a blue ribbon in heterosexuality. "Luke, honey. You know I can tell when you're lying to me, right?"

My throat goes dry.

If only my lies were as uncomplicated as she thinks they are.

"I'm just saying . . . ," Mama continues. "*Whoever* you're hanging out with, you don't have to hide it from me. I know the Bible has some unrealistic expectation for young people these days. But your step-daddy and I aren't completely out of touch. Forty percent of teenagers are sexually active in high school. I read that on Facebook."

"Oh my God, Mama. It ain't like that."

"If you're not comfortable talking about sex," she says, tilting her head, "maybe that's a sign you're not ready to be having it."

"Vanessa and I aren't . . ." I stop myself. "Can we please drop this?"

She puts her gloves up in surrender. "Okay. But if you need to talk, I don't want you to think you can't come to one of us."

I doubt she'd be saying that if she knew what really happened last night.

"You sure you should be doing all this housework?" I ask, pointedly changing the subject.

"Dr. Collier agreed it'd be good for me to be more active a few hours a day. Besides, this house is a mess."

"Well, will you at least let me help?"

"No." She picks her cloth back up from the floor and shoos me away with it. "You do enough around here."

As Mama starts to dust the top of the sideboard cabinet, I notice the past-due bill is still sitting there, along with another stack of mail. Who knows how many other bills are waiting in there. It's been months since Mama's seen a paycheck. And Gabe and Amelia seem to clean out our cupboards faster than I can get paid every other week. I want to ask Mama about it, but I know it'll only cause her more stress.

"At least let me bring that to the basement," I say, pointing to the box of Christmas decorations still sitting in the corner. There's no way I'm letting Mama lose her balance on those creaky old stairs and have to go back on bed rest again.

Mama looks at the box. "Christmas decorations go up in the attic."

"Since when?"

"Since your stepdaddy reorganized the basement. Just leave it for him. You know how particular he is about where everything goes up there."

"It's okay, Mama." I grab the box before she can protest. "I don't mind."

After giving Mama a quick kiss on the cheek, I head upstairs and pull the ladder down from the hall ceiling. No one hardly ever goes into our attic. The light bulb doesn't even turn on when I yank on the shoestring that's attached to it.

Thankfully, there's a shaft of light coming from a window at the far end of the room. Making my way through the dust particles that are floating in the air, I find the other Christmas decorations and place the box with them. The floorboards creak beneath my weight, and I worry about crashing through the ceiling. But before I leave, a set of old suitcases catches my eye.

Crouching next to them, I take out my phone and shine a light on the stickers they're covered in: *The Sugarloaf Lounge. Bucky's Honky-Tonk Saloon. The Grand Ole Opry.* These must be Nana's. I don't know why I didn't think to look up here sooner. Our roof leaks so much I assumed we kept anything of value in the basement.

There are three suitcases in total. I open the largest first, careful not to break the cracked leather straps that hold it shut. There's a musty patchwork quilt sitting on top. I look underneath it, hoping to discover something better, but all I get is another quilt.

The next suitcase contains old bath towels and a hot water bottle, which doesn't leave me much hope for the final one.

This last suitcase is more circular—a hatbox, I think. When I open the lid, my heart leaps in my chest. It's filled with photos. I grab one off the top. The paper's curling around the edges and the coloring is faded, but I can tell right away it's my nana. Her long blond hair's swept to the side and she's wearing a checkered shirt tied at the waist. She's got her guitar with her, like it was supposed to be some kind of publicity shot but whoever's behind the camera is making her laugh too much.

I start going through more photos: Nana performing onstage. Nana standing outside a tour bus. Nana posing with fans.

I can't get over how young she is. She was probably my age here. And she looks so happy. I don't understand why Mama would keep these hidden away. Doesn't she want to remember Nana like this?

I get my answer soon enough, when I find photos of Nana and Wanda Jean. I've seen pictures of them together before—there's a few floating around online. But these are different. More personal. They're doing normal-people stuff: Sitting on a front porch swing. Peering over the railing of the Jackson Hollow Bridge. Blowing out the candles on a birthday cake.

Did Nana regret losing her best friend?

Did Wanda Jean ever forgive her?

Reaching for another photo, my hand brushes against something else. I pull out an old journal. There's a doodle of flowers on the cover, and the pages inside are filled with the same handwriting I found on the piece of paper the locket was in. These must be lyrics, too. Flipping to the back of the journal, I find more folded-up squares of paper tucked inside. There must be *dozens* of songs in here.

There's an ache in my chest. I think about Emmett performing Nana's song at the open mic, and how good it was. What about the rest of these songs? Did she mean to keep them hidden away? Or was she never allowed to perform them? I guess after the scandal with Wanda Jean and Wyatt blew up, no one was interested in hearing what she had to say. That doesn't seem fair, though.

"Luke?" Mama's voice travels up from the hallway down below. "Everything okay up there?"

"Yeah, Mama. Just finishing up."

I carefully return everything to the suitcase. I'll come back for those later. But for now, I keep the photo of Nana with her guitar.

Once I'm back downstairs, I head to my bedroom and shut the door. In the bottom drawer of my dresser, hidden under my jeans, is the picture of Emmett and me kissing in the photo booth. Hopefully Nana won't mind hanging out with us for a while. I know she wasn't the biggest fan of Wanda World. But this way, she'll finally have some company.

Chapter

24

EMMETT

Fun fact: There are 86,400 seconds in every day. Which means, if I sent Orrin the link to my demo two days ago, right after I added Verna's song to it, then I've had to sit through 172,800 seconds of not hearing back from him.

Look, it's not like I expected him to listen to it right away. But he didn't even respond to confirm he received my email. *What if he didn't get it? What if it went to his spam folder? What if he heard my demo and was so disgusted by it, he lit his computer on fire and gave up being a talent scout?*

"Emmett! Put your phone away. We're going to miss our cue."

I set my phone back down on the wooden crossbeam behind one of the stage flats. It's my hiding place for it during the show. Every time I step offstage, I run over here to check it. One of these times, I swear, there's going to be a reply from Orrin. Even if it's not the one I want to hear, it's better than being left in the dark like this.

As Jessie and I secure the two halves of our costume together and rush to make our entrance on time, I remind myself how lucky I am to be in this show. It's funny—at the beginning of summer I had to pinch myself every time I walked out onstage. And now . . . well, it feels more like a job. That's not to say the Jamboree isn't still fun. But compared to performing at the Rusty Spur? Compared to having an A&R scout hand you his business card? It's like having a bowl of cantaloupe for dessert when you know there's also chocolate cake.

To make matters worse, today's one of our dreaded three-performance days. Which doesn't leave me enough time to visit Luke during my breaks. After our first performance is over, I sit at my dressing room table, obsessively refreshing my inbox some more.

When my phone finally dings with a new message, I almost lose it. Until I see it's only a 20 percent off coupon from BigBeltBuckles .com.

"Everything okay?" Avery asks, looking up from his physical therapy textbook.

I set my phone down with a sigh. "I still haven't heard from the scout."

"Hasn't it only been, like, a day?"

"Two days, Avery. *Two*."

He chews on the cap of his highlighter, shaking his head. "I hate to break it to you, but when Hayden was poached, it was because of a performance he did at an open mic *last* summer. The record label didn't offer him a contract until about nine months later."

"*Nine months?*"

My phone dings again. It's Luke, asking if there's any news yet. Which is another reason I'm anxious for Orrin to get back to me. Luke found some more of his grandma's songs to sell. Which is great for him. But until I start making some connections in this business, I'm not sure how much I'll be able to help.

I lower my head onto the makeup table.

"This is killing me."

When I look back up, I catch Cassidy in the mirror, shooting me a dirty look from across the room. Not that I blame her. Besides being ungrateful, I'm also being rude to the rest of my castmates. No one else had a scout come up to them after the open mic.

Although Cassidy did make a point to tell me Foothills Records was more of an indie label, therefore implying it wasn't worth her time. She also claimed Grady had promised to put her in touch with somebody from Sony Nashville. Which, on behalf of Aunt Karen, made me want to politely ask her to get off Grady's nuts.

After texting Luke back and refreshing my inbox for the millionth time, I take Orrin's business card out of my pocket. Not that I need to look at it. I've studied it so many times I can recite it from memory.

"Fuck it," I announce. "I'm calling him."

Avery looks up from his textbook. "Calling who?"

"The scout."

"Emmett, my dude. I'm not sure that's a good idea."

"It's fine," I say. "He gave me his phone number. If he didn't want people calling him, then he wouldn't have put it on his business card."

"Uh, maybe you want to take a minute to think this over?"

"I have thought it over. And I already know what I'm going to say."

Before Avery can talk me out of it, I leave the dressing room and head back upstairs. My heart races as I unlock my phone, unsure whether I have the nerve to really go through with this. But then I look up at the painted backdrop of the Great Smoky Mountains that hangs backstage. This is where I ran into Wanda Jean during our show. This is where she told me I had grit. And Wanda Jean is *never* wrong.

I dial the number. My palms sweat as the phone begins to ring.

And just as I worry I'll have to leave a voice mail, someone answers: "Orrin Merrick."

"Hi. Mr. Merrick. I'm sorry to bother you. This is Emmett Maguire. You heard me perform at the Rusty Spur the other night?"

The line is silent. My heart sinks.

"Mr. Maguire. Yes. How are you?"

Mr. Maguire? Are you freaking kidding me?

"I'm good. I just . . . I wanted to make sure you got the demo I sent?"

There's a pause. Maybe he's double-checking his email. Or maybe he's attempting to strangle himself with the phone cord.

"Yes, I received it. But I haven't had time to give it a proper listen yet."

"Oh, that's okay," I tell him. "I don't want to rush you. I was just worried it got lost. Sorry, I realize you're a busy person. But, well . . . I'm very determined to make it in this business. I know I'm supposed to be patient and play it cool. I'm just finding that impossible to do."

Honestly, I'm proud of how much restraint I'm showing. Because what I really want to do right now is scream: "JUST PUT ME OUT OF MY FRICKING MISERY, DUDE."

"You're in Jackson Hollow, right?" Orrin asks.

"For the summer. Then I go home to Chicago."

More silence. Followed by what sounds like a few clicks on a keyboard.

"Well, I'll tell you what, Mr. Maguire. I'm going to be passing through Junesburg on Friday. If you can make the drive up there, I could probably squeeze you in for a quick cup of coffee. Do you think you'd be free in the morning?"

I can't believe he's asking me that. As if I'd have to check my schedule first. "Yes," I reply, hoping he can't tell how hard I'm smiling through the phone. "I can make that work."

After another excruciating 172,800 seconds, Friday morning is finally here. And my day begins with a surprise: Mom and Dad sent flowers with a note about how proud they are of me. It's nice to know I have their support. And maybe it's naive, but I have a good feeling about my meeting with Orrin today. If he was going to reject me, wouldn't he have done it over the phone? Or by email? Why go to all the trouble of meeting me just to crush my dreams in person?

Although Junesburg is only an hour north of Jackson Hollow, and I'm capable of using my phone's GPS, Aunt Karen insists on driving me. She claims that if I'm going to sign a contract today, I'm still a minor and will need parental consent. I tried to remind her that not only is she *not* my legal guardian, but the chances of me being offered a contract on the spot are extremely slim.

"Well, what if he's an ax murderer?" Aunt Karen asks.

"Um. What?"

"He could be luring you here under false pretenses."

"Aunt Karen. We looked him up ahead of time. He's legit."

She turns her blinker on as we exit the freeway. "You don't think it's easy to build a fake online persona? Clearly you've never been on any dating apps before."

As we cruise through downtown Junesburg, I try to take everything in. This could be a pivotal moment in my life. I don't want to forget a thing. The main street is filled with historic brick buildings. There are antique shops, and fashion boutiques, and a store for handcrafted wood carvings called "Birch, Please!"

When we arrive at the coffee shop I'm supposed to meet him at, there's an open parking spot on the street right out front. Another good sign! As Aunt Karen parallel parks, I spot Orrin through the large picture window. He's sitting at a table with his laptop open and his phone glued to his ear.

"Okay," Aunt Karen says. "In all seriousness, if something about this doesn't feel right, we can leave at any time. You don't have to agree to anything if it's not one hundred percent what you want."

It's nice of her to worry, but I've done my research. I know what red flags to look for. Besides, this meeting feels a lot more informal. Like maybe it's the first step to *eventually* getting signed.

"I'm glad you're here with me," I tell Aunt Karen. Which is absolutely true, and makes this next part all the harder to say. "But, um, would you mind if I talked to Orrin alone? I don't want it to seem like I'm a little kid, you know?"

She smiles, brushing my hair out of my face. "If that's what you want, then yes. I'm just so proud of you. You're really going to be somebody someday. No—you already *are* somebody. I hope you know that."

I give her a hug and exit the car before either of us can get all misty-eyed. When I enter the coffee shop, Orrin's still on his phone. I feel like I should order something, but the last thing I need is caffeine. I already have enough energy coursing through my veins.

Spotting me, Orrin waves me over, and I take a seat across from him as he wraps up his call. He sounds busy. Saying things like "I'm not comfortable with those margins." And "Marketing needs to get their heads out of their asses, then." When he's done, he sets his phone down and takes a sip from his mug. A drop of coffee hits his shirt, blossoming into a stain.

It puts me at ease a bit, knowing he's human.

"Mr. Maguire," Orrin says, offering me his hand.

"Mr. Merrick," I reply, shaking it. "Thanks again for meeting with me."

"Well, I have to tell you, I liked your tenacity. If you wanna make it in this business, talent's only part of the equation. You also need to possess a willingness to never give up."

"All I've ever wanted is to be a country singer," I tell him. "I can't imagine giving up."

He studies me for a second. "Son, may I ask how old you are?"

"I'm seventeen. But I've been taking guitar lessons since I was a kid."

He nods. "We could probably pass you off for about two years younger. Which is good. I'm not saying it's right, but this industry is obsessed with youth. A talented fifteen-year-old's more exciting than a talented seventeen-year-old."

Shit. Maybe I should've had Aunt Karen come in with me after all.

"I'm a straight shooter," Orrin says, finally closing his laptop. "So I'm gonna give you my assessment. I listened to your demo a few times. Your singing's great. There's not much we'd have to change there. But your other songs, well, they need work. I liked the one I heard at the Rusty Spur better."

A massive lump forms in my throat. I try to swallow it down, but it feels like the size of a grapefruit. He liked Verna's song. Not mine.

"Your biggest challenge, however, is going to be your online presence. If I present you to my label, they're going to want to see that you have a sizable audience already. Now, I didn't have much time, but I did manage to dig around a bit. The numbers on your YouTube channel aren't dismal. But they're nowhere close to where they need to be."

Fuck the grapefruit. The lump is a bowling ball now.

"If you want my professional opinion," Orrin continues, "you need to find your niche. I think you should focus on songs with an old-school feel. Some people try crossing over to pop. But anyone can sing that crap. If you stick closer to country's roots, I think you can build some credibility for yourself. It might take longer to grow your audience, but it'll pay off in the end."

My fingers grip the bottom of my chair. This obviously isn't what I was hoping to hear. But if I want to improve as an artist, I have to be open to criticism. Besides, if I take a step back and think about what he's saying, he makes some good points.

"Of course, then there's also the matter of your pronouns."

"Oh," I say, surprised by his inclusiveness. Maybe my own prejudices are showing, but I assumed someone like Orrin wouldn't think to ask.

"My pronouns are he and him," I say.

The middle of his forehead squishes together, as though I started speaking in tongues.

"What?" he asks.

"My gender pronouns. They're he and him."

"I'm talking about the pronouns in your songs," he says. "You sing about kissing other boys. Not girls. That's going to be a problem for a lot of country fans."

Up until this moment, the coffee shop has been filled with noises—people talking, milk steaming, ambient music playing overhead. It all turns to static. My plan wasn't to be a country music star. My plan was to be a *gay* country music star.

"Listen," Orrin says, waving his hand as if he's swatting away a fly. "I don't have a problem with gay people. My wife's hairdresser is gay, and he does an outstanding job with her hair. But if we look at this realistically, your target audience is going to be teenage girls and middle-aged women. If you're singing a love song, you've got to be able to sell the fantasy to them."

I get a sour taste in my mouth. "So what are you saying? I can't get a recording contract unless I lie to everyone?"

He takes another sip of coffee, considering it. "I don't think you can get a recording contract until you expand your platform. If you could get one of your songs to go viral, then that's something I could bring to the higher-ups. But that's not gonna happen if you sing about kissing boys. I'd be happy if you could prove me wrong. I really would."

"What do you consider going viral?" I ask, already dreading the answer.

Orrin scratches his goatee. "If it happens, you'll definitely know."

If I weren't so shocked, I'd probably burst into tears. The worst part about everything he just said is that, if I take a second to think about it, I know he's probably right. Realizing that makes me want to run out of the coffee shop and throw myself into oncoming traffic. But that's not going to fix the problem. And so, in the interest of not burning the only connection I've made so far, I tell Orrin I'll take everything he said into consideration and thank him for his time.

"Let's keep in touch," he tells me.

"Sure," I say, hoping he means it.

When I head back outside, Aunt Karen's waiting for me on a bench. She looks hopeful, like she's convinced something good has already come of this.

"Well?" she asks, standing up.

I could tell her the truth.

Or I could take Orrin's advice and start selling the fantasy.

"No recording contract," I say, keeping my voice upbeat. "But our meeting went really well. I know exactly what I have to do now."

Chapter

25

LUKE

For the past week, César's been training me on side dishes: Creamy grits. Buttery sweet corn. A giant tub of tangy pimento cheese we serve like scoops of ice cream. But for today's lesson, we're finally going off-menu. I'm learning how to make tortas ahogadas, which translates to "drowned sandwiches." It's a lot more complicated than it sounds, though. And since César's from Guadalajara—where this dish was invented—and he's having me fix enough plates to feed everyone our family meal, there's added pressure to get it right.

Since our supplies are limited to the food we serve at Granny's Cupboard, it's not an exact version. Instead of the traditional type of bread—a "bolillo," according to César—I'm using baguettes that will soon go stale. And we have to settle for the restaurant's pulled pork over real carnitas. But I made the sauce from scratch, and César even brought in some special peppers for me to use. No, not peppers. *Arbol chilies.*

"Stomachs are growling," César teases as he passes by.

Lifting my sliced baguettes off the flattop grill, I check to make sure they're slightly toasted on the inside. Next I slather on some refried beans, stuff each one with pork, and douse the sandwiches in a generous pool of the sauce I made.

As I finish off the plates with some onions and a wedge of lime each, Paulo, Bjorn, and the other chefs crowd around me, ignoring the stream of order tickets that are spitting out of the printer. I'm almost too nervous to eat with them. But César says an important part of being a chef is knowing how to critique your own food.

"Well?" he asks, waiting for me finish my first bite.

It takes my taste buds a moment to recover from the intense heat of the chilis. But the sauce has a nice smoky flavor. And I like how it softens the bread without taking away all the crunch. Still, César always finds something that can be improved on.

"Seasoning?" I venture.

He nods. "You're still under-salting your beans, güero. Better to be bold than timid."

I wish my palette were as refined as his. But it's not like anyone's stopped eating. So I guess I'll take that as a compliment.

Before we can finish, the service doors swing open and Rodney barges in with a stack of dirty dishes. "What are y'all doing standing around eating?"

The cooks pay him no mind. Rodney may be the manager, but he's definitely not the one who runs this place.

"Staff meeting," César replies, crossing his arms.

Rodney frowns, turning his attention to me. "Luke, the dining room's a mess."

"Sorry, sir," I say, trying not to smirk. "But my shift ended two minutes ago."

When I enter the employee locker room, Vanessa's sitting on one of the benches, watching something on her phone. It's always a bit jarring to see the servers, who are forced to dress like Colonial milk-maids, using modern technology.

"Hey," I say, throwing my dirty apron in the hamper.

Vanessa's too distracted to respond. I unbutton my dishwasher shirt and toss it in my locker. Now that Mama's up and about again, I have to be extra careful not to wear it home.

"Hey," Vanessa says. "Isn't this your friend?"

My heart thumps against my rib cage as it becomes clear to me what video she's watching. Emmett asked if he could upload his performance of my nana's song to his YouTube channel. I figured if more people saw it, it might increase our chance of selling it.

I suddenly feel naked. And not because I'm standing here shirtless. It's different to know someone's watching it. *Someone I know.* I'm proud of Emmett. And I'm proud of my nana. But I guess I didn't realize I'd be sharing them with the rest of the world.

"What friend?" I ask, pulling a clean shirt over my head.

"That guy who came in here to see you. He works in the Jamboree?"

"Oh. Him."

"I wonder if *he* needs a stylist," Vanessa says. "He's so cute, I wouldn't even have to touch his hair."

I don't respond, hoping she'll drop it.

"Maybe we should go see his show," she suggests.

My stomach clenches. "Uh . . . ," I say, trying to find my way out of this. "I don't really know him. He's just some random guy who started talking to me."

I regret the words as they leave my mouth. But Vanessa's my only friend right now. And if she finds out why I really broke up with her, then I can kiss that goodbye.

"Did you at least get his number?" she asks.

"Nope." I pretend to look for something in my locker, hoping I sound a lot more casual than I feel. "How'd you find his video anyway?"

"Some of the other servers were talking about it. He's good, right?"

I shut my locker and tell Vanessa I've got to run. On my way out, I glance over her shoulder at the video, and it's like someone punching me in the gut. Emmett's more than good. He's the best. I hate myself for not being able to say that.

Arriving in the employee parking lot, my guilt over downplaying my relationship with Emmett only sinks its claws in deeper. Because there he is, a few parking spots away, patiently waiting for me. I hate that I can't run over there and give him a kiss. And ask him about his meeting with the talent scout. And tell him more about finding the rest of my nana's songs.

Instead, we get into our separate vehicles and drive over to his aunt's house first. I don't like making Emmett sneak around like this. But as my run-in with Vanessa just proved, it's too dangerous for us to be seen together at the park.

Once we get to his aunt's house, we can finally be ourselves. It's still a little awkward, knowing his aunt knows about us. But it's not like she's changed how she acts around me. Part of me wonders if Vanessa would be the same if she knew. Or Keith. Or Amelia and Gabe.

Maybe they wouldn't change. But they'd *know*.

And then I'd be asking them to keep a secret from Mama.

Once Emmett and I are alone in his bedroom, he pulls me in for a kiss and wastes no time in getting down to business. "So," he says, plopping onto his bed. "Did you bring the songs?"

"That's really the first thing you want to talk about?" I ask, surprised.

"What d'you mean?"

"Emmett. You're seriously not gonna tell me about it?"

He gets a worried look on his face, as if he's trying to remember if he did something bad.

"*Your meeting with the scout?*"

His face relaxes and he falls back into his pillows. "Oh. That."

"Yeah, that." I climb onto the bed and lie down next to him. "The thing you've been freaking out about all week."

He sighs. "I already texted you everything that happened."

"You said he gave you some advice for your career. That's it. Usually when you text me, I have to speed-read to keep up."

"Well . . . that's basically the gist of it. I didn't want to bore you with the details."

"I'm your boyfriend. I pretty sure you get to bore me with whatever you want."

He looks up at the ceiling, like he's suddenly interested in the light fixture. Something's wrong; I wish he'd tell me what.

"Are you disappointed he didn't offer you a contract?" I ask.

"No. I wasn't really expecting that."

"Then what?"

He pushes himself up on his elbow and looks at me. If I was expecting a teary confession, I don't think it's coming. If anything, he looks more focused and determined than ever.

"The scout thinks I should pretend to be straight."

I laugh. Because that's absurd. If you're comfortable and supported in the life you were meant to be living, why go back to pretending to be someone you're not? Lying to everyone and always having to watch your back isn't healthy. I should know.

"But you're gonna be country music's biggest gay superstar," I say.

He shrugs. "I don't know. He might have a point."

"Hold on. . . ." I sit up, too. "You're really considering it?"

"If I want to sell records, I have to appeal to a broader audience. I mean, there's a reason there are hardly any gay country singers. Guys want songs about getting mud on the wheels of their pickup truck or dating some all-American girl who wears bikinis and drinks beer. And girls, well, they mostly want songs where they're the object of affection for that masculine, truck-loving cowboy."

I shake my head. "But what about you? You're the biggest country music fan I know. And those aren't the kinda songs *you* want."

He picks at his bedspread. "I'm not saying it's right. But it's the way this industry works. I wish I could change it. But I'm a performer at an amusement park. I should just be thankful someone's taken an interest in me."

Hearing Emmett say that feels wrong. He's always so confident about who he is. Is he really going to listen to the first person who tells him no?

"It doesn't have to be a permanent thing," he tells me. "But this could really jump-start my career, you know? If I play by their rules, I have a better chance of getting a recording contract and building my audience. And if my first album does well enough . . . well, then maybe I can switch to a different label. One that's more in line with my vision."

I want to be a supportive boyfriend. And if anyone has the drive and determination to make this work, it's Emmett. So I guess I should trust he knows what he's doing. Besides, it's not like I'm in a position to judge someone for not wanting to disclose their sexuality.

"Okay," I say. "But if you get a fake girlfriend, it better be written into your contract that you still get to have endless make-out sessions with me."

"Definitely," Emmett says, smirking. "You're totally going to be my secret side piece."

I force myself to laugh. Despite the pang in my chest that knows that, technically, I'm the one who already has to keep our relationship a secret.

"Seriously, though," Emmett says. "You're not going to think I'm a sellout if I go through with this?"

"No." I brush aside any lingering doubt. "You'll do what it takes. I admire you for not giving up."

He looks relieved, like he needed me to say that.

"Thanks," he says, leaning forward to give me another kiss.

"Get ready to thank me some more," I tell him, grabbing my backpack off the floor.

I take out my nana's journal and the folded-up squares of paper, making a pile in the middle of his bed. Emmett's eyes go wide.

"Whoa. I know you said you found a lot. But this . . ."

"This is the mother lode," I say.

He opens the songs one by one, taking his time with them. I like watching him smile as he reads. My nana's lyrics must've sat in that suitcase for decades. It's nice they finally get an audience.

"Luke, these are amazing."

"They are?"

"Yes. Are you sure you want to sell them?"

I grab at my shirt, feeling Nana's locket underneath the fabric. I guess I wouldn't want them to go to someone who wasn't going to appreciate them. Someone who wouldn't try making them as good as possible. "Or . . . well . . . You could use them."

"Really? You wouldn't mind?"

I pause. Do I really want my nana's songs out there for the world to hear? *Do I really have a choice?*

"They're all yours," I say, hoping I don't sound hesitant.

His face lights up. "We could share the money. Well, if I got an advance from a recording contract, I'd need some of that money for recording sessions. And it might be a while until we see any profit. I'm getting ahead of myself, obviously. But we can find a percentage that works. Fifty-fifty. Or sixty-forty. Whatever you think is fair."

"Yeah," I say. "We'll figure something out."

Emmett smiles and I try not to think about the money. Now that Mama's feeling better, she'll return to work soon. And Keith doesn't seem to be worried about his shift at the plant changing. I want to believe my family's going to be okay. I guess it's just hard to do that, since we've always had to bust our asses to scrape by.

"Huh," Emmett says, looking through the journal. "That's funny."

"What?"

"Your grandma wrote down the lyrics to one of Wanda Jean's songs."

"Why would she do that?" I ask.

"I don't know. Maybe she really liked it."

I doubt it. Unless she wrote it down when she and Wanda Jean were still friends. Emmett starts flipping through the pages. But he's skimming them now.

"Fuck."

"What?"

"A lot of these are Wanda Jean songs," he says. "Except some of the words or verses are changed. Almost like . . ." He stops reading and looks up at me. The color's drained from his face as though he's seen a ghost. I don't understand what's going on, but my heart's racing anyhow.

"Almost like what?" I ask.

Emmett doesn't answer. So I take the journal from him. The lyrics are about someone named Calamity Joe.

"Almost like these are earlier drafts," he finally says, his voice a soft whisper.

We stare at each other for a moment. The journal and pile of paper in the middle of the bed are like a powder keg. And whatever Emmett or I say next might be the match that sets it all off.

"Why would my nana have these?" I ask.

"I'm not sure."

"You don't think that . . ." I pause, trying to figure out if what I'm about to say could really be true. "That my nana wrote some of Wanda Jean's songs?"

Emmett sits up straighter. "We don't know that. Your grandma and Wanda Jean were best friends, right? There could be a totally reasonable explanation for this. We shouldn't jump to any conclusions."

It's too late. The seed's already been planted. Or maybe it's more like a weed taking root. The only thing I can think about now is how Wanda Jean has millions of adoring fans. Millions of accolades and awards. Millions of dollars generated from her amusement park. My nana, meanwhile, died forgotten and poor.

But I can't say any of that to Emmett. He looks like he just found out the Easter Bunny's been teaming up with Santa Claus to poison children. I don't want to make this worse for him. So instead I collect the squares of paper and say, "You're right. I'm sure there's an explanation."

He looks more surprised than relieved.

"So what do we do?" he asks.

"We stick to the plan," I tell him, placing the songs into his hands. "Besides, it doesn't matter who wrote these. They're ours now."

When Emmett and I say goodbye later that night, I can tell something's off. He kisses me and promises we'll talk later. But the second I leave his aunt's house, I start grinding my teeth.

Did Wanda Jean really steal her songs?

Did Nana not care?

That doesn't sit right with me. I'd like to see Wanda Jean's face if she found out someone still had this journal. She should have to own up to what she's done.

On my drive back home, my anger subsides long enough for me to wonder if I'm wrong. Maybe they had some sort of agreement worked out. Maybe Nana thought letting Wanda Jean use her songs was her penance for stealing Wyatt.

Whatever the plausible explanation is, I'm so consumed with

trying to figure it out that when I pull into our driveway and park next to Keith's truck, it doesn't even register with me. It's not until I get inside the house that I realize Keith isn't at work. He's sitting at our dining room table with his head cradled in his hands, and Mama's next to him, trying to soothe him as she rubs his back.

"What's wrong?" I ask.

They both look up. Keith tries to speak, but his voice cracks. He takes a second to compose himself. When he tries again, his voice is even and strong. "The union had to make some compromises. But I don't want you to worry. Everything's gonna be fine."

"What kind of compromises?" I ask, the pit of my stomach already filling with dread.

Mama forces a smile. "Luke, honey . . ."

"No. I wanna know."

"Thirty hours a week," Keith tells me. "It's enough to keep our insurance."

"How can they do that?" My cheeks flush with heat. There's a familiar stinging in my eyes, but I try to push my emotions back down. "I thought the union was supposed to protect you. Don't they care about the families that depend on—" I stop, covering my face before Mama and Keith can see me burst into tears.

One of the chairs scoots back. Keith's arms wrap me in a hug, which only makes me want to cry more. Keith's never been afraid of showing physical affection. And that's great. But I don't want to be weak right now. I want to be strong and hold myself together like he can.

"Hey," Keith says, placing a hand on the back of my neck. "There's no point in getting upset. I can find a part-time job, okay? We'll make it work. I haven't let this family down yet, have I?"

He hasn't. And even though he's technically my stepdad, I couldn't ask for a better father than him. But that's not the point. The point is *none of this is fair*. The auto plant screwed Keith over. Just like Wanda Jean screwed over my nana.

My family has shit luck, and I'm extremely tired of it.

Chapter

26

EMMETT

I've only had one hangover in my life. It came after the closing night cast party for our spring musical, *Grease*. There were Jell-O shots, tequila shots, and shots of something that stained my teeth blue. Because when it comes to partying, theater kids do *not* mess around. I woke up with a throbbing headache and a mouth that felt like I'd been sucking on cotton balls.

Waking up this morning, however, and remembering what Luke and I may or may not have discovered last night, feels eminently worse. Wanda Jean cannot be a fraud. It goes against the nature of everything she teaches: *Believe in yourself. Be true to yourself. Never be afraid to show the world who you are.*

How could she spread that message to her fans while also deceiving them? It's not possible. There has to be a reason why Luke's grandma had those songs. I just . . . can't think of what that would be yet.

Grabbing my phone from the nightstand, I check to see if I have any texts from Luke. Something felt off between us when he left last night. He said it didn't matter about the songs, but I'm not sure he believed that. He was never a fan of Wanda Jean to begin with. This can't be helping.

There's nothing from Luke. Just a few notifications for my latest

YouTube video. They're probably from Aunt Karen. She's been creating fake profiles and leaving comments in an attempt to direct more traffic to my page.

I set my phone back down, not wanting to depress myself further. I was hoping my video would've had more views by now. It got a decent number of hits when I first uploaded it. I made sure to tag the Rusty Spur, and Jessie and Avery were nice enough to share it with their followers. But after a few days, the traffic slowed to a trickle. The number of views plateaued at around 1,500. Which isn't nothing, but it's not even a fraction of what I need for Orrin.

Dragging myself out of bed, I make my way to the kitchen and pour myself a giant bowl of cereal. I don't know if it's possible to self-medicate with Cinnamon Toast Crunch, but I'm certainly going to try.

Just as soon as I sit at the table, Aunt Karen comes in from the garage. "Hey, Em?" she says, looking at her phone. "Who's Shane McAnally? I feel like I've heard that name before."

"He's a songwriter and producer. You've probably heard a lot of the stuff he's written. He's also gay."

"So if he tweeted out your video, that'd be a big deal, right?"

I drop my spoon; milk splashes out of my bowl.

"What?"

Aunt Karen squeals, bursting with pride as she reads: *This reminds me of my days performing at the Rusty Spur. Except I'm pretty sure this kid is better than I was at that age.*

She holds out her phone. "Look, he ended it with a winky-face emoji!"

It takes me a second to process what's happening. Shane McAnally listened to my song? And he liked it enough to tweet about it? I run over to see for myself. As soon as the shock wears off, I click on the video to see how many views I'm up to. Six digits would be amazing. But I'd settle for five. Honestly, anything above 20,000 and I'm sending this to Orrin.

When I see the number, my heart sinks.

3,422.

It's disappointing, but I try not to let it get me down. It's still cool to get the attention of someone who's successful in this industry—someone who also happens to be gay. Shane McAnally liking my song should count as a bigger validation than hitting a certain number of YouTube views. I just wish the record labels could see it that way.

Scrolling farther down, I read my new comments.

sparkle pony girl: omg. this song. i'm crying. seriously. ilysm.

Janice Tarwater: Finally, a young person who knows how to sing a real country song.
You're better than half the crap they play on the radio these days.

Shauna G: My husband and I recently ended our marriage. I feel like this song was written just for me. Do you have an album coming out? I've been playing this on repeat.

My eyes grow damp. People like my performance. It makes them feel something. Screw the record labels. I don't need to go viral to be a "real" musician.

Though Orrin was right about one thing. He said if I stuck to country music's roots, I could build some credibility for myself. People aren't just responding to my singing. They're responding to Verna's lyrics.

After finishing my breakfast, I jump into the shower and try to figure out my next move. Before I can finish rinsing the shampoo out of my hair, however, I hear Aunt Karen scream like she's being stabbed.

I stumble out of the shower and throw on the fluffy pink bathrobe hanging on the back of the door. Leaving a trail of wet footprints behind me, I return to the kitchen, where Aunt Karen is clutching her chest. When she speaks, her voice comes out in a whisper.

"*Eyeballs.*"

"What?"

She points to her phone, which is sitting on the table. I pick it up. It's still open to Shane McAnally's Twitter page. Underneath his tweet about me, someone responded with the eyes emoji, like they're interested in my song. When I realize who it's from, I get light-headed.

"Kacey Musgraves?"

This can't be real. So I ask again, just to be sure.

"*Kacey. Fucking. Musgraves?*"

Standing there in a fluffy pink bathrobe, with Aunt Karen looking over my shoulder and shampoo still dripping from my hair, I click on the link to my video and watch as the number of YouTube views starts to grow. And grow. *And grow.*

Walking into the dressing room later that morning, I promise myself I'm going to concentrate on the show and not obsessively check my phone. I don't want to be that obnoxious cast member who rubs his good fortune in everyone's face. But I can't help myself. As soon as I see Jessie and Avery, I blurt out what happened and we check how many views I'm up to.

6,372.

6,509.

6,889.

The numbers don't stop climbing. By the time we finish our first show of the day, I'm well past 10,000. Which are more views than I've ever had before. Jessie uses lipstick to start a tally on our dressing room mirror, updating the total every time I hit another thousand. Even Cassidy seems genuinely impressed.

I'm glad they're all happy for me. But the person I really want to share this with is Luke. We have plans to meet during his break. The wait is killing me, but I'd rather tell him in person. I want to see the look on his face when I show him how many people have listened to his grandma's song.

Luke's a few minutes late in getting to our secret meeting spot. And when he does show up, his eyebrows are pinched together, like his mind is elsewhere. Even the kiss he gives me feels like an afterthought.

"Is everything okay?" I ask.

"Yeah. Just tired from my shift."

I bite back my smile, knowing I'm about to cheer him up big-time. "Guess how many views we're up to."

"Huh?"

"The video. From the open mic." My phone might as well be on fire in my back pocket. I want to show him already. "Guess how many people have seen it."

"Oh. Um, a hundred people?"

"Luke. *Seriously?*"

"I don't know. Two hundred?"

Oh my God. He could be guessing all night. I take my phone out and watch his eyes grow wide with surprise.

"Thirty thousand people?"

"Really?" I peer over his shoulder. "It was only at twenty-five thousand the last time I checked."

Only 25,000. Who am I right now?

Luke shakes his head. "How's that even possible?"

Taking a seat on the edge of a rusted old carousel, I give him a detailed replay of everything that's happened since this morning: Shane McAnally. The pink bathrobe. The millions of goose bumps I had when I saw Kacey Musgraves's tweet.

"So this Kacey person helped more people find your video?"

"Yes," I say. "*Wait*, do you not know who Kacey Musgraves is?"

"Should I?"

I laugh. "No. In fact, I think I love you more because you don't."

It's not until I see the panic flicker across his face that I realize what I said.

"Oh. I mean . . ."

I sit up straighter, holding my breath. Fuck it. Why shouldn't I tell him I'm in love? We've seen each other just about every day since our first kiss. And summer won't last forever. I don't want to go back home and regret *not* saying it. Of course, there's always a chance he won't say it back, which would suck. I practice the words in my head, to see how they feel. But just as I make up my mind to tell him, Luke speaks first:

"My stepdad's hours at the plant got cut."

It takes me a second to recover.

"Shit. I'm so sorry. Is he okay? Are *you* okay?"

"I don't know," he says, turning his head from me. "My family's in trouble. It's always been a struggle to pay the bills on time. But it's never been this bad. I barely got any sleep last night."

"This happened yesterday? Why didn't you tell me sooner?"

Not to make this about myself, but I can't believe Luke let me go on and on about my YouTube channel when he obviously had more important things to worry about.

"I had to figure out what I was going to do first," he says.

"Is there anything you *can* do?"

"I thought of something. But it's kind of a long shot." He pauses, looking down at his sneakers, which are covered in dried dish soap. "Also, I'd need your help to pull it off. And I'm not sure how you're gonna feel about it."

"Okay. I try not to sound alarmed. "What did you have in mind?"

He absentmindedly grabs at his shirt, where I can see the outline of his grandma's locket underneath the fabric. "You know how we found my nana's songs? And you said some of them seemed like earlier versions of Wanda Jean's songs?" He pauses, squirming in his seat. "What if we made a copy of everything and confronted Wanda Jean about it? If those really are my nana's songs, then my family deserves some compensation."

My stomach feels queasy. In the distance, the screams from the nearby roller coaster suddenly seem like an omen.

"You want to *blackmail Wanda Jean?*"

He shakes his head. "I don't wanna demand money from her. But think about it. Wanda Jean's made a fortune from some of those songs. If she's a good person like you say she is, well, maybe she'll offer to help my family."

I try to take a breath, but it's like the wind's been knocked out of me. I know Luke's worried about his family. And that he's protective of his grandma. But I'm sorry, that still sounds like blackmail.

When I'm finally able to speak, I hate how whiny I sound: "But there still might be a good explanation for this!"

"I get that she's your hero," he says. "And I'm not saying she's a bad person. But if those are my nana's songs, then this will be her chance to make things right. My family needs help. That's the only reason I'm considering this."

I look away, ashamed of how selfish I'm being. "It's not like you can just make an appointment to see Wanda Jean," I say, hearing the crack in my voice. "She's been kind of a recluse for the last decade or so."

"But you said Grady's in charge of her appearances at the park, right?"

I nod, afraid of where this is going.

"If you find out when she's gonna be here next, then we could try talking to her."

"Luke, I don't—"

"Emmett, please." His voice is soft. Embarrassed, almost. Like he doesn't want to be doing this. "I know I'm asking a lot of you," he says. "If you need some time to think about it, that's okay. You don't have to answer right away."

I force myself to look at him. His eyes look sad enough to merit their own country song. How could I say no? I love Luke. Of course I want to help him. But I also love Wanda Jean. Which is ridiculous since I don't really know her. But I know her music. And I know what she's meant to me all these years. How can I possibly destroy the person who helped shape who I am?

I don't have an answer.

So I don't give him one yet.

Before we head back to work, Luke kisses me goodbye. And for a second, it makes me feel like everything's going to be okay. But then we go our separate ways, and I can't erase the look of disappointment that lingers on his face.

Chapter

27

EMMETT

The following afternoon, I give my worst performance in the Jamboree since my first day of rehearsal. I'm half a beat behind everyone during our big line-dance number, and at the end of the finale, when we're supposed to throw our cowboy hats in the air and catch them, I toss mine right into the audience.

Afterward, sitting at my dressing room table with a pound of cold cream on my face, I feel like a complete failure. Which is the exact opposite of how I should be feeling right now. Taking out my phone, I reread the email I received from Orrin this morning:

Dear Mr. Maguire,

I shared your video with some of my colleagues. While there are many different opinions on what constitutes "going viral," we all agreed that amassing over 50,000 views in a matter of days was a great accomplishment. If you had a larger number of subscribers, or a proper management team behind you, there's a good chance we could get you to where you need to be. As always, I can't make any promises. But I'm going to run some more data and will be in touch again soon. In the meantime, keep working on those songs like we talked about.

Sincerely,

Orrin Merrick

A&R Scout, Foothill Records

My eyes sting. And not from the cold cream. I haven't shared this news with anyone yet. Not Jessie and Avery. Not my parents. Not even Aunt Karen. As soon as I read it, I knew I wanted Luke to be the first to know. But if I talk to Luke, I'll have to give him my answer about Wanda Jean.

I think that's why I was so distracted during the show today. Because I know what answer I have to give him. And the answer I *have* to give isn't the answer I *want* to give. Wanda Jean's my idol. I love her music and what she stands for.

But Luke is my boyfriend.

How can I choose anyone over him?

Washing the cream off my face doesn't leave me refreshed like it normally does. I have to follow through with this before I can lose my nerve. Luke's shift is ending soon. If I leave now, I might catch him on his way out.

When I get to the dumpster in the back of the restaurant, I text Luke that I'm here. I still don't want to confront Wanda Jean. But at least I know I'm doing the right thing.

As soon as the back door opens, however, I see I'm doing the *wrong* thing. Luke isn't alone. I could be wrong—because the last time I saw her, her hair was under a funny lace cap—but I'm pretty sure that's his ex-girlfriend, Vanessa.

Her hair's down now, and she's wearing a stylish green romper that complements her skin tone. The first thing that pops into my head is: *Wow, they made a cute couple.* The second thing is: *Does Luke wish he were straight so he could still be with her? Would his life be easier then?*

I know I should run. But I can't stop watching them. Vanessa touches Luke's arm, laughing at some story he's telling. Luke gestures wildly with his hands, clearing enjoying himself. As soon as he sees me, though, everything stops moving—his hands, his mouth, his feet.

Vanessa also stops, following his gaze toward me.

"Hey," she says. "You're that musician."

I steal a quick glance at Luke. He looks absolutely terrified.

"Uh . . . ," I say.

"I saw your video." She walks over to me. "You know, your performance at the Rusty Spur? You were so good! I'm Vanessa, by the way. Sorry we weren't properly introduced the last time you were here."

She offers me her hand and I shake it, instantly liking her. I don't care how shallow it makes me; flattery never gets old.

"Emmett," I say. "And thank you."

She twists a strand of hair around her finger, smiling coyly. "So, Emmett, you hang out around dumpsters often?"

"Um, no. I was just . . ."

"Vanessa," Luke interrupts. "We should get going. They might close soon."

She gives him a funny look. "Um . . . ? Frosty Freeze stays open late all summer. Emmett, you should join us. We're getting ice cream."

I look over at Luke, hoping he'll give me some sort of signal that it's okay. But he just stands there. I can practically smell his fear.

"Thanks. But I can't," I lie. "I have another show tonight."

Vanessa's expression turns serious. "Okay, fine. I was trying to play it cool, but I'm just going to come out and say it. . . ."

My heart stops.

Can she tell something's up?

Does she know about me and Luke?

"I'm a stylist," she says. "But technically I don't have any clients yet. I asked Luke to model for me, but it was like trying to baptize a cat."

Relief washes over me as I try not to smile. I can only imagine how well that went.

"If you're interested," Vanessa continues, "maybe we could help each other out? I'd style you for free and you could let me use you in my portfolio. That way, if one of us makes it big, the other person can totally exploit our connection for their own personal gain." She laughs. "I'm kidding. But only sort of."

I glance at Luke again, but his eyes won't meet mine. So I panic, saying what I think she wants to hear, in hopes that they'll leave sooner. "Yeah, that sounds great."

"I'm so glad we ran into you," she says, taking out her phone. "After I saw your video, I *knew* we had to talk. But of course Luke didn't have your number. I swear, that boy would only keep a landline if he could."

As Vanessa and I exchange numbers, it slowly sinks in what a bad idea this is. I mean, I'd love to hang out with her. She seems really cool and it'd be amazing to have my own stylist. But I'm guessing Luke told her he didn't have my number for a reason. Which, if I'm being honest, stings.

Luke's not ready to be out yet. And I don't want to push him. But if he *were* out . . . well, then he could've introduced me to Vanessa sooner. And it wouldn't be a big deal for the three of us to get ice cream together. Then maybe I'd feel like I'm a part of *his* life, instead of only having him be a part of mine.

"I should get going," I say.

It's foolish, but I'm still hoping Luke will change his mind and invite me to go with them. Instead, he gives me a stiff head nod and says, "Nice seeing you."

Nice. Seeing. You.

Three words. Each one twists into my chest like a knife. Not that any of this should come as a surprise. I knew Luke would have to keep me a secret. But knowing something is different than experiencing it. I didn't expect it to hurt this much.

I blink back my tears as they leave. I know I should text Luke and tell him I'm sorry for showing up at his work again. But what about me? Don't I deserve an apology as well?

As I continue to stand by the dumpster, I catch a whiff of something rancid. It's like the rotten cherry on top of my garbage sundae. Wanda World is supposed to be a fun, happy place. And here I am, choking on slop fumes after my heart's been stomped on.

Just as I decide to finally leave, I hear my name. I look back to see Luke running toward me. "I don't have much time," he says, trying to catch his breath. "I told Vanessa I left my phone in the kitchen."

I don't know what to say. So I start with the obvious.

"Luke, that was really awful."

"I know. I can't tell if she suspects something or not."

"No. I mean you pretending like you hardly knew me was awful."

"Oh. Sorry." He pauses. And for a second, I wonder if I'm making this into a bigger deal than it needs to be. But Luke's not done talking yet: "I told you not to show up at my work for a reason. I knew something would happen."

"I texted you first," I say.

"Yeah, and I obviously didn't see it."

"Okay. Fine. Then I'm sorry, too."

He sighs. "It was a mistake. I'm sure you didn't mean it."

For some reason, that twists the knives in even deeper. I came here to tell him that—despite not wanting to—I'm willing to help him blackmail Wanda Jean. I came here because I love him. How can that be a mistake?

"You should get back to Vanessa," I say, not bothering to hide the annoyance in my voice.

"Emmett. Don't be that way."

I shrug, as though I don't know what he's talking about.

"You're upset," he says. "Just tell me what's wrong."

"Everything's wrong, Luke! That felt really shitty, okay? I know you can't tell Vanessa I'm your boyfriend. But you were acting like you were afraid of me. Or worse, like I didn't exist."

His face softens. He takes a step closer. "I'm sorry, I panicked. I wasn't trying to make you feel that way. I swear."

His apology sounds sincere. And it should be enough. But something inside me can't let this go. "I've decided to help you confront

Wanda Jean about your grandmother's songs," I tell him. "I'll try to get her schedule from Grady. It's not something I *want* to do. But it's something I'm *choosing* to do. Because you asked me to. I guess I just want to feel like you'd make the same kind of sacrifice for me."

His eyebrows push together. "Is that what this is about? I'm not making sacrifices?"

"That's not what I meant," I say.

Except it *is* what I meant. And I hate myself for saying it.

"So I have to prove myself now?"

"No. Of course not."

His jaw tightens. His nostrils flare. "I'm sorry being with me is such a burden for you. Would it make you feel better if I came out to people? Is that what I have to do?"

I've never seen Luke get angry before. I've clearly set off something in him, and I wish I could undo it. Of course this would be easier if Luke were out to certain people. But how can I seriously ask that of him?

"Just forget I said anything, please."

"Maybe I should tell Vanessa the truth about us," he says. "I'm sure she'd love to find out I was lying the entire time we were dating. But, hey, at least she can take comfort knowing everything's okay now, because I'm finally with someone I can be myself around."

He stares at me, and I don't know what to say. When he speaks again, his voice is quieter, but with a sharper edge. "Or how about I tell my family? Yeah, that way my mama can put her rosary to good use as she tries to pray the gay away for me."

"Would . . ." My words catch in my throat. "Would she really do that?"

"Yes, Emmett. This may come as a surprise to you, but not everyone's got the luxury of being out."

If he meant to make me feel like an asshole, it worked. I didn't know that about his mom. I know hardly anything about his family. And I guess now I know why. I don't want to put Luke in any more danger of being found out. Maybe he's right. This is too dangerous. I'd never forgive myself if one of his coworkers walked out here and saw us.

"You should leave," I tell him. "Before Vanessa starts to suspect something."

"Shit. I should text her."

He takes out his phone. But when he looks at the screen, his face drops.

"What is it?" I ask.

When he doesn't answer me, I imagine the worst. *Did Vanessa come back and see us? Did she text Luke and tell him she knows?*

"Fuck," he whispers, clearly shaken.

"What happened?"

Luke looks at me, his eyes wide with fear.

"My mama's in the hospital. She collapsed."

"*Oh my God.* Is she okay?"

"I don't know. My stepdad said they just got there."

A sharp pang stabs at my heart. Now I really want to take back everything I said. Luke has a lot going on in his life. I shouldn't be mad his entire world doesn't revolve around me. What kind of boyfriend does that?

"I have to go," he says.

Luke takes off running, not even giving me a chance to respond.

"Wait, let me come with you." I hurry after him, trying to catch up. "Nobody has to know I'm your boyfriend. I could just be a friend. Or your coworker."

Two ladies from the candy shop—dressed in frilly pink aprons and matching caps—pass by and say hello. I stop and give them a friendly smile, waiting until they're out of earshot before continuing my chase.

"At least let me drive you there," I call after him. "I won't even go into the hospital."

"It's fine," he calls over his shoulder, not slowing down.

"Luke," I shout. "It's *not* fine. You shouldn't have to do this alone!"

He finally stops, turning around to face me.

"Emmett. You can't."

"Please," I beg. "Don't shut me out."

I'm not asking for him to make a sacrifice. I'm asking for him to make a compromise. One that will let me feel like I can be there for him. Even if it means waiting in the parking lot, where no one else can see me.

Luke looks at me for another second, but I can tell his mind is already made up.

"I'm sorry," he says. "I have to put my family first."

It's selfish, but as he takes off running again, my heart aches. He's never going to change. Not for me. Not for himself. The only thing I can do for him now is stand there. And watch him leave without me.

Chapter

28

LUKE

As I pace around the hospital room, my eyes keep landing on the tray of food sitting next to Mama's bed. I don't have to lift the beige plastic lid to know she hasn't touched any of the crap under there. What Mama needs is a real meal. Not some unseasoned chicken or runny mac 'n' cheese. I wish I could cook for her right now. I wish I could do *something*.

"How long's she been asleep?" I ask.

"Not long," Keith replies. "We came up here after her CT scan. The preliminary results looked okay. But they're waiting for the attending to review everything before they start her on steroids."

That's another thing to hate about hospitals. The waiting. I take a seat in the chair next to Mama's bedside. Except for the bandage around her head, Mama looks peaceful. She's propped up on pillows and tucked snugly away in crisp white sheets. Underneath the bandage, however, there are five fresh stitches.

No one was around when Mama fell. Keith had run out with Gabe and Amelia to pick up supper—*supper I should've been fixing for them*. Mama was conscious but groggy when they returned home and found her lying there. They think she must've got dizzy and lost her balance while walking down the stairs.

Keith hovers over Mama on the opposite side of the bed. He has dark circles under his eyes and a worried crease in his brow. Now that he's going back to working a shorter day shift at the plant, he's already applied for overnight work at the Shop & Save, restocking the shelves. He works so hard for our family, but Mama getting sick again is beyond his control.

"She's gonna be fine," Keith assures me. "They'll probably keep her for a day or two of observation."

I want to believe him. But this isn't Mama's first time in the hospital. And it won't be her last. You can learn to manage your MS, work with your doctor to try out different medications, sign up for experimental drug trials, and hope you spend most of your time in remission. But it's not like you're ever going to be cured.

Mama's flare-ups are usually small. She just has to slow down and let her body rest for a few days, but then she's back on her feet and you'd never know she's living with a chronic illness. This spring, though, it took her months to recover. And if she's had another relapse so quickly, it could be a sign she's getting worse.

The door to Mama's room flies open. "Luke," Gabe says, rushing in with a candy bar in each hand. "You're here!"

"Hey," I whisper. "Mama's sleeping."

While Gabe runs over to give me a hug, Amelia hangs back in the corner, keeping to herself. Now that she's getting older, I think she's starting to understand how serious Mama's condition can be when something bad happens.

Soon the attending arrives and pulls Keith out into the hallway. I suddenly find myself envious of Gabe, who's oblivious to anything but his candy bars. *What if Mama has to stay in the hospital for a while?*

What if our insurance doesn't cover all of it? Thankfully, Keith returns a few minutes later and tells us Mama's CT scan came back clear.

"Why don't y'all go home and eat your supper now," he says. "Your mama would kill me if she knew I let you raid the vending machines."

"But I wanna stay with Mama," Gabe whispers.

"She'll feel better knowing y'all are back home," Keith tells him. "Y'all can FaceTime her before you go to bed. I promise."

"Come on, buddy," I say, giving Gabe a squeeze. "We can visit Mama again in the morning. Maybe sneak in some doughnuts."

On our way out, as I wait for the woman at the front desk to validate my parking ticket, my phone vibrates in my pocket.

Hey, sorry to bother you.

I wanted to see how your mom's doing.

His texts hit me like a punch. If I close my eyes, I can still see the look on Emmett's face when I acted like I hardly knew him. That was an extremely shitty thing to do. But I didn't have a choice. Just like I didn't have a choice not letting him come to the hospital with me. I can't imagine Emmett sitting with me at my mama's bedside. It'd raise too many questions. Besides, the person I am around Emmett is not the same person I am around Vanessa and my family. I have to keep those two worlds separate.

Before I can respond to his texts, the woman stamps my ticket and Gabe grabs on to my hand. We walk with Amelia to the parking ramp, and for the whole ride home, Gabe can't stop asking about stitches: *Do they hurt? Will they be there forever? Is it like the time Mama fixed a hole in my sock?*

When we finally pull into the driveway, I tell Gabe I'll let him stay up past his bedtime if he runs inside and changes into his pajamas right away. His eyes go wide and he dashes out of the car. Amelia undoes her seat belt but doesn't move. She's hardly said a peep all night.

"Hey," I say. "You know you don't have to worry about Mama, right? If the doctors didn't think she was gonna be okay, they would've said so."

Her bottom lip quivers.

"Bean. What's wrong?"

She doesn't correct me for calling her Bean—she must be really upset.

"It's my fault Mama fell," she says.

"Mama got dizzy. You know that can happen when she has a flare-up."

She sniffles. "But it's my fault she was on the stairs in the first place. My soccer jersey was dirty and I told her she needed to wash it. If she hadn't done laundry and brought everyone's clean clothes upstairs, she never would've had to come back down!"

"Come here," I say, wrapping my arm around her. "Mama's been up and down those stairs every day since she got off bed rest. She could've fallen at any time. Nobody thinks this is your fault. Especially not Mama."

The fact that Amelia lets me hug her for as long as she does is a miracle. But soon enough, she dries her eyes and goes back to being an impenetrable wall of sarcasm and middle school angst. When we get inside, I ask her to change into her pajamas as well. She complies. But not without an eye roll first.

Standing at the bottom of the stairs, I try to find where Mama fell. Sure enough, there's some dried blood on the base of the banister, so I get some soapy water to clean it up. Even though I told Amelia she shouldn't blame herself, this feels like my fault. I've been so busy with Emmett lately that I haven't been able to take care of everything at home. If I'd kept up with the laundry, Mama might not be in the hospital.

After Amelia and Gabe come back downstairs, I reheat the take-out they picked up with Keith and we sit in front of the TV to eat. I try to take my mind off Mama. But three bites into my burrito, something Amelia said finally hits me: *Mama brought clean clothes upstairs.*

If Mama was doing my laundry, she might've put clothes away in my dresser. What if she saw the pictures I'm hiding in there? The one of Nana when she was younger. And worse, the ones of Emmett and me in the photo booth.

"I'll be right back," I say, trying not to panic. I'm probably overreacting. But as I run up the stairs, my heart pounds faster. All I can think about is Mama finding that picture of Emmett and me kissing.

When I get to the top of the staircase, my heart stops.

My bedroom door's open.

Running into my room, I head straight for the dresser and pull open the bottom drawer. The photos are tucked under my jeans, just like I left them. I stand back up. Mama left my clean clothes out on top of my bed. My secret's still safe.

Sitting on the edge of my mattress, I hold the photos to my chest and wait for my heartbeat to return to normal. Nothing happened. *But it could've.* I need to find a better hiding spot for these.

Before I can think of where to put the photos, something else catches my eye. On top of a pile of neatly folded shirts, I see the Wanda World logo. *Fuck.* My dishwashing uniform. I've been so careful about keeping it in my locker at work until I was ready to do laundry. I must've slipped up and brought one home.

Does Mama know I work at Wanda World?

If she saw this, she's gotta know.

How could I be so careless? I look at the photos of Emmett and me again. If I slipped up about working at Wanda World, I could easily slip up about having a boyfriend, too. Keeping these photos was a mistake. I need to get rid of them. And anything else that puts me in danger of being found out.

My phone buzzes in my pocket.

You're probably mad at me.

But I'm worried about your mom.

Please let me know if everything's okay.

Reading his texts, my chest goes tight. Like there's too much weight pressing down on me. It's not just a set of photos that could expose my secret—it's choosing to be with Emmett in the first place. I try to take a breath and tell myself I'm wrong. But I can't ignore the truth. Emmett's only here for the summer. No matter what, he'll be leaving soon. My family, on the other hand . . . how can I risk losing them?

I take one last look at us kissing, then close my eyes.

I know what I have to tell Emmett.

And I know how much it's going to hurt.

Chapter

29

EMMETT

The best part about performing at Wanda World is that we never have a bad audience. People are so excited to be here that they applaud for literally everything. Cassidy or Jameson sing one of their solos? Applause. Jessie and I spin around in our Calamity Joe costume? Applause. We do our big line-dance number, stamping our boots so loudly and in such perfect unison it sounds like claps of thunder? Standing freaking ovation, every time.

Of course, the worst part about performing at Wanda World is that when you're phoning in your performance like I am this afternoon, you feel like a total dick. The smile on my face is stretched so wide it hurts, but there's no real emotion behind it. I used to get such a rush performing in the Jamboree. But now, as I promenade around the stage, I'm just going through the motions. None of this means anything anymore.

Hip bump left. Hip bump right.

Did Wanda Jean even write these songs?

Clap. Paddle turn. Clap.

Does Luke want to break up with me?

Tuck your thumbs into your belt loops. Try not to cry.

When we get to the end of the song and do our big hat toss, the audience applauds like we just cleared the oceans of all plastic and achieved world peace. My smile grows wider as I take my final bow with the rest of the cast. But as soon as I exit the stage, I run off to the wings and sob behind a curtain.

I try not to think about my fight with Luke. About the texts he sent me last night. The ones that are already seared into my brain:

Mama's okay. Just a few stitches.

I think I need some space for a couple of days.

Until I figure stuff out.

When he sent that, I wanted to respond and ask what exactly he meant by "space." But I didn't. Because I'm too afraid of the answer.

By the time I pull myself together and head back downstairs, the dressing room is almost cleared out. Everyone's excited to get out of here and have a night off from the park. Everyone but me. I take my time returning my costumes to the rack, then stare blankly at my reflection in the dressing room mirror.

"Emmett," our stage manager says. "You're moving slower than Christmas. I need to get home before Poppy Seed and Tipsy start to worry."

Poppy Seed and Tipsy are her cats.

Since the stage manager and I are the only ones left, I suggest that if she wants to lock up, I'll be sure to close the door behind me on my way out. I can tell she has her reservations. But, thankfully, her love for Poppy Seed and Tipsy exceeds her distrust of an unsupervised teenager.

Once I have the place to myself, I open the drawer to my dressing table and take out my phone. I've been afraid to check it all day. Part of me is hoping I have a new text from Luke. And part of me is hoping I don't. Being in limbo is better than being dumped, I guess.

Not wanting to prolong my agony, I unlock my phone and steel myself for the worst. But there are no new messages.

I slump forward, cradling my head in my hands. The worst part about this is I have no one to blame but myself. I shouldn't have shown up to his work yesterday. I shouldn't have given my phone number to Vanessa. I shouldn't have asked to go to the hospital with him. But I couldn't help myself. I'm in love with Luke. It's not like there's a switch I can flip, one that turns my feelings on and off whenever it's convenient.

I'm not like Luke. I don't understand how he could hold me in his arms the way he did that first night we spent together, and then be so cold to me in the parking lot. He was like two different people.

Despite wanting to stay immobile for the rest of the night, I force myself to get up. I refuse to let this destroy me. Luke made it clear he's always going to put his family first. And even though it hurts, I can't fault him for that. What I can do, though, is try to protect myself. I need to start putting my music first again. Like it was before I met Luke.

Ironically enough, just as my romantic life's starting to crumble, my music career is finally taking off. I received another email from Orrin this morning. He wants me to drive back to Junesburg tomorrow to meet with him and one of his colleagues at a recording studio there. Before they present my music to the executives at the label, they want me to lay down some new tracks. Orrin says their equipment will give me a higher-quality sound. But I'm sure he's also expecting me to change the pronouns in my lyrics so the executives will think I'm straight.

After turning off the lights in the dressing room, I grab my guitar and sneak back upstairs. It's always a bit strange to be in the theater after a show. If it weren't for the empty pop bottles and stray pieces of kettle corn, you'd never guess that less than thirty minutes ago hundreds of people were crammed in here. Beyond the top row of bleachers, the sun is starting its descent. The sky will be dark in another few hours, which means I'd better get to work.

Taking a seat on the lip of the stage, I open the zippered pocket of my guitar case and pull out Verna's journal and the loose squares of paper. Luke said I could use these songs. But it feels very weird to be doing that now. I mean, I don't know what's going to happen between us. What if he breaks up with me and wants them back?

I unfold one of the sheets. They're good lyrics. And Luke said his family could really use the money. So maybe he'd still be okay with this? I know I should feel bad about trying to pass off someone else's lyrics as my own—and there's definitely a part of me that does. But I also know this industry won't give someone like me a fair shot. So I need to grab hold of every advantage I find. Besides, Wanda Jean already stole some of these songs. And if she couldn't make it to the top without some help, then what chance do I have?

I look through the journal first. There are songs about growing up in Jackson Hollow, songs about leaving home, and songs about falling in love. A lot of these have already been recorded, though. So I start going through the loose sheets. These must've been written later, after Wyatt left Verna. Because they're all about heartbreak.

A picked flower will wilt
Paper yellows with time
You can't stop the seasons from changin'
Foolish me, thinkin' you'd always be mine

Beautiful things don't last forever
Every sunset makes me wanna sigh
I thought if I wrote you into a love song
Maybe part of us would never die

Yeah, I wrote you into this love song
Stainin' the notes with tears as I cry
I wrote you into this love song
'Cause I still ain't ready to say goodbye

When I try setting the lyrics to music, it's amazing how easily the chords come to me. The words might be Verna's, but the emotions behind them . . . those belong to both of us. She wrote this song for Wyatt. And I'm singing it for Luke.

After I teach myself one song, I move on to the next. I string until my fingers are callused and numb. Until it's too dark to read anymore. By the time I'm done, I have almost a dozen new songs. Which should be plenty for Orrin to choose from.

As I gather my things and walk backstage, a sliver of light catches my eye. The door leading down to the dressing room is propped open with a piece of cardboard. Which is strange, since I definitely didn't put that there.

I head back downstairs, hoping it's just the janitorial staff. But when I get to the door that leads into the dressing room, I hear voices. One belongs to Cassidy. The other—a man's—sounds familiar, but I can't quite place it.

"What are you doing?" Cassidy says. "Don't use your car keys!"

"Hold on. I learned this trick in college."

"Check the drawer by the microwave. There's one around here somewhere."

Opening the door a crack, I spy Cassidy sitting on top of one of the dressing tables. She's holding a bottle of wine and two plastic cups. I can't see whom she's talking to at first. But when they finally come into view, I realize why I know his voice.

"Found it," Grady says, holding up a corkscrew.

He uncorks the wine and pours some into each cup. I can understand *what* my eyes are seeing, but not *why*. It doesn't make sense for Cassidy and Grady to be hanging out together, especially this late at night.

"My hero," Cassidy replies, leaning in to give him a kiss.

Before their lips can touch, I let go of the door. It makes a clicking noise as it shuts. *Shit*. I don't know if they heard that, but I'm not sticking around to find out. I bound back up the stairs, taking them two at a time.

It's not until I'm back in the employee parking lot that I process what I saw. Cassidy leaned forward to kiss Grady. I don't know that Grady kissed her back. He might've stopped her. He might have reminded her he already has a girlfriend. A really awesome one who happens to be my aunt.

Given the wine and the clandestine meeting spot, that outcome doesn't seem likely. But for Aunt Karen's sake, it's what I'm choosing to believe, at least until I can come up with a more reasonable explanation. One that won't break her heart.

Chapter
30
LUKE

Sitting at Mama's bedside again this morning, I can't stop fidgeting. I'm even more on edge than when I was here last night. The good news is the doctors don't think it was another relapse, and Mama's clearly doing better: She's awake. She's sitting up. She's brushing a dusting of powdered sugar from her hospital gown. The bad news, of course, is that she knows I've been hiding something from her.

"You want some more juice, Mama?" I ask, unable to sit still any longer.

"I want another doughnut," Gabe says, playing with the cords hanging down from the heart rate monitor.

"You've already had two," I tell him. "And quit messing with those. Why don't you go sit with Bean?"

"No thanks," Amelia says, absorbed in her iPad over on the couch.

"I'm still hungry," Gabe whines.

"Then we can get you something from the cafeteria," I tell him.

"But I don't like the cafeteria."

"You haven't even been there yet."

Amelia sighs. "When will Daddy be back? I need my headphones."

Keith went home to shower and grab a clean change of clothes after spending the night here. Before he left, he made Amelia and Gabe promise they'd be on their best behavior. It clearly didn't take.

"Ready for blastoff," Gabe says, pressing the buttons on the side of Mama's bed. Amelia groans and turns the volume on her iPad to full blast.

"Enough," I snap. "Amelia, take Gabe to the cafeteria." Gabe opens his mouth to protest, but I don't dare give him a chance. "Or the gift shop. I don't care where y'all go. Just give your mama some peace." I grab a twenty-dollar bill from my pocket—the only cash I have, but if that's what it costs to get them out of here for a few minutes, it's worth every cent.

Amelia snatches the money from me and heads for the door. Gabe follows her, asking if he gets to ride in the elevator again.

"Sorry, Mama," I say, finally pouring her some juice.

She smiles, smoothing down the hair sticking out from under her bandage. "I don't mind. It's usually so quiet around here."

She's right about it being quiet. In TV shows, hospital rooms are full of beeping machines and people shouting "stat!" But here, there's only a faint hum from the air conditioner. Sitting back down, I realize my mistake. Gabe and Amelia were a good distraction. Now that it's just Mama and me, we might actually have to talk about something. Like what a Wanda World uniform was doing mixed in with my laundry.

"You need anything else?" I ask. "A second pillow? Something to read?"

"No, honey. I'm fine."

Another silence settles over us; my heartbeat whooshes in my ears.

Is she gonna ask about the uniform? Or is she waiting for me to confess?
Maybe I should go check on Amelia and Gabe. Maybe she'll take another nap.

"You tired, Mama? I can hit the lights."

She waves her hand like she's batting away my question. "What I'm tired of, is having all the attention on me. Why don't you tell me what's going on in your life? We haven't seen much of you this summer."

Her tone is warm. Unsuspecting.

Yet that statement feels *very* weighted.

"Yeah," I say. "Things are . . . good."

Mama looks directly at me. "There something you wanna talk about?"

I try not to break eye contact, but Mama's stare is too much. We really shouldn't be talking about this right now. But it doesn't look like she's leaving me much of a choice.

"Well . . . ," I say, swallowing back my fear. "I, um, quit my job at the factory and started working in a kitchen instead. I'm only a dishwasher for now. But the head chef's been teaching me a lot, actually."

I sneak a peek at Mama, hoping to see a smile or some hint of excitement on her face. But her mouth's pulled into a thin line. She already knows where this is heading. Might as well get the worst part over with.

"The restaurant's in Wanda World. I wanted to tell you sooner, but I was worried you'd be upset."

She closes her eyes.

"I'm sorry, Mama. I wasn't planning for it to happen. But Vanessa got me the job. If I thought I could find another restaurant to work at . . ."

Her eyes snap back open. "I don't care if you're working at Wanda World. I care that I had to find out about it by doing your laundry. How long's this been going on?"

"Since the beginning of summer," I say, looking away again.

"Why didn't you tell me?" Her voice is stern. Disappointed.

"Because I know how much you hate anything to do with that place. Country music and Wanda Jean ruined Nana's life—you've been hammering that into my head since I was a kid." My voice trembles, but I can't help it. "I didn't tell you I was working there because I couldn't stand to let you down. I made a mistake, okay?"

"You don't need to get so worked up," she tells me. "I'm just trying to understand."

"Whatever." I look down at the floor. "It doesn't matter. I'm gonna quit anyhow."

Working at Wanda World was a mistake. I should've stayed at the factory. I don't know what made me think I could be a chef. What made me think I could sneak around with Emmett and be whoever I want.

"No one's saying you gotta quit," Mama says.

I look back up at her, not believing for a second that she really means that.

"Honey, I think you might be overreacting."

I'm overreacting? She's the one who wouldn't ever let us go there, who kept Nana's pictures hidden in the attic, as if they were something to be ashamed of. I know I should let this go, but I can't. I'm tired of never being able to talk about this stuff.

"Really," I say. "So it wouldn't bother you *at all* if I was working at Wanda World?"

"It doesn't matter what I think," she says. "You're seventeen. You should be allowed to do what you want. I just want you to be honest." She leans forward, fussing with the pillows behind her back. "It makes me wonder what else you might be keeping from us."

Her words zap the fight right out of me.

What does that mean?

Does Mama suspect something?

I shift in my chair, trying not to let my panic show. Telling her about Wanda World was bad enough. There's no way I can tell her the truth about everything else. Because it's not like I can quit being gay if that upsets Mama, too. It doesn't work that way.

It's not a great feeling, constantly hiding part of myself from her. But I'm not the only one who's keeping secrets around here. If she wants me to be honest and open with her, then it should go both ways. Everyone's been so careful around Mama since her last big flare-up. Like she's fragile and might break. I know I shouldn't argue with her and risk upsetting her even more. But I'm worried that if I *don't* say something, things are only going to get worse.

"Mama, is our family in trouble?"

Her mouth drops into a frown. "What d'you mean?"

"I found the overdue property bill. We haven't paid it yet, have we?"

She sighs. "That ain't something for you to worry about, Luke."

"If we're gonna lose our house, I think I should be worried."

"We're not . . ." She pauses. "Your stepdaddy and I are taking care of it."

I knew it. It's just as bad as I thought.

"I might be able to help," I say, leaning forward. I wasn't planning to tell her about this yet. But, well, she asked for transparency.

"Remember when I went into the attic last week," I say. "I found a bunch of Nana's songs in an old suitcase up there. At first I was thinking we could sell them as memorabilia. But after looking into it more, I discovered a lot of the songs Nana wrote have actually been recorded by Wanda Jean."

Mama's expression doesn't change.

"Don't you get it?" I ask. "Wanda Jean stole some of Nana's lyrics. And we have the proof. That's gotta be worth something."

Her face softens. "Honey, I love how you're trying to help your family out. Really, that means the world to me. But it's best you leave your nana's things alone. There's no reason to go digging into the past."

"If Nana wrote those songs, she deserves the credit. Wanda Jean should have to own up to what she did."

"Luke, trust me. Your nana would want you to leave it alone."

"How d'you know?"

"She was *my* mama," she says, a little too sharply. "I lived under the same roof as her since the day I was born. I think I know what she'd want."

"I'm sorry, Mama. It's just . . . you never talk about her."

"Well . . ." She pauses, looking tired as she smooths out the top half of her blanket. "Your nana was a complicated woman. She loved me fiercely. I know she did. But a lot of days, she was too bitter at the world to let it show."

"Why? Because Wyatt left her?"

She nods. "Because Wyatt left her. Because Wanda Jean got famous. Because she felt country music had turned its back on her. Your nana was dealt a lot of tough blows. There's no arguing with that. But after a while . . . I don't know, she gave up trying to move on."

Mama touches the cross she always wears on her necklace. "Sorry, Mama. May you and God forgive me for speaking ill of the dead."

I think about the song Emmett sang at the open mic. *Empty rooms in an empty home.* Except the home Nana lived in didn't stay empty. Mama was there. And eventually, I was, too. Didn't we count for anything?

"I have many good memories of your nana," Mama says. "But there are also some not-so-good ones. Which is why, when your father left, I knew I had two options. I could stay sad and bitter—which, believe me, I wanted to do. Or I could try to move on."

She smiles, looking at me. "I'm glad I chose the latter. I know your brother and sister drive you up a wall at times. But I can't imagine our family without them."

"Me either, Mama."

She holds out her hand. "Promise me you'll forget about your nana's songs. Leave them in the past. That's where they belong."

Maybe she has a point. Country music's only been trouble for our family anyhow. I never should've given Emmett those songs to begin with. I'm glad they helped him find that scout. But the thought of them being out in the world for everyone to hear—I guess I didn't think about what that'd be like. What if Mama heard one of those songs? It'd just upset her all over again.

"Okay," I say, giving her hand a squeeze. "I promise to leave it in the past."

Mama tries to smile again, but her face is pale and drained of color, like talking about this has really taken it out of her. I shouldn't be agitating Mama; she needs to focus on getting better.

Soon Gabe and Amelia come bursting back into the room. They're all smiles as they present Mama with a teddy bear from the gift shop. It's holding a big red heart that reads "Get Well Soon."

As Mama gives them each a kiss, I want to believe I meant what I said, that I'll leave the past in the past. But when I think about Wanda Jean using my nana's songs, I still feel the anger churning around inside me. It's red. And hot. And bitter.

Maybe I'm just like my nana.

Maybe I'll never be able to let this go.

Chapter 31

EMMETT

Not everyone can pull off wearing a maroon fedora. But the receptionist at the recording studio is making it look easy. In fact, with her cropped T-shirt and gold hoop earrings, she looks more like a recording artist herself than someone who should be stuck working behind a desk. Peering up at us from under a curtain of wispy bangs, she instructs Aunt Karen and me to take a seat while we wait for Orrin.

The waiting area is just as stylish. Instead of a watercooler, there's a silver platter with bottles of water on it. I don't know why I find that so impressive; I just do. It's like I've reached a level of professionalism where I'm no longer expected to drink from cone-shaped paper cups. That's ridiculous. But judging from the framed records hanging on the wall—Rhiannon Giddens, Gillian Welch, Mickey Guyton, Margo Price—a lot of big-name artists have also sat here.

"How are you feeling?" Aunt Karen asks.

"Like I'm going to throw up."

"Well, I'm sorry, but I'm going to have to say something mushy and embarrassing now. . . ." She leans in closer, lowering her voice. "From the moment I first held you in my arms, I knew you were going to be something special. I have no doubt you're going to walk into that room today and blow them away with your talent. But even if you don't, it doesn't change anything. It's not the end result that makes you special. It's how hard you've worked to get there. Going after your dreams isn't easy; take it from someone who's selling tote bags out of her garage."

Hearing her say that should make me feel better. Except when I look at Aunt Karen, all I can think about is Grady and Cassidy in the dressing room. I should've told her when I got home last night. But I convinced myself it was better to wait. Not better for Aunt Karen. Better for *me*. I didn't want any distractions before my meeting with Orrin.

Of course, now the guilt is eating away at me.

Which has become its own kind of distraction.

"Aunt Karen . . . ," I say, trying to decide if this is really the best time and place to tell her. Her eyes are wide with excitement. I don't want to fill them with tears.

"Would you mind coming into the studio with me?" I ask. "I'd feel better knowing you were there."

She gives me an enthusiastic hug. Which only makes me feel worse. Thankfully, Orrin arrives soon and escorts us to one of the recording rooms. Junesburg might be a small little town in the middle of nowhere, but when we walk into the control room, you'd never be able to tell we weren't in Nashville. Everything's modern and clean. There's dark wood paneling, soft overhead lighting, and a massive recording console that probably cost more than our house.

Two middle-aged men sit in front of the console. Orrin introduces me to them as Bill Mooney, a producer acquaintance of his, and Travis, the sound engineer. "They're here as a favor to me," he explains. "So let's make good use of their time."

I clutch the handle to my guitar case a little tighter, suddenly very glad Aunt Karen came with me.

Travis helps me get set up in the studio. He makes sure the condenser mic is at the right height before heading back into the control room to test my levels. I strum a few chords to try to familiarize myself with the way sound travels around the space. Once we're ready to go, I place Verna's lyrics on the music stand in front of me and tell myself this is no different than singing on the empty stage last night.

"Let's start with the song I heard at the Rusty Spur," Orrin's voice says from over the monitor. "And don't worry about being perfect."

I tap my toes to set the rhythm. When I start playing, I try not to look through the window to the control room, where four pairs of eyeballs are staring back at me.

"Stop." This time it's Travis's voice on the monitor. "Closer to the mic, please."

I take a step closer.

I start over.

Bill Mooney, the producer, leans over and talks to Orrin. "Hold up," Orrin says. "Don't rush it. Try slowing the tempo a bit."

I take a breath.

I try again.

When I get to the part about empty rooms in an empty home, it's not hard to channel Verna's loneliness. I just imagine what it'd be like if Luke never talked to me again. And this time, I finally make it to the end of the song.

"Really great," Orrin tells me. "And now that you're warmed up, let's try it again."

I sing the song twice more. Thankfully, Orrin's satisfied with the results. He tells me to hang tight while they listen to the playback. As the men huddle around the control panel, Aunt Karen stands behind them and gives me an enthusiastic thumbs-up.

I return the gesture. But then, as I pull the music stand closer to get ready for my next song, I start thinking about Luke again. I still haven't heard from him since he texted me. It's only been two days. But it's felt like two lifetimes.

"Okay," Orrin says. "I think we're all happy with that. Let's hear what else you've got for us."

I try to clear Luke out of my head, but I can't. I don't understand why he's keeping his distance from me. I get that his mom's sick. And he's not ready to be out yet. But I just wanted to be there for him. Why does it feel like I'm being punished for that?

It's not fair to ask Luke to endanger himself to make me feel less hurt. But I'm tired of all the lies. Grady cheating on Aunt Karen. Wanda Jean not writing her own music. Me, having to act like I'm a stranger whenever Luke is around someone he knows.

"Emmett?" Orrin asks, snapping me back to the recording studio.

"Sorry," I say. "I'm ready."

I reposition myself in front of the microphone. But as soon as I look at the lyrics for my next song, my mouth goes dry. *Isn't this lie just as bad, if not worse?* How can I be mad at Wanda Jean for stealing Verna's songs when I'm doing the same thing? I told myself it was okay because I was helping Luke. But that's not what this is about anymore. Luke's not even talking to me right now. I'm not in this recording studio for him. I'm here for myself.

I look back up at the control room. Aunt Karen's still smiling, waiting for me to begin. She thinks I got here because I'm determined and talented. And while I may be both of those things, that's not why I'm in this room today. I'm in this room because Verna wrote better songs than I can, and I was willing to lie and pretend they're mine. I want a recording contract so bad it hurts. But if I get one, I want to feel good about it. Not guilty.

Orrin comes back on the monitor: "Son, I hate to rush an artist. But we've only got this room for another thirty minutes."

I nod, knowing I have to sing something. It just can't be Verna's lyrics. I start playing the first chords that pop into my head. I haven't practiced this song in a while, and I'm worried I won't remember all the words. But soon enough, my confidence takes over.

So just turn around
With your boots
And those jeans
Ain't looking for no man of my dreams

Orrin stops me. But this time, instead of playing God from the control room, he joins me in the studio.

"Emmett." He motions me away from the mic. "What song is this?"

"It's called 'Dream Cowboy.' I wrote it earlier this summer."

"I thought we had an understanding," he says. "I can't produce something like that."

I want to stand my ground, but there's already a quiver in my voice. "Why? What's wrong with it?"

"Country music isn't ready for a song about two men."

"But it could be," I say, pleading. "Country music is capable of change. Look at Lil Nas X. Or Brandi Carlile. Or Brandy Clark. They all managed to break through."

"Yes, but—"

"How can you say country's not ready for a song about two men when no one's given us one?" My heart's pounding—there's no going back now. "There could be an audience for it. But we'll never know if the record labels and radio stations keep saying no."

Orrin sighs, glancing over at the control room. "If I bring a song like this to my executives, they're going say you're not the kind of artist we're looking for. I'm sorry, but it's a waste of my time."

Tears sting my eyes. Wanda Jean said you have to believe in who you are. And, yeah, maybe she's a fraud. But that doesn't mean I have to be one, too. If I'm lucky enough to have my own fans someday, I don't want them to love me for a lie.

Orrin looks me square in the eyes. "Don't blow this opportunity, son. Most artists have to pay for studio time. I'm doing this as a favor to you. Because I believe in your potential."

I look at Verna's lyrics on the music stand. I don't know when I'll get another chance like this. Maybe I never will. Which is why saying no seems like the absolutely wrong decision to make. But then again, so does saying yes.

"I appreciate everything you've done for me," I say, grabbing Verna's lyrics as my tears start spilling out. "But you shouldn't ask people to change who they are."

If Orrin says anything to me on my way out, I don't hear it. It's like I'm walking through a vacuum where nothing else exists. No cool receptionist. No bottles of water on a fancy silver tray. No Aunt Karen, whom I totally forget about until I'm back in the parking lot.

"Emmett, wait!" I turn around to see her running after me. "What happened?"

I don't know where to begin, so I blurt out the first thing that comes to me: "I didn't deserve to be in there. Those weren't my songs."

Aunt Karen frowns. "What are you talking about?"

Not wanting to hang around the recording studio, I ask her to drive me someplace else. And as we sit in a parking lot at a gas station down the road, I tell her about how Luke found the songs in his attic. How Wanda Jean had stolen them from Verna. How Luke wanted me to get the schedule from Grady so we could confront her about it.

"Not that it matters anymore," I tell her.

"Why not?"

"Luke asked for space," I say, choking back a sob. "I think he wants to dump me."

"Oh, Emmett. I'm so sorry."

Aunt Karen opens her glove compartment. As she reaches for a napkin to hand me, I catch a glimpse of her feather tattoo. The one she got so she could still feel free while being tied down. More tears spill down my cheek. I should've told her about Grady as soon as it happened. It was selfish of me to wait.

"There's more," I say, sniffling.

Aunt Karen nods.

"I saw something. Something I have to tell you about." Wiping my cheeks dry, I crumple the napkin in my hands and take a breath. "Grady was in the dressing room with Cassidy late last night. They were drinking wine and I'm pretty sure they kissed."

Aunt Karen blinks, and without any emotion in her voice, she asks, "Is Cassidy the blond one?"

"Yes."

"I need you to step out of the car for a minute."

"I'm sorry," I say, feeling terrible all over again. "I should've told you when I got home. I wanted to, but—"

"Emmett," she says, stopping me. "I'm not mad at you. But I need to do something right now and I don't want to scare you."

"Uh . . ."

"Please. You'll know when it's safe to enter again."

I step out of the car as directed. After I shut the door and take a step back, Aunt Karen grips the steering wheel and lets out a primal scream. She slumps back in her seat when she's done, and I take that as my cue to get back in.

"I knew it," she says, slowly shaking her head. "I knew something was off. But I didn't want to believe it. For once, I thought everything was finally working out for me. I mean . . . *fuck*. I bought a house here. What am I supposed to do now?"

"Aunt Karen, I'm really sorry."

She looks at me. "No. Grady never should've put you in that position. Besides, it's better I find out now. I mean, can you imagine if—"

She sits up straight. I wait for her to finish her sentence, but she just starts the engine instead. We leave the gas station and drive all the way home in silence.

When we pull into her driveway, Aunt Karen runs inside. I give her a moment, unsure whether she wants to be alone or not. When I finally enter the house, she's in her office, kneeling on the floor with the folder from Villa Delphine Luxury Resort and Spa.

"That fucker," she says. "He wasn't planning a beach wedding.

He was applying for a job in their entertainment division. This is an employment contract."

She tosses the folder.

Papers fly everywhere.

When she looks up at me, her eyes are wet. But there's also determination in them. "So," she says, tightening her jaw. "You still need access to Wanda Jean's schedule?"

Chapter

32

LUKE

Sitting alone in my truck, with only the rain and a six-pack to keep me company, I've come to a startling realization: *I might not hate country music.*

Some of the songs are surprisingly catchy. Especially the party anthems. It doesn't even matter if you don't know any of the lyrics. When someone sings about red plastic cups and drinking on a Friday night, all you want to do is crank up the volume and sing along.

Then there are the sad songs. Songs about trying to forget someone. Songs about crying into your beer because you can't. You'd think they'd make me feel worse. But, actually, it's nice to know I'm not alone in going through this.

Heavy raindrops pelt against my windshield as I crack open another beer. I guess it's fitting that I drove here tonight. When Emmett and I had our first kiss, and I told him I wanted to open my own restaurant someday, it made this parking lot feel like a place for new beginnings. But now, much like the boarded-up windows of the abandoned diner in front of me, it feels like a place for endings.

I need to break up with Emmett. It's the only way to protect my family. I can't risk Mama finding out the truth. I've already upset her enough with my job at Wanda World, and bringing up Nana's songs.

Besides, it's not like my relationship with Emmett was going to last forever. I'm just speeding up the inevitable.

It's been two days since I texted him. I don't want to drag this out; the right thing to do would be to tell him in person. But how can I look Emmett in the face and honestly say I don't want to be with him anymore?

I take another swing of beer and grab my phone. I could just text him and get this over with now. Except Emmett means too much to me to end things that way. And I'm not nearly drunk enough to be *that* big of an asshole.

I should probably just head back home, but I'm in no condition to drive. And while I'd normally walk the few miles back into town, it's raining so hard tonight that I'd be better off in a canoe.

Picturing myself canoeing home makes me giggle.

Shit. I am drunk.

With my phone still out, I text the only person I can think of who wouldn't judge me right now. Ten minutes later, when Vanessa's headlights cut across the parking lot, I regret my decision. I was a shitty boyfriend to her when we were dating. Now that we're friends, I'm not sure I'm treating her any better. I shouldn't be asking her to clean up my mess like this.

Vanessa's car pulls up next to mine and we roll our windows down. "Luke," she shouts over the downpour. "What the hell are you doing?"

I hold up my beer. "Staying hydrated."

She rolls her eyes. "Okay. How about you let me drive you home now?"

"But you just got here," I say, hearing the fuzzy slur of my words.

Before she can protest, I open my door and scoot over to the passenger side, ignoring the crunch of empty cans beneath my boots. Vanessa tosses a rain jacket over her head and makes a dash for my truck.

"It smells like a frat house in here," she says.

"Nice to see you, too."

"Seriously, Luke. I'm—" She pauses. "Are you listening to country music?"

I switch the radio off. "What? I'm buzzed. Okay?"

She takes out a brown paper bag from under her raincoat. "Here. You should probably put something else into your stomach."

As soon as I open it, the smell of buttery fresh biscuits hit my nostrils. "You're a genius," I say, tearing into one.

Vanessa takes a biscuit for herself. "The kitchen was asking about you, by the way. They want to know when you're coming back."

I've only missed two shifts. And since Mama's been in the hospital, Rodney couldn't be a jerk about it. I told him I'd be back tomorrow, but there's no way I can keep working there. Not only because of Mama. For my own sake, too. I don't want to risk running into Emmett after I break up with him. It's best I cut Wanda World out of my life altogether.

"I'm not going back," I say.

"What?" Vanessa replies, mid-chew. "Why not?"

"Mama found out I was working there."

"She's making you quit?"

"I want to quit. I'm gonna ask for my job back at the factory. It paid better anyhow."

"I thought you hated working there," she says. "And what about your training with César? You're just going to give up on that?"

I reach for my beer, only to find I finished it already.

"It's not a big deal," I tell her. "You gave up on your fashion internship, right?"

"That's different."

"How?"

She slumps back into her seat. "Because. It just is."

"Ah, very illuminating."

"I couldn't afford to go, okay?"

"*What?*" I'm unable to hide my surprise. "You never told me that."

She pulls on the drawstring to her raincoat, frowning. "I was embarrassed."

"Vanessa. You know my family. If anyone gets what it's like not to have money . . ."

"Yeah, that's *why* I was embarrassed. Living in Nashville for the summer would've been expensive. My parents were supposed to help. But when they discovered the shopping spree I went on beforehand, they made me return all the clothes I'd bought for the internship and said I had to get a real job instead. It's my own fault I couldn't go."

"Oh."

"I know it makes me sound spoiled," she says. "But I wasn't being materialistic. I bought those clothes because I wanted to be taken seriously. I was afraid if I got to Nashville and people found out I was from Jackson Hollow, they'd think I was some small-town hick."

"No, that makes sense," I tell her. "And I'm sorry you couldn't do your internship. For what it's worth, I don't think you're spoiled."

She sighs. "Well, if I'm being completely honest, I might be a *little* spoiled. But nothing humbles you faster than having to wait tables at Wanda World. Do you know how many times I've picked up a napkin only to find someone blew their nose in it?"

"So you're not only working there for the free biscuits, then?"

"Please. I'm *mostly* in it for the free biscuits. The character building and personal growth are just side benefits."

Outside, the rain's still coming down in sheets, making the inside of my truck sound like we're going through a car wash. Earlier tonight, I didn't think there was enough beer in the world to get me to stop thinking about Emmett. But now that I've polished off an entire six-pack, the sharp edges have finally started to blur.

"Okay," Vanessa says, turning toward me. "I came clean about my internship. Now do you want to tell me why you're sitting in your truck, in the middle of nowhere, drinking alone?"

I shrug. "Do I need a reason?"

"Luke Reginald Barnes."

"*Not* my middle name."

"Is it because of your mama?" she asks, softening her tone.

"Mama's fine. They're discharging her tomorrow."

"That's great."

I nod, hoping we can drop it. But I make the mistake of looking over at her. Vanessa's hair is wet from the rain and her lips have the tiniest curl of a smile. Like she knows if she waits long enough, I'll eventually crack.

My cheeks grow warm and I have to look away. It doesn't take beer goggles to know Vanessa's attractive. If this were a few months ago, and I was still desperate to prove I could be with a girl, I might've tried to kiss her. But a lot has changed since then. I know what I want now.

I want to stop hurting Vanessa.

I want to stop trying to be something I'm not.

"Well, I'm not going to force it out of you," she says. "But if you ever need to talk, I'm here. Things feel different between us now. In a good way, I mean. It makes me kind of sad it couldn't have been like this when we were dating."

"Yeah," I say. "Me too."

Vanessa deserves to know the truth. And now that I'm breaking up with Emmett, it'd be nice to have someone else I can be myself around. But I don't know how to do that without hurting her, so I keep my mouth shut.

"I don't know if this rain's gonna let up," Vanessa says, peering up through the windshield. "Should we make a run for my car?"

I tell her yes. But as soon as I open my door, I freeze. Vanessa's the closest friend I have. But how close can we ever really be if I keep deceiving her like this? If I exit my truck, I'll be choosing a lie over her.

"Wait," I say, closing my door again. "There's something I need to tell you."

Vanessa looks at me. I try to take a breath, but my chest is too tight. I don't know if I can do this. I don't know if I *should* do this. Would I tell her if I were sober? Probably not. But maybe that's why I need to do it now.

Vanessa reaches out to touch my arm.

"Luke. Whatever it is, you can tell me."

I search for the courage to say the words out loud. But the only thing I find is more fear. When Emmett talks about being gay, it seems so natural. He's proud of who he is. And he should be. But when I think about myself that way, those two words—*I'm gay*—feel like they can only be wrapped in shame.

Since I still can't bring myself to say it, I try working my way around it.

"It's about Emmett and me," I tell her.

Vanessa takes her hand away. "Oh. Okay."

"He's not just some guy I ran into at the park. We were sort of, um . . . dating."

Vanessa doesn't say anything at first. In fact, so much time passes that I start to question if I really said it out loud, or just imagined it. When she finally speaks, her voice is hollow.

"I should've known," she says. "I could tell something was up between you two. But then I thought, no, Luke would've told me if there was."

"I'm sorry. I wanted to tell you. But I was afraid."

Her face is completely blank. I could understand if she were confused. Or shocked. Or angry. But neutral? This seems worse.

She crosses her arms, staring straight ahead at the dashboard. "This is a really fucked-up way of telling me. No matter what I say right now, I still have to drive you home afterward."

"It's okay," I tell her. "You can be mad."

"*I know.* I'm not asking for permission."

"Vanessa, I didn't mean to hurt you. . . ."

"How long have you known?"

When I speak, my throat goes tight, like I have to squeeze the words out. "I don't know. I think part of me always knew. I just didn't want it to be true."

She looks up at the ceiling. Her eyes are glassy, and I feel like an asshole for making her cry. I also feel like an asshole for *not* crying. What's wrong with me that my feelings are always buried so deep?

"I'm sorry I was such a terrible boyfriend," I say.

She closes her eyes. "You don't have to beat yourself up. It's not going to fix anything."

"You deserved better."

"Stop." Her eyes flick back open. "I wanted to be with you, Luke, okay? Our relationship wasn't meaningless. Not for me."

I wanted to be with her, too. But I knew it could never work. And instead of telling her that, I built a wall between us, waiting until she became frustrated enough with me that it led to our breakup. I thought telling her the truth would've been too hard. But trying to tear that wall down now feels even worse.

"It wasn't meaningless for me, either," I tell her.

Which, apparently, is the wrong thing to say. Vanessa buries her face into her hands, letting her hair fall in front of her face. "God, I'm such an idiot. These past two months, they felt different. And I thought maybe we'd . . ."

She stops herself.

She sits back up and tucks her hair behind her ears.

She takes a breath.

"I should be a supportive friend right now. And I want to be. But I just . . . I can't. Not yet. This is a lot to take in."

"Yeah," I reply. "I know."

Outside, the rain finally starts to let up. I could probably walk back home, save Vanessa the trouble. But it doesn't feel right to leave her like this, so instead I turn the radio back on. Another sad song is playing. A heartbreak song. And since that feels a little too on the nose, I move to turn the dial.

"Wait," Vanessa says, stopping me. "I like this song."

I nod, turning it up. Listening to country music with Vanessa feels . . . strange. But I guess that's how things might have to be between us for a while. And maybe that's okay. It's better than lying and always feeling guilty around her.

After the song ends, Vanessa turns to me. "Can I ask you something?"

"Sure."

"Why'd you and Emmett break up?"

"We haven't yet," I say. "Not technically."

"But I thought you said . . ."

"I'm *planning* to break up with him," I tell her.

"Why?"

"It's complicated."

Vanessa doesn't say anything. But she doesn't have to. I know what I'm doing; I'm building a wall again. And so, in the interest of not shutting her out anymore, I tell her everything. I get the sense she doesn't agree with my reasons for breaking up with Emmett, but she doesn't try to change my mind, either.

"Just promise me this," she says. "At least tell him the truth. He deserves that much."

I know he does. But I couldn't bring myself to be honest when I broke up with Vanessa. What makes me think I'll be able to do the right thing this time around?

Chapter

33

EMMETT

Arriving at the end of the hiking path, I take a moment to catch my breath and appreciate the view before me. Maybe it's just the altitude, but looking down on Jackson Hollow, I suddenly realize how Wanda World is both *very* big and *very* small. Big, because it's home to forty-two rides, including six roller coasters; employs thousands of people; and welcomes over two million visitors a year. And small, because next to the Great Smoky Mountains and the endless green valleys that stretch across Tennessee, it's really just a dot on a much larger map.

When I first found out I'd be performing here this summer, I thought it was the greatest thing that had ever happened to me. But now that I've been here awhile, now that I'm looking down at the park as a whole, I can see how my time here will probably only count for a much smaller fraction of my life.

Maybe that's why Luke chose this spot to break up with me. That is, assuming he's going to break up with me—which I most definitely *am* assuming. If he wanted us to stay together, he would've said so. Instead, he sent a "hey, can we talk?" text and instructed me to meet him at the top of this lookout point.

I take a seat on a nearby bench and check my phone.

Great, I can't believe I showed up early to my own breakup.

I really hope I'm wrong. Because after what happened at the recording studio yesterday, I can't handle any more devastation. It sucks I blew my chance with Orrin. But I can always write more songs. And if I'm lucky, I might catch the attention of another scout someday. But if Luke ends things with me, that's it. I don't want to replace him with anybody else.

Pebbles crunch in the dirt behind me. Glancing over my shoulder, my heart hitches in my chest. Plain white T-shirt. Tight blue jeans. Well-worn cowboy boots. He has no right to be this good-looking right now. Couldn't he at least have worn something baggy? Like a trash bag?

"Hey," Luke says. "You got here early, too."

"Um. Yeah."

As he makes his way toward me, I don't know what to do with myself. Do I stand? Would it be weird to give him a hug? What about a kiss? Oh God, what if I've had my last kiss with Luke already and I didn't even know it?

"Sorry if this is kind of awkward," he says, sitting next to me on the bench.

"Yeah. Maybe we should just pretend we're naked."

"Uh . . ."

My face starts to burn. "It was supposed to be a joke. Like when a performer gets stage fright and they picture the audience in their underwear? Never mind. That was the worst possible thing I could say."

He laughs. It fills me with the tiniest bit of hope.

"How's your mom?" I ask.

"Better. She came home from the hospital this morning. The doctors aren't sure what happened. Which isn't surprising; you rarely get answers with MS. But at least she's got her energy back now."

"I was worried," I say.

"Sorry, I should've told you sooner."

"No, it's okay. You had a lot going on."

In the distance, a blue haze rests over the Smoky Mountains like a blanket. Aunt Karen says it's fog rising up from the vegetation. Like the mountain's releasing a breath of air. I know I have lofty ambitions for my life: make my way to Nashville, sign a recording contract, become country music's biggest gay superstar. But right now, I'd settle for remaining in Jackson Hollow. I could keep working at Wanda World. Play more open mics. *Stay with Luke.* I can feel him next to me, bouncing his leg, working up the nerve to speak. He can't break up with me. I'm not ready for this to end yet.

"Emmett, I—"

"This is a really great view," I say, accidentally interrupting him.

"Oh, yeah."

"Sorry, I didn't mean to—"

"No, it's okay."

A silence falls over us. There may as well be a dark cloud hanging above our heads. Except, instead of a storm, it's an impending breakup that's about to pour down on us. Luke opens his mouth again and I steel myself for the worst.

"Emmett, I owe you an apology."

Wait—is that a ray of sunshine breaking through?

An apology is not a breakup.

An apology is a bandage, meant to heal what's broken.

"I feel terrible about what happened the other day," he says. "I shouldn't have acted the way I did when Vanessa and I ran into you."

"I get it," I tell him. "You were trying to protect yourself."

"But it wasn't fair to you."

No, it wasn't. And the other day, in the moment, I was upset. But now that I've had to time to step back and see things in perspective, the only thing that matters is being with Luke. If that means going back to meeting in secret and acting like strangers when we're in front of other people, I'll do it. I'd rather have Luke on his terms than not at all.

"The truth is . . ." He pauses. "You scare me sometimes, Emmett. I like who I am when I'm around you. And it makes me wonder if it could be like that with everyone."

I want to tell him yes, it could.

But Luke's situation is different from mine.

"And that's why . . . ," he continues, clearing his throat to hide the crack in his voice, "I have to stop seeing you."

His words hit me like a brick. I knew summer wouldn't last forever. But I didn't think I'd have to worry about that yet. Not when we still have time left.

"I'm sorry," Luke says. "I know this isn't fair to you, either. But I started getting careless. My mama found out I was working at Wanda World. If she found out I had a boyfriend, too . . . it'd break my family apart."

My chest tightens; I can't get my words out fast enough. "We could be more careful," I say. "What if we only met at the park?"

"I quit the restaurant this morning."

"*What?*"

"Emmett, it isn't easy for me to say this. But my mind's made up. I never should've let things get this far." He turns his head, like he can't even look at me.

"Don't do this," I say. "Please. We can figure something out."

"No. We can't."

I get that he has to be discreet around his family. But how can he throw away what we have together? It doesn't make sense.

"Is this really what you want?" I ask.

"It doesn't matter what I want. It's what I have to do."

I close my eyes.

But that doesn't stop the first tear from spilling out.

"It's not like we were gonna be together forever," he says. "It's better we end things now. It'll be less messy, you know?"

"Luke, this was always going to be messy. I'm in love with you."

My confession surprises me. But it's true. I do love him. And I'm not afraid to say it anymore. I just wish I'd been able to tell him sooner—when it still mattered. If Luke wants to break up with me, I don't think I can stop him. He's made his decision. And it's not like I can force his family to change how they feel. Or ask him to choose me over them.

Next to me, his posture stiffens.

"I'm sorry," I say, opening my eyes. "I'm sure you don't want to hear that right now. But if this is the last time I get to see you . . ."

My voice catches.

Fuck. *Is* this the last time?

I take a breath and try again: "If this is the last time I get to see you, I would've regretted not saying it."

Luke still won't look at me. With his chin up and his shoulders squared, he's as stoic as ever. But I know him. He's not as impenetrable as he seems. Underneath all that armor, he's a mess of emotions like everyone else.

"Emmett . . ." There's a tremble in his voice. He pauses before speaking again. "I wish I could say those words back to you. But I'm not . . . It's just . . ."

I nod, trying not to fall apart as another tear rolls down my cheek.

"It's okay," I tell him. "You don't have to say anything."

It's better that he doesn't. I'd rather believe he can't say those words because he doesn't love me. Because if the opposite is true—he *does* love me, he just can't bring himself to say it yet—I'll never be able to move on from him.

Luke stays silent, and it's like part of me is dying inside. I thought I understood what it meant to have your heart broken. Like when you tear up while listening to a really sad country song. But I was so completely wrong. Because this . . . the ache that's in my heart right now—no song has ever made me feel this devastated before.

34

LUKE

The words are stuck in my throat. I know how badly Emmett wants to hear them. But I can't bring myself to say them. Because I'm not sure if they're true. I like Emmett a lot. More than I ever thought possible. But I can count the number of people I've said "I love you" to on one hand. And they're all family, so I didn't really have a choice in the matter.

With Emmett . . . love feels too scary. I wish I could blame Whizzer and Bulldog, or some of the guys at school, or even my mama, for making me think it's not okay to have those kinds of feelings for him. But, really, the loudest voice has always been my own. I told myself I could never be in love like that. And now I don't know how to stop believing it.

"I should go," Emmett says, wiping away his tears.

My heart tugs in my chest. I want him to stay. I want to explain why I can't say those words yet. But that would just prolong our breakup and make this all the harder to do. So I nod, pushing my feelings back down.

Emmett picks his backpack up off the ground. Unzipping it, he pulls out Nana's journal and the little squares of paper. "Here," he says, offering them to me. "I wanted to give these back."

"You don't need them?" I ask, surprised.

He shakes his head. "They don't belong to me."

"So? That didn't stop Wanda Jean from using them."

There's bitterness in my voice. But Emmett doesn't flinch.

"I know," he says. "And I'm sorry I tried to defend her when you first told me. Your grandma deserves the credit for these songs. Which is why I can't use them, either. If I ever make it in this business, I want to know I got there because of my own talent. Not someone else's."

A tiny flicker of relief blossoms inside me as I take the stack back from him. I know using the songs was my idea, but Mama's right. It's better to leave the past in the past. I can put these back up in the attic now, where they belong.

"You didn't need these songs anyway," I say. "You'll make it. I know you will."

"Thanks," he replies softly. "I hope so."

I wait for Emmett leave, but he doesn't move from the bench. It's torture. Because the longer he sits here next to me, the harder it becomes not to try and take back everything I just said about breaking up with him.

"I wasn't sure if I should tell you this or not," Emmett says, "but I know when Wanda Jean's going to be at the park again."

"What?" I ask, unsure what that has to do with any of this.

"I saw her schedule. We could still confront her about your grandma's songs."

Oh. That.

"It's not a good idea," I tell him.

He looks at me, and there's determination in his eyes again. "This isn't some ploy for us stay together. I'll admit I was only going along with your plan before because I was afraid you'd be mad if I didn't. But now I'm doing this for myself. It doesn't matter if she's my hero. I need to know the truth."

"I appreciate you telling me that," I say. "But I talked to my mama. She wants me to forget about all of this."

"Well, no offense to your mom, but Verna was *your* grandma."

"So? What does that mean?"

"It means you should also have a say."

I look down at the journal. The thing that's filled with my nana's words. Words that were recorded by someone else, or never at all. Words that have been hidden away from the world and long since forgotten. I used to think naming a diner after Nana was the best way to keep a part of her alive. *What if there's a better way?*

Tracing my finger along the doodles of flowers on the cover, I open my mouth to speak. But my words are stuck again.

"Tell me," Emmett says. "What do *you* want, Luke?"

Chapter
35
EMMETT

The first time I visited the museum at Wanda World—*Forever &*
Always Yours: The Wanda Jean Stubbs Story—my eyes immediately
filled with tears. It's hard not to get emotional when you're staring up
at a giant mural of the woman who inspired you to not only write and
sing your own music, but also take your dreams seriously.

Arriving at the museum this afternoon, however, I'm having a
very different emotional reaction. The mural is painted on the side
of the building, where Wanda's fiery orange bouffant takes up half of
it. Her larger-than-life smile is matched by the park-goers who stand
in front of her, posing for pictures that will surely end up in scrap-
books and on holiday cards. I envy their innocence. They still think of
Wanda Jean as a legend. Not a fraud who stole someone else's songs
and passed them off as her own.

Making my way around to the front entrance, I'm met by red velvet
ropes and a line of people waiting to get in. There's a new exhibit opening today: a hologram of Wanda Jean that will welcome visitors when
they enter the museum. The park's doing a big press event for it. And
since the real Wanda Jean is going to be there as well, access is limited.

I don't know what Aunt Karen said to Grady. (She probably didn't have to say much, considering the Cassidy situation, which he didn't deny.) But I now have around my neck a pass that will get me into the ribbon-cutting ceremony.

When I finally get inside, the main lobby is packed. It's an impressive space—two stories tall, with giant banners hanging down from the ceiling that depict Wanda Jean at different stages in her career. There are newspaper reporters; a camera crew from the local TV station; and important-looking people from the corporate offices, who invited as many of their friends and family members as they could score an extra ticket for.

In the center of the lobby, additional ropes and a team of square-jawed security guards are positioned around the exhibit. Which, as of right now, is just an empty glass box with a big ribbon around it. The buzz of excitement in the room, however, is palpable. It's rare for Wanda Jean to make a scheduled appearance like this.

I check my phone.

Why hasn't Luke texted yet?

This past week has been tough. I've lost count of how many times I reached for my phone, only to remember Luke and I broke up. Seeing him today will be strange. Before I met Luke, my music was always enough to keep me satisfied. But now that I've made room for someone else, now that I know what it's like to be in love, it's as if there's this giant Luke-sized hole in my life.

Squeezing past a group of women in pink Wanda World T-shirts, I head farther into the museum. I walk past the replica of the one-room shack Wanda Jean grew up in. Past the display cases filled with her numerous Grammys, CMA, and ACM awards. Past the mannequins dressed in her sparkling, bejeweled stage costumes.

After walking past her massive wig collection, I slip through an unmarked door, propping it open with a museum flyer. A long hallway with fluorescent lighting leads me to another door. This one's marked "Emergency Exit Only." I take a deep breath as I push it open, hoping it's not connected to a security alarm.

Warm Tennessee sunshine hits my skin as the smell of chlorine from the nearby log flume wafts by. There's no alarm. But there's also no Luke.

Did he change his mind? Was the thought of seeing me again so awful he couldn't bring himself to go through with it?

I check my phone again. The ceremony's supposed to start any minute now.

"Emmett."

I look up. Luke's running toward me with his backpack. My heart twists. Maybe I'm the one who can't go through with this. How am I supposed be around him and not shatter into a million little pieces?

"Sorry," he says. "I'm here."

I nod. Because I don't trust my voice not to tremble. Luke follows me inside and we hurry back down the hallway. When we get to the other door, he reaches out, like he's going to touch my elbow, but stops himself.

"Wait . . ." He takes a step back. "How's this gonna work?"

"I don't know. There's a lot of security, though. I figure our best shot is to try to get her attention on her way out. I'm hoping if you show her your grandma's journal, she'll recognize it."

He clutches the straps of his backpack, like we're about to jump out of an airplane and they're attached to our only parachute.

"We have to at least try," I tell him.

"I know. It's just . . . I don't like people knowing I'm Verna's grandson."

"Wanda Jean's the only one who has to know."

"Yeah. Well, her especially."

The pained look on his face is too much for me to take. I hate seeing him like this. I hate that I can't give him a hug right now.

"I get this isn't easy for you," I say. "But I'll be right by your side. We'll do this together, okay?"

He nods and we sneak back into the museum. When we get to the lobby, it's even more crowded than before. I tell Luke we should try moving closer to the front. But suddenly, Wanda's song "Forever & Always Yours" plays from the speakers above. A massive cheer rises from the crowd.

"Come on," I say.

Luke freezes.

"We have to go," I tell him.

"There are too many people." He slides the backpack off his shoulder. "I can't."

Something changes in the air. People's necks crane and the collective focus of the room shifts toward the back. With an additional team of security guards surrounding her, Wanda Jean enters. She's wearing a sparkling silver dress that may as well have been made from disco balls. The sleeves are dripping with beaded fringe, which creates a hypnotic swishing movement as she lifts her arm to wave.

The crowd absolutely loses it.

"Please," Luke shouts over the noise. "I need you to do this for me."

He holds out the backpack.

Luke may have dumped me, but that hasn't changed how I feel about him. I'd do anything he asked me to. Including this.

Taking the backpack from him, I get a lot of dirty looks as I try to push my way to the front. (Not to mention a few elbows.) By the time I finally make it up there, Wanda Jean's safely behind the ropes and someone hands her a microphone.

"Howdy, y'all!" she says, flashing a smile that's almost as big as the one on the mural outside. "Can I just say what an honor it is to have so many incredible fans joining me for this special day?"

Everyone cheers. And even though I know what Wanda did to Verna, I feel myself falling under her spell all over again.

"When I was a lil' girl growing up in the holler," she says, "I never could've imagined they'd create a replica of me someday like the one y'all are about to see. Heck, in our tiny cabin, we didn't even have a mirror!" She laughs. "It's true. If you wanted to see what you looked like, you had to run half a mile down the road and peer into the crick!"

The audience is eating up her story. But what if that's all it is? *A story*. If she lied about writing her own songs, who knows what else isn't true.

"But enough about the good ol' days. Let's get on with the show!" Wanda Jeans motions to one of her security guards, who steps forward with a giant pair of scissors.

"Now, I know y'all came to see me do some ribbon cutting today," she says. "But I'm gonna let Cyrus here do the dirty work. I just had my nails done. And, sugar, they weren't cheap." She laughs again, showing off her manicure. "Just because we didn't have mirrors growing up doesn't mean I'm not vain now!"

The security guard cuts the ribbon, and the audience applauds as the hologram version of Wanda Jean materializes in the glass box, waving and throwing out an excited, "Howdy, y'all!"

"Hey," the real Wanda says. "That's my line!"

The hologram continues: "I'm so glad y'all stopped by my museum during your visit here at Wanda World. This place holds some of my dearest memories. Whether I was singing for the toadstools and fireflies in the holler, or onstage at the Grand Ole Opry, I was always meant to be performing. What gives me the greatest pleasure, though, is being able to share my gift with those who matter most to me. That's you: my fans! Without y'all, I don't know where I'd be." The hologram pauses. "No, really. Technology like this is expensive!" She laughs. "But seriously, y'all mean the world to me. So take a look around, hum a little tune, and please know I will be *forever and always yours*."

The hologram sings the last few bars of "Forever & Always Yours," which sends the crowd into another round of enthusiastic applause.

"Not bad, right?" the real Wanda Jean asks. "Now if only they could smooth out some of the wrinkles on my human face, too."

As Wanda Jean cracks more jokes and poses for publicity shots, I formulate my plan. I need to be at the back of the exhibit, so I can get her attention as she exits. She'll be surrounded by security. But if she sees the journal, she might stop and hear me out.

Squeezing my way around to the back, I pull the journal from Luke's backpack. But before I can get any farther, a hand comes down in front of me.

"Sorry, we need to keep this area clear."

One of the security guards is blocking me. "It's okay," I say, flashing him my pass from Grady. The guard, who's at least twice my size, doesn't even blink.

"Son, you need to back up. Now."

"But I work here," I tell him, hoping I sound official enough.

He touches his earpiece, ignoring me. I glance over at Wanda Jean. She's blowing kisses to the crowd and waving goodbye already.

"Okay, look." Time to switch tactics. "I need to talk to Wanda Jean."

"Yeah. You and everyone else."

"No. Really. I know someone who's related to Verna Rose. And it's important I talk to her. She'll want to hear what I have to say."

He laughs. "*Verna Rose?* Most people at least pretend to be a long-lost cousin or related to one of her hairdressers."

"I'm not making this up," I say.

Wanda Jean turns to leave, which sets her security team into motion. The guards form a circle around her. And before I know it, we're met with a rush of people.

Everything's moving too fast. As Wanda Jean's escorted away, fans shout to get her attention. They're snapping pictures on their phone and waving memorabilia they hope to get signed. When Wanda Jean finally gets close enough, I hold the journal up and try yelling her name. But it's pointless. I'm swallowed up by the crowd.

My heart sinks as she moves toward the exit.

There's no way I can get to her now.

"Wait!" a voice booms across the lobby.

The hairs on the back of my neck stand up. I turn around, trying to locate where it came from. Looking up, my jaw drops. Luke's leaning over the railing on the second-floor balcony. He's holding up something silver and shiny, which catches in the light.

"This was my grandmother's locket," he shouts.

The bodyguards are still trying to escort Wanda Jean out. But some of the people around me have stopped trying to get her attention. They're staring at Luke, too.

"Her name . . . This locket . . ."

The lobby goes quiet. Luke stops and takes another breath.

"My nana was Verna Rose."

Chapter
36
LUKE

I don't know how Emmett does it. How he finds the courage to get up onstage, stand under a bright spotlight, and perform for a room full of strangers. Because if there's one thing I don't enjoy—*and this point is hitting especially hard right now*—it's being the center of attention.

The entire lobby is staring at me.

The entire lobby just heard me confess that Verna Rose was my nana.

The entire lobby is waiting for me to say something else.

I didn't think this far ahead. As my heart continues to hammer away, I realize what a terrible idea this was. I should've stayed downstairs, hidden in the back of the crowd. It's just . . . all my life, I've chosen staying safe over taking a risk. I didn't want to regret not doing something this time.

Of course, now that I *did* do something, I'm not sure it mattered. Wanda Jean's being ushered away by her security team. But before she disappears, I swear, she turns her head and looks up at me.

A chill runs through me as I take a step back from the railing. After having Wanda Jean take up so much space in the way my family remembers my nana, it's like seeing a ghost. I slip the necklace into my pocket and try to shake it off. I need to get out of this museum and far away from Wanda World. But suddenly, everything starts to spin. My arms are pinned behind my back and someone's pushing me into a wall.

"You got any weapons on you?" a voice barks in my ear.

After a thorough pat-down, the security guard who accosted me turns me back around. He's so in my face, I can smell the cinnamon gum he's chomping on.

"You're done here, buddy," he tells me.

"Okay," I say. "I'm leaving."

He grabs me by the arm, escorting me to the stairs.

"Is this really necessary?" I ask.

"You know how many weirdos we get at the park? People trying to get attention for themselves by causing a scene."

"I'm not lying," I say. "Verna Rose really is my nana."

He sneers. "Yeah. And mine's Loretta Lynn."

People stare at us as he leads me back downstairs. I keep my head down, not wanting to suffer any more humiliation. But when I hear my name, I look back up to find Emmett pushing his way through the crowded lobby. I break free from the guard, making my way toward him.

"I can't believe you did that," Emmett says.

"Me either."

"I'm sorry my plan didn't work. There were too many people."

"It's okay," I tell him. "I know you tried."

We're both slightly winded and smiling. For a second, it's easy to forget we've broken up. But soon the smile drops from Emmett's face.

I follow his gaze, looking over my shoulder. My security guard friend has returned.

"Relax," I tell him. "We're going."

Emmett and I turn to leave, but the guard's quick to cut us off again. "Hold up." He touches his earpiece, listening to whoever's on the other end. "Yeah, I got him. He's not going anywhere."

"Look, I'm not a danger to the park or anything," I say. "I swear."

The guard puts his hand back down. "Wanda Jean wants to see you."

"*Holy shit*," Emmett says. "Are you serious?"

"Not you." The guard points to me. "This one."

I look at Emmett. He tries to hide his disappointment with a shrug. But this was his plan, and I know how badly he wants to know the truth. There's no way I'm doing this without him. "He's coming with me," I say.

The guard rolls his eyes, touching his earpiece again. "There are two of them." He pauses, eyeing Emmett. "Nah. Just some scrawny kid."

Emmett's too busy biting back a smile to be offended.

"Let's go," the guard says.

He leads us out of the lobby and into an elevator, which we ride all the way to the top floor. When the doors open again, we step out into a giant loft space that appears to be both an office and a dressing room. There's a long conference table, racks of costumes hanging in clear garment bags, and framed posters of Wanda Jean on the walls. In the middle of the room, through a large arched window, there's an impressive view of the park.

"Take a seat," the guard says.

Emmett and I pull out two chairs at the conference table. Now that some of the adrenaline has worn off, neither of us knows what to say.

"This is weird, right?" Emmett whispers, hugging my backpack against his chest.

I don't know if he means waiting for Wanda Jean or sitting here together after we've already broken up. But the answer is yes.

The elevator dings again. When the doors open, Wanda Jean walks into the room with two more of her guards. Without missing a beat, she gives us a big, friendly smile. I can't tell if it's genuine or part of her act.

"Nelson," she says, addressing the guard who escorted us. "Did you offer our guests here something to drink?"

"Uh . . . no, ma'am."

"Y'all need anything?" she asks.

We both shake our head.

She turns back toward her guards. "At ease, boys. Y'all can take a breather."

"Ma'am," Nelson says. "I'm not sure that—"

"Bless your heart for doing your job so well," Wanda Jean says, cutting him off with another smile. "But you forget Jackson Hollow girls aren't helpless. I can take of myself. I'm sure of it."

Nelson's cheeks grow pink. He steps back into the elevator with the other guards and the doors close behind him.

"Now then," Wanda Jeans says, clasping her hands together. "Assuming no one's here for an autograph, y'all will have to excuse me for a moment. This outfit wasn't made for sitting."

As she makes her way across the room, the beads on her dress jingle and clank like a pocket full of loose change. Wanda Jean disappears behind some curtains; I look over at Emmett. He's got that look in his eyes. The one he had when we were at the swimming hole and he explained why he loved country music so much.

"Don't worry," I tell him. "I'll do all the talking."

It takes him a second to snap out of it.

"What? No. I want to help."

This can't be easy for him. Even I feel the magnetic pull Wanda Jean possesses when she's in a room. But I need to remember why I'm here: to learn the truth about my nana.

When Wanda Jean finally comes back out, she appears to have shrunk. She's wearing a colorful dressing robe and fuzzy pink slippers. But it's not the lack of heels that makes her look a foot or two shorter. It's because she doesn't have a helmet of bright orange hair resting on top of her head.

"Don't look so shocked," she says, touching the scarf that's covering her real hair, which is short and mostly silver. "Everyone knows how much I love my wigs."

When she joins us at the conference table, she studies Emmett for a second. "We've met before, haven't we?"

"I . . . uh . . ." He chokes on his words. "Yes. Backstage once. I'm in the Jamboree?"

She laughs, sounding pleased with herself. "I'm *very* good with faces. Less good with names. But tell me yours anyhow."

"Emmett."

She nods. "Emmett. I'm gonna try to remember that. I wish I could get to know all my employees by name. But, well, there are just too many of y'all."

When she turns to look at me, she loses the crinkles around her eyes from smiling. She doesn't say anything right away. Which makes me uneasy.

"I'm Luke," I say.

"Luke," she repeats, as if trying to determine whether or not it fits.

"I'm sorry I caused a scene earlier. But I really am Verna's grandson. And I can prove it." I go to reach for the necklace, but Wanda puts out her hand, stopping me.

"Oh, sugar. You don't need to prove it. It's plain as day."

It takes me a second to realize what she's talking about.

"Because I look like Wyatt?" I ask.

"Well, there's no denying that." She leans forward, studying me. "But there's plenty of Verna in you, too. You've got her eyes."

She sits back, clutching her robe closed tighter, like she just realized how uncomfortable it'd be to look into Nana's eyes again.

"I guess that makes you Lori's boy, then."

Hearing that name knocks the wind right out of me.

"You know my mama?" I ask.

She shakes her head. "Not exactly. I know *of* her. After your grandmother passed away . . . well, I didn't wanna go poking my nose where it didn't belong. But I did send your mama a letter. Just my condolences, really. Not that I expected a response. I can certainly understand why your family wouldn't want to hear from me."

Mama never mentioned that. Not that I'm surprised, I guess. She's always tried to protect us from anything related to Nana, Wanda Jean, and country music.

But Mama's not here now.

"If you don't mind," I say, shooting Emmett a look, "we were hoping to talk to you about my nana."

Wanda Jean places her hands on the conference table, before changing her mind and folding them in her lap instead. Without the massive wig and loud, shimmery dress to hide behind, she seems a lot less confident. Nervous, even.

"What do y'all wanna know?" she asks.

Emmett unzips the backpack and pulls out the journal.

"We want to know why you stole her songs," I say.

Wanda Jean looks at me, then at the journal, then back at me. Instead of any recognition or guilt, there's only confusion in her eyes.

"I'm sorry," she says. "I'm not sure I understand."

"You don't recognize this?" Emmett asks, waving the journal.

She looks at it again. And then I see it. Something flashes across her face. "Is that . . . but where . . . ?" She brings her hand to her chest, feigning shock. "My goodness, I don't think I've seen that in almost fifty years."

"I found it with my nana's things," I tell her.

"Is that so?" She shakes her head slowly, really trying to sell her incredulousness. "Ain't that something? I had no idea she kept it."

"Of course she had it," I say. "It was her journal."

"Oh, sugar. There's been a misunderstanding. That's *my* journal."

Emmett drops it onto the table, startling everyone. "Bullshit. I've seen your signature a thousand times," he says. "The handwriting in here's too messy. It has to be Verna's. You took her songs and passed them off as your own."

I didn't expect Emmett to be so mad.

Wanda Jean, on the other hand, seems almost amused.

"I hate to break it you," she says. "But not everything about me is real. My hair, my nails, my signature . . . that's all part of Wanda Jean, the Performer. She's who I am when I need to entertain my fans. But *that* handwriting, those pages . . ." She points at the journal. "That's the Wanda Jean who grew up in Jackson Hollow and wrote all her own songs, hoping like hell she'd get a chance to perform them someday."

"But why would my nana have your journal, then?" I ask.

"Well . . ." Her eyes roam the room, like she's searching for an answer. "That journal's from when I was around your age. Your nana and I were still friends back then. I suppose it could've gotten mixed up with her things somehow."

"But what about these?" Emmett pulls the loose squares of paper from the back. "These songs aren't from when you and Verna were friends. Here, this one. *Empty rooms in an empty home.* Verna clearly wrote this after Wyatt left her. And the handwriting matches what's in the journal."

Something in Wanda Jean's face changes. "May I see that?"

Emmett looks at me. I nod.

Wanda Jean takes the paper and holds it delicately, like she's afraid it might disintegrate. Her eyes turn glassy as she reads the lyrics.

"I never knew she kept them," she says, her voice barely above a whisper.

"What are you talking about?" Emmett asks.

She sets the paper down. "I'm sorry, Luke. But your grandmother didn't write this song. I did."

As much as I don't want to believe her, there's something about the way she's looking at me that makes me think it's true. She's not being defensive. Or overconfident. If anything, she seems sad to admit it's hers.

Emmett, however, isn't buying it. "But if you wrote this about Wyatt, how'd it end up with Verna? It doesn't make sense."

Wanda Jean slides the paper back across the table. "Boys, I'm truly sorry if any of this has upset you. It happened a long time ago; I'm not sure it's worth worrying about now." She pushes her chair back, as if she's about to stand. "If there's anything else y'all need, I can get a member of my team to—"

"It's worth it to me," I say. "What aren't you telling us?"

She pauses, gripping the armrests of her chair, before lowering herself back down. "Sugar, I ain't sure it's my place to tell."

"Please," I say. "I know hardly anything about my nana."

She looks at me. Like, *really* looks at me. I force myself not to look away. Whatever she has to say, I want to hear it. I *need* to hear it.

"I didn't write that song about Wyatt," she says.

Her answer just hangs there for a minute.

"Okay . . . ," Emmett says. "But that still doesn't explain why Verna had it."

Wanda's eyes soften. Like she's asking my permission for something. But I have no idea what. I just want to know the truth about my nana. Why couldn't she move on from Wyatt? Why weren't Mama and I enough to make her happy? Why'd she hang on to some old love song Wanda Jean wrote? Why didn't—

Goose bumps prick my skin.

Oh. That's why.

"I wrote that song about your grandmother," Wanda Jean says, confirming my suspicion.

The room goes fuzzy as I try to piece everything together. *Wanda Jean was in love with Nana. But did Nana . . . was she also . . . ?* All this time, I thought I was wrong for not being like the rest of my family. But what if I wasn't the only one? What if there were two of us?

"Should I continue?" Wanda Jean asks.

I nod slowly, still in shock.

"Well, I hardly know where to begin." She pauses, lacing her fingers together like she's getting ready to pray. "When your nana and I were your age, it wasn't acceptable for two women to be together. Not in this business. And certainly not in this town. Your granddaddy knew the truth about us, though. And when he agreed to be my manager, we decided he should become my husband as well. So people wouldn't ask questions."

I glance over at Emmett.

His jaw is practically on the conference table.

"Our arrangement worked for a while," Wanda says. "But as time went on, as I started to do more press and give more interviews, I got tired of pretending. I just wanted to be with your nana. Even if it meant sacrificing my career."

The video of Nana and Wanda performing at the Grand Ole Opry pops into my head. They sang that duet. "Gotta Keep a Smile on Your

Man." But offstage, they were living a completely different life.

Wanda sighs. "Of course, Wyatt wasn't too keen on me telling the truth. He couldn't have cared less about losing me as his wife. But losing me as his client?" She lets out a bittersweet laugh. "Well, that man certainly had a good sense for business. As soon as he realized I was serious, he started working on your grandmother. He promised to turn her into a bigger star than I would ever be. Unfortunately, that wasn't a promise he could keep. He soon left her to chase after other women and the bottle."

She pauses, pressing her lips together. "That would've made it easier, though. If your nana had left me because of her music."

"Why did she leave you?" I ask.

"Because Wyatt offered her something I couldn't: a chance at being normal. You see, when I was with Wyatt, our marriage was nothing more than signatures on a piece of paper. I could be with Verna, and he could run around with any woman he wanted. But when Wyatt offered to marry your nana, she saw an opportunity to change herself."

"Why?" I ask, even though I already know the answer.

"Your grandmother had a strict upbringing," Wanda says. "A lot of us did. And even though I know she loved me, she still thought it was wrong for us to be together."

So she married Wyatt and got pregnant with Mama. But it wasn't Wyatt she was heartbroken over for the rest of her life. It was Wanda Jean.

"What about these?" I ask, pointing to the squares of paper.

"I sent those songs to your nana," Wanda Jean explains. "I told her

I wouldn't record them without her blessing. But she never responded to any of my letters. So after a while, I took the hint and stopped sending them."

"But you recorded other songs," Emmett says. "Some of your biggest hits are about Wyatt and Verna running off together."

"It's true. I put a lot of my anger into my music. I suppose it was another way of trying to get Verna's attention. If she wasn't reading my letters, then maybe she'd hear one of my songs. But not all of them were angry."

I can see Emmett cycling through her lyrics in his head. "*My love for you is not a cage,*" he says. "*It's a flame. Burning bright. One I'll never let die.*"

Wanda Jean smiles, her eyes damp with tears again. "*So spread your wings, my lil' darlin'. And fly, fly, fly.*"

"But you stopped," he says. "You haven't released any new music since—"

"Since Verna passed." She shrugs very matter-of-factly. "I didn't see the point anymore. Almost every song I wrote, I wrote for her."

Maybe that's why we never played country music in our house. Maybe Nana couldn't bear to hear what Wanda Jean was trying to tell her.

"But your fans," I say. "Didn't you want them to know the truth?"

She pauses, taking a moment to consider her response. "What I put into my music . . . that's up to me. Nobody owes their story to the world. I only told the things I wanted to be heard. Some of the details may've been left out. But the emotions, those were always real."

"And you never fell in love again? Not after my nana?"

It's a personal question to ask. But to Wanda Jean's credit, she doesn't shy away from answering.

"Well, I haven't been alone all my life. I guess that's one way of putting it. And I suppose I've loved other people. But, no, it's never been the same as it was with Verna."

Her answer makes me sad. Not only for Wanda Jean and Nana. But also, selfishly, for myself. What if I'm making a mistake with Emmett? What if I never find somebody else who makes me feel the way he does?

Reaching into my pocket, I pull my nana's necklace back out. "I guess this was from you, then, not Wyatt?"

Wanda Jean closes her eyes and nods.

I set the heart-shaped locket on the table and slide it toward her. "I think my nana would want you to have it back."

Her eyes snap open. "No. I couldn't."

"It's okay," I say. "I don't need it anymore."

She looks at the locket. I can tell she wants to pick it up, even if just to hold it again for a second. "Sugar. Are you absolutely positive?"

"Yes. I am."

When I started wearing it, I thought it was the only connection I had to my nana. But now I know we're connected in other ways. Besides, I think Nana *would* want her to have it. If she hated Wanda Jean after all those years, I doubt she would've kept it tucked safely away in one of her songs.

Wanda Jean picks the locket up, placing it in her palm. She stares at it for a moment before letting out another laugh. "Dang it. I knew I should've washed off my makeup. Y'all are about to see more of the real Wanda Jean. And let me tell you, she ain't always pretty."

A streak of mascara runs down her cheek.

She doesn't bother wiping it away.

By the time Emmett and I finally leave the museum, the temperature outside has dropped. The sun's dipping behind the mountains and visitors have begun their mass exodus toward the maze of parking lots. They leave behind empty soda cups and poorly folded-up maps, making the park look like a ghost town.

"That was intense," Emmett says, stopping in front of Ye Ol' Tannery, where you can get your name carved into a leather Wanda World key chain.

"Yeah," I say. "It was."

"Are you okay?" he asks.

"I think so. Are you?"

He nods. "Yeah. I guess."

The scent of funnel cakes and cinnamon rolls still lingers in the air around us. Looking up at the Bone Rattler and the Smoky Mountain Scrambler and all the other rides—which are backlit by a sky the same color as the bright pink taffy they sell in the gift shop—I realize this may be my last time at the park.

My last time seeing Emmett.

I don't want to make the same mistake my nana did and keep pretending to be someone I'm not. But on the other hand, if I start living my life the way I want to, I'm afraid I'm going break my mama's heart. *Twice.* Once when I tell her the truth about me. And once when I tell her the truth about Nana.

"So," Emmett says. "What do we do now?"

I give him the only answer I can.

"I've no idea."

As Emmett and I continue walking, I keep looking for a sign. Something that will tell me what to do. I listen closely to the music playing throughout the park, hoping one of Wanda Jean's lyrics might help guide me. But nothing comes to me. And soon enough, we arrive at the employee parking lot, safety lamps flickering on above us, ready to go our separate ways.

Chapter

37

LUKE

Sitting at our kitchen table a few days later, with a stack of Nana's cookbooks next to me, I'm unnerved by how quiet our house is. Keith's working his new shift at the plant, Amelia's at soccer practice, and Gabe and Mama are out back. Even our refrigerator—which is well past its warranty and makes strange humming noises—is silent right now.

I'm supposed to be planning what I want to make for supper this weekend, but my mind's elsewhere. Ever since Emmett and I talked to Wanda Jean, there's something she told us that I can't get out of my head. When I asked why her songs didn't tell the entire truth about her and Nana, she said nobody owes their story to the world.

If I don't want to ever come out, I don't have to. That's my right. Nobody else should be able to make that decision for me.

But at the same time, I'm not Wanda Jean. I'm an aspiring chef in Jackson Hollow. The world's not exactly asking for my story. But what about the people who do know me? *My world.* Do I owe anything to them?

I look over at my phone, which is also silent. I told Emmett I needed more time to figure things out. I miss getting texts from him.

I miss being with him. But even if we got back together and kept our relationship a secret, it'd only be a temporary fix. He'd still have to leave at the end of summer. I don't know if I can stomach breaking up with him twice. Maybe it's easier this way.

I unlock my screen and pull up our messages. I try to imagine myself deleting them, just like I did with Cody's. But I can't. Because Emmett means too much to me. He loves me. The *real* me. And I . . . well, it's possible I'm also in love with him.

The back door swings open, slamming into the wall like it always does, and Gabe rushes in, excitedly telling me about the toad he's got cupped in his hands.

"Go upstairs and put that in your aquarium," Mama instructs him. "I don't wanna find any surprises in the bathtub this time."

Gabe runs off; Mama moves to the sink, attempting to scrub the dirt out from under her fingernails. She missed planting anything in the garden this spring. But now that she's home from the hospital and feeling better again, she's already put in cucumbers, radishes, and mustard greens for the fall.

"Still trying to decide on your menu?" she asks.

"Huh?" I say, taking a second to remember why the stack of cookbooks is next to me. "Oh. Yeah. I guess I got distracted."

Mama smiles. "How'd this family get so lucky that you picked cooking as a hobby?"

I wasn't expecting it, but her words slice right through me. Cooking's not just a hobby for me anymore. It's something I'm taking seriously now. I want to go to culinary school, and work in a restaurant, and cook good Southern dishes that would make my nana proud.

Mama should know that about me. But she doesn't, because I guess I haven't talked about it very much. Not like I have with Emmett. Or even Vanessa. Are those the only two people I'm ever going to let in?

Nobody owes their story to the world.

But maybe it's not about *owing* your story.

Maybe it's about *wanting* other people to know.

How can I tell Mama, though, if it means her finding out I'm gay? What if she can't ever accept that part of me? She might not love the person I want to be. The person I already am. Telling her could ruin everything.

"What's that look for?" Mama asks, drying her hands off with a dish towel.

My throat goes tight. There's a stinging in my eyes.

"Luke?"

My chin trembles as I try to hold back the tears. I hate crying in front of people. Not because I think "real" men shouldn't do it— though I've definitely been taught to think that's true. For me, it's more about staying in control. Once that first tear slips out, it's harder to keep the rest of your feelings in check.

It's too late now, though. I choke out a sob, covering my mouth.

Mama rushes over, kneeling next to my chair. "Luke, honey, you're scaring me. What's the matter?"

I want to tell her, but I can't. The tears won't stop. They're hot and wet and streaming down my cheeks. My body starts to shake, and it's as though every emotion I've ever tried to keep inside me is bursting out at once.

"Luke, baby. Tell me what's wrong."

I try to speak, but my words come out in a moan.

Mama wraps her arms around me, whispering over and over again:

"Just tell me.

"Just tell me.

"Just tell me."

Chapter

38

EMMETT

Looking out into the packed amphitheater tonight, it's like I'm seeing the Jamboree through a whole new set of eyes. The smiles on the sea of faces seem brighter. The occasional flash of the camera phone, less annoying. It doesn't matter how many times I've done this show. Now that I know the truth about Wanda Jean, the *real* story of what happened between her and Verna Rose, it's an even bigger honor to be performing her songs.

Wanda Jean has always been a trailblazer. Maybe she had to keep certain aspects of her life hidden from the public, but that doesn't diminish the power of her music. A song doesn't always have to be true. But there should be *truth* in it. An emotion you can connect with. Lyrics that articulate something you believe. A progression of chords that makes you *feel* something. For me, Wanda Jean's music has always had those things.

She makes me want to be a trailblazer, too. I'm determined to let my songs tell the kind of stories she couldn't.

Of course, the other reason it feels like I'm seeing the show through a whole new set of eyes is because *I'm literally seeing the show through a new set of eyes*. With the summer more than half over already, I've been promoted to the front half of Calamity Joe.

Left turn, right turn.

Two steps forward.

Spin. Whinny. Spin.

My new role may not be as exciting as being discovered by an A&R scout or recording in a professional studio. But when the weight of that lasso hits my shoulders and the audience breaks into enraptured applause, it still makes me smile.

"Sweet biscuits and gravy," Cassidy says, popping her head out from under our costume after we've waddled off the stage together. "Don't they ever dry-clean this thing?"

I shrug. "You get used to the smell after a while."

To Cassidy's credit, she doesn't roll her eyes or scowl. "Whatever," she says, fluffing her hair back into place. "I guess I'll be thankful for this when I'm famous and need a funny anecdote for the talk show circuit."

Once she's liberated herself from the back end of Calamity Joe, Cassidy takes off to change into her next costume. I'm not sure if she or Grady ever found out I was the one who saw them kissing in the dressing room. But after Aunt Karen dumped Grady for being a cheating jerk, they officially started dating. So I guess Cassidy can't be *that* mad at me.

"That has yet to get old," Jessie says, running off the stage in her rodeo getup. "Did you hear how much they loved us? I thought they'd never stop clapping."

"They loved *you*," I correct her. "You're owning that song. Especially the yodel."

"Hey!" Avery pops his head through a side curtain as Jessie sets her lasso on the prop table. "You sounded amazing out there."

Jessie takes a quick look around, then leans forward to give him a kiss. Avery disappears through the curtains with a big grin on his face.

"I didn't know *that* was happening," I say.

Jessie shoots me a look. "It's not. I mean, *it is*. But we're keeping it casual for now."

"So I guess you stopped saying no to everything, then?"

She shrugs. "Maybe I just started saying yes to the right things."

After Cassidy and Grady's relationship went public, Jessie and Avery confronted Miss Trish, asking her why the girlfriend of the senior VP of entertainment management had all the best parts, while the other cast members, including the two non-white ones, were stuck in the chorus for the majority of the show.

According to Avery, Miss Trish acted all defensive and hurt. She claimed that promoting diversity was already a "core value" of the park, and that roles were assigned to people based on seniority and talent. When Avery pointed out that he and Jessie had been performing in the show just as long as Cassidy had, and therefore Miss Trish must be implying that they weren't talented enough, she finally relented and gave them each a solo.

Recasting two of our musical numbers doesn't fix the diversity problem in the Jamboree, but there's no denying that the show has only improved with the recent changes. Hopefully the rest of the industry will also learn to diversify more. There's a big appetite for country music out there. The people who are allowed to succeed the most in performing it shouldn't all have to match one skin tone. One gender. One sexuality.

Whether or not the record labels and radio stations are ready for a gay country singer is beyond my control. But here's what I *can* focus on for the time being: I can keep writing new songs. I can keep posting them to my YouTube channel. I can keep putting myself out there, demanding to be heard.

"Emmett," Jessie whispers, tossing me my cowboy hat. "We're on."

Right. I can also run back out onstage to sing and dance my ass off with the rest of my castmates. Which is exactly what I do.

Afterward, once our costumes have been put away and the stands are all cleared out, I stick around with Jessie and Avery to eat greasy park food and prepare for the next open mic night at the Rusty Spur.

"No pressure, y'all," Avery says. "But this is our last chance."

"*For the summer*," Jessie replies, throwing a cheese fry at him.

It's hard to believe summer will be over soon. This past week's been tough. I haven't seen Luke since our confrontation with Wanda Jean. He said he needed more space to figure things out. Wanting to respect that, I've poured all my time and energy into songwriting. I've written love songs, heartbreak songs, and everything-in-between songs. Even if I don't catch the attention of another scout, I'll at least be heading back home with plenty of new material.

"Emmett," Avery says. "You should go first."

"Why me?"

"Because. You're the one who recently deleted a YouTube video with over fifty thousand views. You obviously need the most help."

"I still can't believe you did that," Jessie mutters, shaking her head.

"I told you. It wasn't my song."

"Dude," Avery says. "Just credit the songwriter next time."

"They didn't want to be credited."

I can't lie, it nearly killed me to delete that video. Especially since I could've gone viral and racked up fifty *million* views if people found out I was singing a long-lost Wanda Jean song, one about being in love with Verna Rose. But I didn't think it was right to put their story out there. Besides, if I want to make it in this industry, I'm going to need my own hit songs. I might as well start working on them now.

"Fine," I say, picking up my guitar. "This is still a work in progress. The verses could be stronger. And I haven't figured out the bridge yet."

"You're stalling," Jessie says.

She's right. This my first time performing this song for anyone, and I'm kind of nervous. But maybe that's a good sign. I take a breath and go for it.

> They say boys will be boys
> Then teach us all the rules
> Always drink your beer from the bottle
> Never be the first to back down from a fight
> And son, ain't no shame in adjusting the family jewels
>
> Maybe I'm not like most boys
> But I'm no stranger to being tough
> I've had to keep my chin up
> And be the bigger man
> Even when they tell me I'm not man enough
>
> But what if the bravest thing for me to do
> Was to tell the world how much I loved you
> Then maybe real men would cry
> And cowboys could kiss

Yeah, real men would cry
And cowboys could kiss

As I strum the final chord and listen to the vibrations of my guitar echo across the amphitheater, my cheeks go warm. Not because I'm embarrassed by the content, or being falsely modest. But after performing Wanda Jean's songs all summer, I guess I've forgotten what it's like to put myself out there and perform one of my own.

"I love it," Jessie says.

"Yeah," Avery says. "It's different from your last one. But in a good way."

We take turns workshopping our songs for a while. And after we're done, and all the cheese fries are gone, Jessie and Avery start packing up their guitars.

"I'm going to stick around for a while," I tell them.

On their way out, Avery and Jessie wait until they think I'm not watching, then hold hands as they leave. Once they're gone, I take a seat on the edge of the stage and run through my song again. It might be a work in progress, but I'm feeling pretty good about what I *do* have. So I take out my phone, prop it against my guitar case, and hit record.

"Hey, y'all. It's Emmett. Are my *y'alls* sounding better? We elongate our vowels back in Chicago. We also call soda 'pop.' Anyhow, I wanted to share a song I've been working on. It's not finished yet. But I've always been a bit impatient. I'll upload the final version when it's done. So be sure to hit subscribe down below. Oh, yeah . . . this song's called 'Cowboys Could Kiss.' And, um, I wrote it for someone special."

After playing my song, I watch the video back and upload it to my channel.

It might not be perfect.

But it's real.

As I put my guitar back in its case, my phone buzzes.

DID YOU SEE IT???

BE SURE YOU'RE SITTING DOWN.

I have no idea what Aunt Karen is talking about, but her enthusiasm makes me smile. Breaking up with Grady wasn't easy for her. She thought she'd finally found someone she could settle down with. But just because Grady was an asshole, it doesn't mean she can't still grow roots. Instead of running off to a new city like she's done in the past, she's decided to stay here and keep Jackson Hollow as her home. She even got a new tattoo to celebrate—a little burst of fire in honor of her favorite Wanda Jean lyric: *Darlin', even a wet blanket like you can't put this flame out.*

My phone buzzes again and a link to a YouTube video appears. The preview shows Wanda Jean all done up in another sparkly dress and fabulous wig. I click on it, allowing her to fill my screen.

"Howdy, y'all! Thanks for checking out my new video. I've said it a million times, and I'll say it a million more . . . I wouldn't be here if it weren't for my fans. Truly, y'all give so much to me." She pauses, allowing a mischievous grin to sneak across her face. "However, there's something I haven't given y'all in a while. And that's new music."

Holy shit.

Aunt Karen was right. I'm glad I'm sitting down.

"Of course, I never stopped writing music," Wanda Jean continues. "I just took a break from recording it. About a dozen years, to be exact." She laughs, putting her hand to her chest. And that's when I see it. She's wearing the locket.

"When I wrote this new song, well, I knew I had to share it with y'all right away. I hope it might clear up some of the rumors and misconceptions people may've heard about me over the years."

She rubs the locket between her thumb and finger, taking a moment before looking into the camera again. "I really do hope y'all enjoy this song. It's called 'The Sweetest Rose.'"

I pause the video.

My hairs are standing on end.

If this song is what I think it is . . . If Wanda Jean is coming out to everyone, then I'm going to have to work *a lot* harder to become country music's biggest gay star.

Looking out at the empty seats in the amphitheater, I can't help but laugh. I've always been a little too ambitious. But I like that about myself. I'd rather dream too big and come up short than dream too small and regret it. Maybe I won't get *exactly* where I want to be. But that doesn't mean I shouldn't try.

Before I can listen to Wanda Jean's new song, a notification pops up on my phone. I have a comment on my video already. When I click over to my page, my heart starts pounding.

Luke (Not Reginald) Barnes: Great song. Sounds even better in person.

I look back up. I was wrong; the amphitheater isn't empty. Sitting in the top row, in the exact same spot where he heard me practicing my Dream Cowboy song earlier this summer, is Luke. As he makes his way down toward the stage, I push a stray curl out of my face, hoping I don't look as panicked as I feel.

Is he here to get back together?

Or end things for good?

Luke doesn't say anything. He just stops in front of me, making my heart feel as though it's about to burst right out of my chest. It's getting dark out. But the lights are still on in the amphitheater, and it's impossible to miss the damp tears on his cheeks.

"I've never seen you cry," I say.

He stares up at me, taking his time before speaking.

"No one's ever written a song for me before."

I grip the edge of the stage, suddenly feeling way too vulnerable. "Don't tell me what you thought about it. I honestly don't think I could handle that right now."

"Emmett. I'm really sorry."

My stomach drops. "Oh. You hated it."

"No—not that. I'm sorry for making you wait so long."

"It's okay," I say, even though I've been silently freaking out all week, trying to distract myself with my music. "I know you needed some time to—"

"I loved your song."

"You did?"

"Yes."

God, why do I feel like I'm going to throw up? I love Luke. And I really wish I could reach out and wipe the tears from his face right now.

"What are you doing tomorrow night?" he asks.

"I have a show," I say, my heart pounding wildly.

"And after that?"

"Nothing."

"Good. There's something I want you to do."

"Look," I reply, spitting my words out faster than I can process them. "I don't really know where we stand right now. And I'm not trying to pressure you to make a decision one way or the other. If you want to hang out and be friends, that's cool. But, um, I still have feelings for you. And I don't think that I can just—"

For the first time tonight, Luke smiles.

"Will you please shut up and let me kiss you?" he asks.

I don't have to give him my answer. He pulls me down into him, and as soon as our lips meet, it's as if nothing's changed. I immediately get that roller-coaster feeling again. Like I'm slowly inching my way toward the top. I'm excited and terrified all at once. Because it's like we're about to hit that first big drop, and I have no idea what comes next.

Chapter 39

LUKE

A lot can go wrong when you're cooking a new recipe for the first time. Maybe your oven runs too hot. Maybe you aren't familiar with some of the ingredients. Maybe you're fixing a big Sunday night supper for your family, but you're so nervous about getting everything just right that you give up and order a bunch of pizzas instead.

It'd be easy to keep making the same kind of food. Recipes you already know. Cooking outside your comfort zone can be scary. But sometimes, taking a risk pays off, and things aren't as scary as they first seem. Who knows, you might even create a dish that everyone likes better in the end.

"Luke," Amelia says. "Is the oven supposed to be smoking?"

Then again, cooking is hard. And sometimes, despite your best efforts, you still burn the corn bread.

I grab my pot holders and yank open the oven door. The top of my corn bread's not even golden yet. Amelia smirks, giving the block of Parmesan another push down the grater. "Just checking to see if you were paying attention."

"Thanks, Bean. Some sous chef you turned out to be."

"Maybe if you actually let me cook something . . ."

No task in the kitchen is unimportant. If the dishes don't get washed, the food's not going out to the tables. But maybe she has a point. She's not a little kid anymore.

"Okay," I tell her. "Scoot on over. You're gonna learn how to make a roux for the creamed spinach."

Not every dish I'm making tonight is new. In the past week, I've made enough creamed spinach to feed half of Tennessee. After quitting my job at Wanda World, I couldn't bring myself to ask for a second chance at the hose factory. Thankfully, I didn't have to. César, it turns out, has connections in a lot of different kitchens. He helped me get a job over in Rayburn, at Pinkie's BBQ. And not as a dishwasher. As a prep cook. I've never been happier to stand in front of a steaming pot of beans all day, or to shred fifty pounds of cabbage.

After helping Amelia achieve the right consistency for our roux, we add in the cheese and spinach. Next I check on my homemade dumplings, which are simmering in a pot of chicken stock.

"These are about done," I say, putting the lid back on. "Turn off the burner in another minute. I'm gonna see how Mama's doing."

As I walk into the dining room, Gabe comes flying around the corner wearing only his swim trunks and a cape.

"Uh, buddy? You might wanna put on a shirt."

"Why?"

"Because. Tonight's kind of important, okay?"

He nods and takes off running again, almost crashing into Mama as she walks into the room with a set of serving bowls. The bowls are turquoise and chipped; they don't exactly match the rest of the dishes

Mama's so nicely set the table with.

"You sure you want these?" she asks. "We've got nicer ones."

"They were Nana's," I say, taking them from her. "I figured it'd be nice to start using them again."

Mama inhales sharply and tucks her hair behind her ears. When I came out to her earlier this week, she couldn't stop crying. I know her church will always be important to her, and that she's probably struggling to reconcile how she can love the both of us. I don't expect her to sort it all out overnight. But to her credit, she's trying really hard to make sure everything's perfect for tonight.

After I came out to Mama, I thought she was going to be in for an even bigger shock when I told her Nana was also gay. But I was the one who ended up being surprised. Mama had always known about Nana and Wanda Jean. Nana had told her. That's why Mama was crying so much. She knew how hard being gay had been for her mama, and she didn't want that same kind of life for me.

"Mama," I say, setting the serving bowls down. "Can I ask you something?"

My chest gets tight. But I'm learning how to push past that panicky feeling I always get. "This might sound silly, but earlier this summer, when you had the TV on in your bedroom, two men kissed on some show. You shook your head, like you didn't think it was right."

That was a statement. But the question buried in there is one I'm too afraid to ask: *Do you wish I weren't gay?* Mama might still love me. But that doesn't mean she wouldn't change me if she could.

"Oh, honey." Her mouth crumples into a frown. "I honestly

don't remember that. But I suppose . . . well, I suppose I probably did." She blinks, casting her eyes toward the ceiling. "It's not that I thought it was wrong, necessarily. It's more that I didn't think it was *fair*. I know times have changed, and two men kissing on TV is normal now, but it still stings that your nana never got her chance to be happy."

Nana never answered Wanda Jean's letters. But she did keep all her songs. So even if Nana thought it was wrong to be gay, there must've been a part of her that wanted to hang on to those memories.

"I'm not sure Nana was able to accept herself," I tell Mama. "I don't wanna make that same mistake. I realize being gay isn't always gonna be easy. But I don't think I'd change it if I could. This is who I am."

A tear rolls down Mama's cheek, but she brushes it away and wraps her arms around me. "Then that's all that matters."

As we break apart from our hug, Keith comes in carrying a tub of vanilla ice cream. I'd asked him to pick some up on his way home from work, so I could serve it with the peach cobbler I made for dessert.

"Oh," he says, stopping as he notices our faces. "You told him the news already?"

"What news?" I ask.

"Uh . . ." Keith holds up the ice cream, making his escape toward the kitchen. "Better throw this in the freezer and wash up before supper."

Mama looks at me. "I wasn't trying to hide anything. I just . . . I needed time to think things through." She presses her lips together. "I finally reached out to Wanda Jean."

I try not to look shocked, but my eyebrows push up. When I talked to Wanda Jean, she said she wanted to help my family in any way she could. And I didn't even tell her about our bills; I knew Mama and Keith would be too proud to accept that kind of help. Still, I thought if Mama at least talked to her, some good might come of it. Even if it was just to get some closure on what happened with Nana.

"It was the strangest phone call," Mama says. "She's real easy to talk to. Within seconds, I'd forgotten I'd spent most of my life resenting her." She shakes her head, like she still can't believe it. "She shared some nice memories of your nana. And somehow, before we hung up, I had an offer to go work for her."

"What? Like *at Wanda World*?"

I try to picture Mama scribbling down people's orders while wearing one of those funny caps. It doesn't seem right.

"The benefits are better than what I'd get if I went back to the Craft Barn," Mama says. "I'd finally have sick-time pay."

"But, Mama, do you *want* to work there?"

"Well . . . one of the things we talked about was the possibility of me working in her museum, where I could also help oversee an exhibit that would be all about your nana. I think maybe I'd like that."

The pictures I found of Nana. The ones that show her smiling and laughing and holding her guitar. They've been sitting in our attic, hidden away for decades. What if other people could remember her like that, too?

"I don't know," Mama says, sighing. "I keep changing my mind, which is why I didn't tell you yet. Besides, I know how special tonight is. I don't wanna distract from that. Whatever you're cooking smells delicious, by the way."

Shit. Supper.

I give Mama a kiss on the head, grab Nana's serving bowls, and head back into the kitchen. Thankfully, Amelia's got everything under control. The same can't be said of me, however. After almost burning myself while getting the corn bread out of the oven, I manage to flick a giant glob of creamed spinach onto my shirt.

"Fuck."

"Language," Amelia teases.

"Get someone to help you bring all this food out," I tell her. "And don't forget we still need butter on the table. Oh, and have Gabe fill everyone's water glass. *No*—not Gabe. He'll spill. Do we have enough ice? I forgot to check."

Before Amelia can respond, I'm out of the kitchen and dashing up the stairs. My fingers fumble as I try to unbutton my shirt. I finally get it off, and the doorbell rings.

"Nobody answer that!" I yell, running back down the stairs as I throw a clean shirt over my head. "Y'all just . . . have a seat in the dining room. *Please.*"

By the time I get to our front door, my heart's pounding in my chest. New recipes aren't the only reason I'm nervous about tonight. But I can't let fear stop me. Nana never got her chance to be happy. I don't want to miss mine. So I take a deep breath, grab hold of the doorknob, and pull.

"Hi there," Emmett says, standing on our front porch.

"Hey," I reply, smiling.

Not wanting my family to see him yet, I step outside and pull the door closed behind me. Since our nearest neighbor lives half a mile down the road, no one would notice if I pulled Emmett in for a kiss. But I'm still too nervous.

"Those are nice," I say, looking down at his feet.

He lifts the leg of his jeans, showing off the embroidery on his shiny leather cowboy boots. "Yeah? You don't think I look like a poseur?"

"Emmett. You can be from Chicago and still wear cowboy boots."

"That's what Vanessa said. She picked these out for me."

"I know," I say. "She texted me earlier and said I'd better compliment you on them."

"Hey, that's cheating!"

I point to the rolled-up tube of paper he's holding in his hand. "What's that?"

"Oh. Um. This?" He shifts his weight. "This is something I very much regret not leaving in my car."

"Sorry, now I'm twice as interested."

He winces. "My aunt said it was bad manners to bring a host flowers, because then they have to worry about finding a vase. So I brought this. I thought it might be funny."

He reluctantly hands it over. Unrolling it, I see it's a poster. *A poster of him.* His name is in big letters across the top, and he's leaning against a beat-up old pickup truck, looking at the camera with what can only be described as "smoldering" eyes.

"My aunt decided that, in addition to making all her Wanda Jean merchandise, she wants to start helping me promote my career."

"I'm *so* hanging this on my wall," I tell him.

"Ha ha."

"I'm serious. It's great. You're gonna sign it for me, right?"

His cheeks turn pink. "Yeah. Of course."

A breeze picks up, rustling the leaves on the giant oak tree in our front yard. Even though I want to stay out here with him forever, I know we can't. And not only because supper's getting cold. I invited Emmett over for a reason. I love him. I know that now. And while I still don't know if I'm ready to say those words out loud, there's something else I can do: I can show him.

"Do you want to come inside?" I ask.

He smiles. "I'd like that."

Opening the front door again, my stomach twists into a knot. Our house has never felt so still. My pulse races as I lead Emmett toward the dining room. I can't tell if it's from excitement or nerves. Probably both. Is it possible for something to feel like both a life-changing event and not a big deal?

I stop before we enter. Emmett's hand finds mine.

"Hey," he whispers. "You can do this."

I give it a squeeze.

"I know."

When I first told Emmett I wanted to be a chef, he said cooking made me an artist. I didn't believe him at the time. But now, as we enter the dining room together, it's like I'm looking at my masterpiece. There's a table full of food. And my family sitting around it. And my mama, who's giving me a big smile, even though she's also kind of nervous.

There's only one ingredient missing now. It's a tricky one. One I haven't worked with before. But it's essential. Without it, I might as well be trying to make bread without dough. An omelet without eggs. Biscuits without gravy.

"Everyone," I say, taking a breath. "I'd like y'all to meet Emmett. My boyfriend."

ACKNOWLEDGMENTS

It's probably safe to say that this book wouldn't exist without Dolly Parton. However, there are a number of other people who were just as instrumental in helping me bring Emmett, Luke, and Wanda World to life on these pages.

My amazing agent, Lauren Spieller, who has advocated for me tirelessly since day one. Thank you for asking why I liked country music so much, and then telling me to "put it in the book." Thank you also to Uwe Stender and the entire team at Triada US Literary Agency.

My brilliant editor, Kristin Daly Rens. Some of my favorite parts of this book exist because of you. Thank you for the amount of care you put into Emmett and Luke's story, and for your guidance, which always left me feeling like I was in the best of hands. On our very first phone call, I said you *have* to visit Dollywood someday. I'm still insisting upon that.

Alessandra Balzer, Donna Bray, and the entire team at Balzer + Bray and HarperCollins. Thank you Christian Vega for your insightful editorial feedback, along with Caitlin Johnson and my copyeditor, Laura Harshberger, all of whom make me look like a much better writer than I actually am. Additional gratitude to Allison Brown, for making my book a real, physical thing, and Shannon Cox and Mitch Thorpe for getting the word out about it.

Chris Kwon, along with Alison Donalty, Jenna Stempel-Lobell, and my illustrator, Betsy Cola, gave me a book cover that still takes my breath away. Betsy, I don't know how you were able to perfectly capture what was in my head, but I do know that looking at your illustration—which I've done an embarrassing amount of—always leaves me with 'kilig.'

I've had many great teachers along the way, including the fellow writers I've taken workshops and classes with. Thank you for all the feedback and encouragement. If I had ten more pages, I would list you all. And special thanks to my mentors, Kimberlee Auerbach Berlin and Diana Spechler, who gave me a better crash course in writing than any MFA program could.

My early readers, starting with my writers group: Emily Helck, Katie Henry, Siena Koncsol, and Michelle Rinke. The only thing I cherish more than your spot-on critiques and fancy snack food, is our friendship. I wasn't kidding when I said none of you can ever leave me. Kit Rosewater, thank you for always lifting me up (and listening to me babble on). Ash Van Otterloo and Erica Waters, thank you for teaching me the ways of the South. Any mistakes belong fully to this New Yorker with strong Midwest roots.

Claudine Quiba and the other readers who reviewed *A Little Bit Country*, thank you for your attentive, thoughtful feedback, which improved my characters and the stories they wanted to tell. Mason Deaver, Jennifer Dugan, Erin Hahn, Katie Henry (again), and Jason June, you have my endless thanks and gratitude for your generosity and kind words.

One of the best parts of releasing a book has been getting to meet so many incredible authors. Thank you to my fellow #22Debuts for sharing resources, sharing fears, and sharing in the excitement. Erik J. Brown, Kristin Dwyer, Anna Gracia, Naz Kutub, and Susan Lee, you have made me laugh way more than I thought humanly possible.

Beth Phelan, thank you for creating #DVpit and opening the door for countless marginalized writers.

My coworkers at the LGBTQ Center, with a special shoutout to the finance department, thank you for sharing me with the publishing world.

Is it time to talk about music again? This book was inspired by my love of female country singers. Dolly Parton, Loretta Lynn, Miranda Lambert, Kacey Musgraves, Patty Griffin, Lori McKenna . . . the list could go on. I didn't really fall in love with country music until after I came out. Thank you for always giving me a home.

My family: Dad, Mom, Mike, Ellen, Maddie, Tori, Molly, Ann, Brian, Ethan, and Declan. Thank you for your unending enthusiasm and support. In both my writing career and my life. I'm lucky to have a family where everyone's welcomed to take a seat at the table.

And lastly, my husband, Danny. Thank you for putting up with my long writing hours, for letting me drag you to Dollywood, and for being my constant source of love and support. You can't have biscuits without gravy. And I couldn't imagine my life without you.